MW00526216

SANTA'S
SECRET

FERN
MICHAELS

SANTA'S
SECRET

KENSINGTON
PUBLISHING CORP.

KENSINGTON BOOKS are published by

Kensington Publishing Corp.
900 Third Avenue
New York, NY 10022

ISBN: 978-1-4967-4682-5

Printed in the United States of America

Prologue

Most class reunions are anticipated with either dread or extreme enthusiasm. It's hard to find a middle ground. Either you feel a kinship with your former classmates and can't wait to catch up, or you realize you probably have absolutely nothing in common with any of them. *Who are these people?*

Francesca "Frankie" Cappella had that very thought as she walked under the banner that read: WELCOME RIDGEWOOD HIGH ALUMNI. She couldn't help noticing the edges on the banner were a little frayed and wondered how many reunions this worn piece of fabric had resided over. She took a deep breath and scanned the room, catching a glimpse of one of the few people she intermittently stayed in touch with. It was Nina Hunter. A well-known actress who had been on a popular sitcom, she and Frankie had bonded performing together in their high school plays. Frankie sang, Nina acted. Delighted to see each other, Nina and Frankie sidled up to the bar, and before long, two of their other high school theatre friends appeared on the scene. Amy Blanchard was the brainiac of the group—not that any of them were mental lightweights, but Amy was brilliant. Back in high school, she was in charge of the staging of their plays. Then there was Rachael Newmark, the dancer, also known for her delight in chasing men.

The four women were quite different in personality except for a few shared traits: they were smart, ambitious, and talented, and all had a passion for their work. It took less than a few minutes for them to find a table, where they huddled and exchanged impressions on how everyone in the room had aged. There were a few who looked like they could be "Real Housewives," with their vacuous eyes, over-Botoxed foreheads, and lips that looked like they had been stung by a school of jellyfish. There isn't anything wrong with trying to keep oneself "refreshed," but too many women went over the top.

Nina had been under much pressure when she was living in Los Angeles and working in the film and television industry. Studio executives either wanted a well-known talent or an ingenue. Nina was well-known, but not well enough to continue an on-screen career as she maneuvered through her thirties. Talent was the least of media moguls' priorities.

Frankie bemoaned that it was the same in publishing. Even though it was a female-dominated industry, the very top positions were held, by and large, by men. Frankie wasn't necessarily interested in climbing the corporate ladder. What she was interested in was acquiring good books, but it seemed like her superiors were less interested in quality than they were celebrity.

Amy was feeling stifled in her job at a biotech company. Sure, she made tons of money, but it was just so boring.

Then there was Rachael. She was the only one who had gotten married and had children, but her marriage was a bust, and she was divorced. She had thought she would spend her days being a socialite—until her husband wiped out her trust fund and reality smacked her in the face. She thought she needed another man, but what she really needed was a job. In her search for a greater meaning in life, she opened a dance studio, which was quite successful, much to her own surprise. Yet, she was still in search of validation from another man, an error many women make.

After an hour of the torture of classmates they no longer had anything in common with, the four women left the past behind and regrouped at a nearby motel, where Frankie and Nina were staying, for an impromptu pajama party. Realizing they were all unattached, they made a pact that if they didn't have dates for New Year's Eve by Thanksgiving, they would do the unthinkable: go on a singles' cruise.

The excursion provided a boon for all of them in different ways. The adventure proved to be one of enlightenment, romance, revelation, and renewal. Nina's career went from being on television to writing for television. Amy went from Silicon Valley tech geek to a professor at MIT. Rachael began working with a world-famous dancer, and Frankie was promoted to executive publisher for Grand Marshall Publishing's cookbook division. She also found romance: "right in her own backyard," as the saying goes. Even Amy's divorced father found love on the same ship on the high seas.

Their seafaring triumph encouraged them to devise a plan to meet again for another New Year's Eve escapade a year later. They agreed on Lake Tahoe, where estranged friendships were rekindled, professional adversaries quashed, and lessons about snowshoeing were learned. The hard way. But persistence, love, and solid relationships prevailed, and a promise of another adventure was made.

Fast forward to the present. Brothers Marco and Giovanni Lombardi are partners in the eponymous family restaurant, Marco's, located in the Flatiron District of Manhattan. It is a modest, neighborhood favorite for dinner and ideal for a casual business lunch. The food is authentic, and the atmosphere is cozy without being overcrowded like some New York restaurants where you're practically sitting on a stranger's lap. There is a laid-back bustle—an oxymoron if there ever was one, but an oddly accurate description. One can feel the passion the Lombardis have invested into the business over the past thirty years. The minute you walk through the door, your senses are immersed in the lush aromas of fine herbs, the distant sound of classical music, and warm lighting that filters through the lemon trees that surround the dining room. Whatever is on your worry list takes a brief hiatus once you are inside.

Marco and his wife Anita live in the apartment above the restaurant, just as Marco and Giovanni had when they were growing up. They are the third generation to be at the helm. They rarely have time to rest, let alone take a vacation. But that was going to change this winter.

The holidays are always frenetic, with private parties and their usual customers. But this year it will be different. Marco and Giovanni decided it is time to give all their employees a break; they will close the restaurant for ten days, from right before Christmas through the New Year so the staff can spend the holidays with their loved ones. The Lombardis will spend time with their family, too, in Italy. Marco's two children are old enough to fly without annoying other passengers, and they will finally meet their cousins and Aunt Lucia.

Their now-widowed mother, Rosevita, had moved back to Italy to be with her long-widowed sister-in-law Lucia. Lucia had never set foot outside of Italy and still lives in the same house where their husbands were raised. It is a modest villa in the hills outside of the city of Salerno, but has ample room for Marco, Anita, and the kids, as well as Giovanni and Frankie. Giovanni was certain he could convince Frankie to spend the holidays with his family as long as he could concoct a plan for her folks.

For the past two years, Frankie and her parents have spent Christmas Eve at Marco's restaurant, and then on Christmas Day, Giovanni would join them at Frankie's parents' house. Giovanni knew Frankie would love to go to Salerno, but he didn't want her to feel any guilt about leaving her parents alone, so he devised an "offer they could not refuse." He would pay for Frankie's family's airfare and secure a spot at a nearby Airbnb. It would be his Christmas present to them.

One morning in late August, over breakfast, Giovanni shared the details of his plans with Frankie. He posed it as a suggestion, hoping Frankie would be amenable. "You know my mama doesn't want to leave Aunt Lucia alone since Sergio moved to Australia, and Aunt Lucia will never set foot on an airplane. Dominic moved to Baronissi, a few kilometers away, to be closer to the school." Giovanni was referring to Lucia's sons. "I was-a thinking, maybe you, me, your family could go to Italy for Christmas. I would pay for all the arrangements."

"That's very generous, Gio, but what about Nina, Amy, and Rachael?" Frankie asked with a slight frown. "We all agreed to plan another trip between Christmas and New Year's."

"*Cara*, we can still celebrate together. You, your family, and I will go to Salerno for Christmas, and we can meet the others in Rome, Firenze, or Napoli. Wherever they wanna, but I have to spend this holiday with Mama. It's *importante*."

Frankie understood the significance of his words. "Okay. I'll figure something out." Frankie got up from the table, rinsed her coffee mug, smiled, and kissed him on the cheek. "Time to put on my bossy pants!"

"You look so good in them!" Giovanni grinned.

She blew kisses to the kitties, grabbed her tote, and hustled her way to her office.

Later that day, she sent a Zoom invitation to the other women and hoped they wouldn't protest her suggestion. She did some research and made a list of scenarios she would run through with them, making the trip as attractive as possible. *Who wouldn't want to spend the holidays in one of the most spectacular countries in Europe?*

And so it began . . . a visit to Italy in search of another new beginning, a peek at a scientific wonder, a glimpse of ancient history, and the secret recipe for Mrs. Lombardi's panettone.

PART I

Chapter 1

Frankie's Pitch

Frankie left work at six and walked down Fifth Avenue, imagining the Christmas decorations that would be in place while she was devouring mozzarella di bufala from real Italian Mediterranean buffalos. Eating the soft, buttery cheese was almost required by law when you were in Campania, with Salerno and Caserta being two of its biggest producers. Speaking of laws, she had read that buffalo mozzarella sold as mozzarella di bufala campana had been granted the status of *denominazione di origine controllata*, a controlled designation of origin for thirty years, authenticating the product. She was salivating just thinking about it.

By the time she arrived at her apartment, Bandit and Sweet P. were patiently waiting right inside the door. She often wondered how they knew she was in the building. Must be animal instinct. "Hello puddie-tats! Did you miss your mommy?" Bandit would invariably walk ahead of her, directing her to the kitchen—if you could call it a kitchen. In New York, a typical kitchen was so small, it was barely functional. Only large enough for one person at a time, there was a compact refrigerator that could only hold a couple of quarts of milk, a dozen eggs, a head of lettuce, and a stick of butter. Don't even attempt to roast a turkey in the miniscule oven they provide. In fact, any type of cooking was nearly impossible. Frankie thought it was a conspiracy between landlords and restaurant owners. Every day, there was a new take-out menu under her door or in the lobby. She often teased Marco whenever she got a new menu from his restaurant.

Bandit was rubbing against her ankles, alternating between one leg then the other as Frankie opened the can of cat food. "I am going to squish you if you're not careful." This was a ritual with them. Bandit made sure Frankie couldn't escape from his dinner plans. Sweet P. was simply happy to have a warm place, a cuddle-buddy with Bandit, and regular meals. "Why can't you be polite, like Sweet P.?" Frankie would often ask. "Look at her, sitting patiently." Bandit would answer with a meow, and head-bump her ankle. It always made Frankie chuckle. "How is it that two little furry creatures can make me so happy?" She placed their bowls on the floor as Sweet P. sauntered in, all ladylike. Even though Bandit was the first to stick his head in his dish, and the first to finish, he never tried to nudge Sweet P. from hers. "Why can't people be this considerate?" Frankie said out loud.

She rinsed the empty can of cat food, placed it in the recycling bin, and washed her hands. Frankie often wondered if the city was actually doing any recycling. Did they really, honestly separate the glass from the metal? Sure, there were machines that could do it, but New York was a small area with a lot of people. A lot. Millions, in fact.

Her cell phone rang, pulling her from her trash can musings. It was Giovanni.

"*Ciao, bella! Come stai?*"

"*Molto bene!*" Frankie answered. She knew she was way behind in learning Italian. Better start practicing.

"Have you spoken to your friends about Italy?" Giovanni asked.

"I have a Zoom call with them in two hours."

"*Bene*. I know someone who has a big house near ours. It's in Baronissi, a few kilometers from my family home. It has four bedrooms, so your friends can stay there if they wanna. It's about an hour to Amalfi, Sorrento, and Positano."

"It sounds very convenient." Frankie was impressed at how much Giovanni was looking after the travel prospects for everyone.

"*Sì*. And only thirty minutes from Pompeii," Giovanni added. "They said we can trade apartments. They come-a here. We go-a there."

"Gio, your accent has been rather apparent lately," Frankie teased.

"*Scusi?*"

"Your accent. Thick. Like a block of Parmigiano-Reggiano," she chuckled.

"Sorry. I'm excited for the plans."

"We still have four months to go." Frankie couldn't help but smile at his enthusiasm.

"Yes, but we have to make-a the plans now. Time will be flying."

"Very true." Frankie paused. "I think I'll be able to convince everyone that Italy would be the best place to spend New Year's."

"And you can tell them about all the fireworks. From Naples to Salerno. The sky is like-a diamonds, rubies, and emeralds." Giovanni sounded like a kid who was about to go on his first field trip.

"So when will you and I leave?" Frankie was tapping her pen, ready to take notes.

"We have to help Mama shop a few days before."

"And?" Frankie was waiting for Giovanni to give her an exact date and time. She was picky that way. "Details, please."

"I'm-a think we should plan to arrive by the twenty-second. We leave the night before."

Frankie checked her desk diary. The office would be closing the following day for the holidays. "Will that be enough time to get everything ready?" She knew not to question Giovanni when it came to planning meals, but she couldn't help herself. "How many people are going to be there for Christmas Eve?"

Giovanni was counting in his head. "Maybe twenty. Christmas Day it will be people coming in and out, so Mama will have food ready for guests."

Frankie was imagining a gastronomic exploration. "Seven fishes on Christmas Eve?"

"*Sì*, of course," Giovanni replied.

"When do you think my parents should arrive?" Frankie sat with her pen poised.

"Maybe the twenty-third. Give them time to un-lag-a the jet."

Frankie burst out laughing. "Jet lag."

"*Sì*. My brain is working like a loco-motion. I cannot translate fast enough in my head," he chuckled.

Frankie thought it was charming. "Alright. You and I will fly out on the twenty-first, and my folks will join us on the twenty-third."

"*Sì*. Perfetto."

Frankie checked the time. "I have to get going. I have a call with the girls in a few minutes. What time do you think you'll be home?"

"Busy night. Maybe ten, ten thirty."

"Okay. See you later. Wish me luck with my pals."

"*Buona fortuna*. I have every confidence you will encourage them to join us in Italy. *Ciao, bella.*"

"*Ciao*, Gio," Frankie ended the call. Everyone agreed to plan a trip, but the *where* hadn't been decided. Rachael suggested Paris. Amy wanted to go to Switzerland, and Nina was longing for a palm tree. If Frankie did what she did best, everyone would be satisfied. She was a planner, and an organizer extraordinaire. It was no surprise Grand Marshall Publishing gave her the Cooking for a Cause imprint. With the celebrity-oriented mentality of her corporate supervisors in mind, she proposed a new concept of curating cookbooks that were attached to a celebrity with a charitable organization. She even came up with the logo: C4AC Books would be sold through the associations, which would then use the book as an incentive for donations. The publisher would also donate a portion of the proceeds to the charity. It was a windfall during the holidays, with every talk show clamoring for celebrity chefs to do on-air cooking demonstrations. It was also exhausting for Frankie and the publicity department. Lots of moving parts. The current year's books would go on sale while the following year's books were being turned in. But once the deluge was over, Frankie could take a little break, which was one of the reasons the trips had been planned between Christmas and New Year's Eve.

This year she would be on an accelerated schedule, with arrangements during the cookbook releases, and the publicity spectacle with four publications hitting the stores the first week of October. Normally publishers do not publish big books up against each other, but cookbooks were always a hot item for gift-giving, and there was nothing more compelling than seeing a live demonstration showing how easy it is to create a fabulous meal, and, for a good cause. Of course, there was a slew of people in the wings slicing, dicing, and prepping at these events, but everyone wanted to see the celebrity chef create their special recipe.

Frankie even was able to get Giovanni onboard. After the trip to Lake Tahoe the year before, and the last-minute emergency dinner they prepared for sixty people, Giovanni decided there was a need for an instructional booklet to help people be better organized when they cooked. With the encouragement of Frankie, Giovanni and chef Mateo Castillo, one of Frankie's authors and founder of the charity, Share a

Meal, created an e-book to teach people how to prep *before* they started to cook.

"They'll begin one part of the meal, but then have to prep the other items while trying to keep track of whatever is in the oven or the pan. It's a mistake many people make," Mateo wrote in the introduction. "Also, invest in a box of disposable nitrile kitchen prep gloves. A box of one hundred will cost less than ten cents apiece. It's safer. But make sure you don't get the baggy type. They slip off and you have less grip. You need good dexterity when you handle kitchen tools."

Giovanni contributed, "To help make cleanup a little easier, cover the counter where you are working with wax paper."

Frankie was the first to note that those little tips would be a favorite among aspiring kitchen wizards. Frankie was a superb ringmaster for her authors, but she was also quite skillful when it came to marketing. Giovanni and Mateo's *Food Prep 101* e-book was used as a free incentive if you bought any C4AC book. It was also available for $1.99 online, with the profits going to the individual charities. It was a great way to continue visibility for the organizations throughout the year, especially during any of the annual holidays when people cooked.

The alarm on Frankie's phone buzzed, reminding her it was time for the Zoom call. Frankie had a habit of setting a timer when she was engrossed in a project. She could easily get lost in whatever she was working on, and before she knew it, she was late for a meeting, or dinner, or most things. She had an old-fashioned wind-up kitchen timer on her desk in her office. It was useful and quite appropriate.

She settled herself in lotus position in front of the coffee table and powered up her laptop. Then she clicked on the buttons enabling everyone else to log in. First up was Nina.

"Sweetcakes!" You couldn't help but smile when you heard the words coming from Nina. "What's happening, babe?"

Her curly hair was pulled back with a bandana, a look she often sported.

"Honey pie!" Frankie responded. "What's shakin'?"

Nina did a little shake of her shoulders. "Just me, toots."

"You sound like Rachael," Frankie laughed, referring to their over-the-top friend who was known for her exaggerated gestures.

"Ah, but I didn't say 'hoochie-coochie,'" Nina joked. "Speaking of hoochie-coochie, there she is!"

Rachael's slim face appeared, with her head wrapped in a fruit-laden turban. She was wide- and wild-eyed as usual, shaking a pair of maracas.

"*Hola, chicas! Arriba! Arriba! Arriba!*" Latin music was playing in the background as Rachael mamboed her way across the screen.

Frankie and Nina were rolling over with laughter. *It's good that some things never change.* Before Rachael finished her footloose entertainment, Amy popped in, and immediately began to bounce in her chair. It was reminiscent of the days when the four of them were working on the high school plays. Pure fun.

Frankie pulled Bandit onto her lap and stood him on his hind legs. Her hands were under the cat version of armpits, swaying his paws back and forth to the music, without any objection from the furry feline. It appeared that he actually was enjoying himself as much as everyone else. Sweet P. looked at them and then at the laptop. Frankie was convinced Sweet P. rolled her eyes. After a few measures, Bandit decided he had enough humiliation and wiggled away from Frankie's grip.

Amy noticed Bandit was now sitting next to Frankie's cell phone. Laughing so hard, she could barely spew out the words, "Look out, Frankie! He's calling the SPCA!"

At that point, all four women were howling; tears were running down their cheeks.

"You guys make my face hurt," Amy giggled. She was finally pulling it together, but a moment later, they looked at one another and burst out laughing again. *Man-o-man, it felt so good. Make that girl-o-girl.*

Once they finally settled down, they brought one another up to speed with work, romance, and family matters.

Three of them had settled into a routine with their significant others, with the exception of Rachael, who drummed her fingers on her desk as she listened to their stories of domestic bliss.

Nina and Richard had a part-time situation. He had two offices—one was in Philadelphia and the other in New York—and split his time between them. Nina thought it was the perfect situation. "I only have to look at his socks on the floor a couple of times a week, instead of every day," she joked.

"Oh, I can't believe Richard would leave his socks on the floor," Amy defended him.

"That's just a euphemism for annoying habits," Frankie chuckled.

"Oh. Right." For a scientist, Amy was often in a fog when it came to pop culture and jargon. She was somewhat of an absent-minded professor. Her reading material usually consisted of technical journals and science magazines. She could tell you the names of the closest asteroids but could barely name any of the Kardashians, much to the relief of Frankie, Nina, and Peter. *Better a brainiac than a social media/celebrity junkie.* Peter was also more cerebral than his friends, which made them well-matched. When Amy and Peter moved into their first apartment together, they transformed the den into a game room with a large square table in the middle to accommodate several jigsaw puzzles at the same time. Since then, they bought a townhouse with three bedrooms, and much more space for many more puzzles. They had gotten quite good at it and joined an international jigsaw club and were gearing up to enter a competition.

"A jigsaw competition?" Rachael asked sincerely.

"Yes, dear. Dancing isn't the only thing where one can compete," Nina teased.

"Yeah, yeah. Blah, blah, blah," Rachael feigned annoyance. Rachael was still looking for "Mr. Right," but at least she wasn't desperate this time. She and Randy, the concierge from Lake Tahoe, forged a strong friendship, and Rachael persuaded her ex-boyfriend, a famous dancer, to help Randy find work on Broadway. Rachael enjoyed spending time with him and his friends dancing at clubs in New York when he wasn't appearing in a show. Most of the time, she was the only heterosexual in the group, which seriously decreased her odds for dating prospects. In all honesty, she enjoyed all their fussing over her. When Nina asked about the absence of potential dating material, Rachael recounted with: "At least someone is paying attention to me!"

Frankie took the reins, as usual. "Okay, ladies. It's time to plan our holiday escapades."

Nina eyed Frankie. "So, babycakes, what do you have in mind?"

She knew Frankie too well to think she'd start a conversation without an agenda, but in a good way.

"Amy, you said you wanted to go to Switzerland."

Amy began clapping. "Yes! I want to go to Geneva to see the Hadron Collider."

"The what?" Rachael knitted her eyebrows.

"Hadron Collider. It's the world's most powerful particle accelerator. It established the existence of the Higgs boson— a subatomic particle thought to be a fundamental building block of the formation of the universe."

Rachael placed her head on her table and pretended to snore.

"Very funny," Amy said, smirking. "You've heard of the Big Bang Theory?"

Rachael lifted her head and was back on camera. "Yes. It was a TV show."

Amy groaned. "Never mind. But it's in Geneva."

Frankie cleared her throat. "I am certain that I am not up for another snow-covered mountain adventure."

Nina huffed, "And I want some kind of palm tree."

"Anyone for Paris?" Rachael suggested.

Then all eyes were on Frankie. They knew she had to have something up her sleeve.

"Italy." It was a statement instead of a question. Before anyone could interrupt, she went down her list of all the reasons why it was a good idea, including Amy's trip to Geneva in her pitch. "We can all meet up on the Amalfi Coast."

"Ooh . . . that sounds lovely," Nina answered.

"And they have palm trees. And olive trees, and lemon trees," Frankie added. "They say the gardens of the Amalfi Coast are some of the most beautiful in the world." She paused for a response.

Nina knew Frankie had more to share. "Spill, girlfriend."

"Giovanni wants to visit his mother for the holidays. He and Marco plan to close the restaurant for ten days so the staff can have a relaxing time with their families."

"Oh, that's so nice," Amy cooed.

Frankie smiled. "Giovanni also found a couple who own a large house a few kilometers from his mother's. They're interested in trading ten days in New York for ten days at their home in Baronissi. They're both professors at the University of Salerno, Baronissi campus. It's well-situated as a home base for day trips; an hour drive to Sorrento and thirty minutes to Pompeii." She waited again.

"So, we don't have to worry about paying for a hotel?" Rachael asked. This time, her eyes were on full alert.

"That is correct. Unless you want to start in Florence or Rome and make your way down the coast."

"This sounds great!" Nina was smiling from ear to ear.

"Plus, we'll be with people who know where to go and what to do, and when to do it," Frankie added. Her gift of persuasion seemed to be well at hand.

"I'm in!" Nina hooted.

"Me too. After Geneva." Amy raised both fists in agreement.

"What about the men?" Rachael realized she would be the seventh wheel.

All eyes bounced from one face to the other.

"What if we have them meet us later in the week?" Frankie suggested. "That will give us girl time."

"And a few days for Rachael to find a boyfriend!" Nina teased.

"Oh, shut it." Rachael folded her arms. "It doesn't matter as long as we can have some gal-pal adventures."

"That's the whole idea. Giovanni is going to be with his mother, his Aunt Lucia, his cousins, and his cousins' kids, and who knows who else will want his and Marco's attention. Plus Anita and the kids."

"Where will you be staying?" Rachael leaned into her camera.

"Rosevita knows Giovanni and I are basically living together. Remember she spent years living in New York. Nothing can shock her."

"And Aunt Lucia? Will she have something to say about it?" Nina asked out of curiosity. "Italian families can be tight and have a lot of influence on each other."

"True. Lucia is her sister-in-law, so I don't know the pecking order in this situation, although I know she's a few years older. She was married to Giovanni's father's brother." She took a deep breath. "I guess we'll have to see how judgey they are." Frankie rolled her eyes. "My folks will be staying at an Airbnb from the twenty-third to the twenty-sixth, and we know that *they* know, and that's who matters to me. Don't misunderstand me. I don't want to cause any strife in Giovanni's family, but as long as both our parents are okay with the arrangements, then *questo è tutto*. That's that!" Frankie stated.

"This is so exciting!" Amy's cheeks were getting rosier by the minute.

"So do you think your significant others would be on-board with this?" Frankie asked.

"I'm sure Richard would enjoy a few days of Italian gastronomy, and a peek at Pompeii and Herculaneum," Nina said.

Professor Amy chimed in, "Did you know it took only twenty-four hours for Mt. Vesuvius's eruption to bury Pompeii in pyroclastic material?" She nodded as if everyone knew that little tidbit of historic trivia.

"Pyro what?" Rachael asked.

"It's a combination of fluidized hot rock fragments and gases. The temperature can reach over six hundred degrees Celsius, or eleven hundred degrees Fahrenheit."

"Let's change the subject, please," Frankie urged and shuddered.

"But just so you know, the Italian government monitors the volcano's seismic activity twenty-four hours a day through the Vesuvius Observatory. We'll be alerted at least two weeks ahead should anything be of concern."

"Thank you, professor. That's a relief," Nina interrupted, knowing Amy could go on about anything scientific.

"Sorry," Amy said, blushing. If there was anyone who was enthusiastic about her work, it was Amy. It was all of them, actually, but she was the only one who could throw facts, figures, and mathematical formulas like Cy Young could throw a baseball. Fast and furious.

"Now, where were we?" Frankie looked down at her notes. "Okay, so the house will be available from December twenty-first to January third."

"There's a producer who I worked with a zillion years ago who lives in Milan now," Nina said. "He's been bugging me to visit. If he's available, I'll fly into Milan on the twenty-sixth, stay for two days, and take a train to Naples on the twenty-ninth. Italia Rail has a high-speed train. Takes about five hours, but I'll be able to see the countryside."

"Five hours doesn't seem like high-speed." Rachael pursed her lips.

"There've been times when it's taken me almost five hours to drive from Ridgewood to Midtown Manhattan, which is only twenty-four miles. And I can tell you, the view from the turnpike overpass ain't pretty," Nina replied.

"You've got a point," Rachael answered.

Frankie turned to Amy's face on the screen. "What say you?"

"I say I shall contact the head of my department and ask him if he would please reach out to someone in Geneva to get me a visitor's pass to the Hadron Collider."

"Perfect." Frankie was grinning. Two down, one more to go. "Rachael?"

"If you gals don't mind, I'd like to invite Randy. He's always fun, and he doesn't start rehearsals for the next play until first week of February."

"That'll give him a month to recover," Nina chortled.

"Ha. Ha. But you're right!" Rachael hooted. "We'll probably go to Rome first and then meet up with you guys."

"*Molto bene*! Then it's settled!" Frankie was delighted and relieved that the trip was coming together. It was important to have all the details nailed down way ahead of time before things got bananas at work. "Okay, so you guys check with *your* guys and give me a schedule."

"Right-o, Bossy Pants." Rachael saluted at her camera.

"I wish you guys wouldn't call me that. It makes me sound so . . ."

"Bossy!" Amy giggled. "And that's why we love you, Frankie. You take the thinking out of it."

"Glad to be of service." She gave a humble nod. "Let's recon in the next two weeks. We should be able to get good airfare if we reserve now."

"Right again," Nina said, and smiled.

"Alrighty! We shall be in touch! Love you guys!" Frankie hit the "leave meeting" button on her screen as the other women's voices echoed the same sentiment.

Frankie stretched and checked the time. Giovanni should be home shortly. Bandit was snoozing under the table. "The mambo tucker you out, little guy?" Frankie asked. He yawned and stretched one of his front paws. Sweet P. was as alert as ever. She had gotten over being skittish at the recurring sounds of sirens and horns blowing, but she remained vigilant.

Back at the restaurant, Giovanni and Marco were doing the end-of-the day true-up procedure of checking the register with the checks. There were always complimentary glasses of wine and desserts for regular customers, and it could be tedious to filter the comps from the totals, especially on a busy night. Once they were finished, Giovanni went upstairs to his old apartment, where he showered and changed before going to Frankie's. He never wanted to stink of grease or have his hair giving off whiffs of scampi. Never. He always wanted to be impeccable. But this wasn't because he sought attention. He was actually very shy. Big brother Marco was always the one in the spotlight, especially with the family—the firstborn son, and all. It never bothered Giovanni, and he often appreciated being in the shadow. Less pressure.

But that also made him less confident when it came to women, even though he was the more handsome of the two brothers. People had said that Giovanni looked like the movie star Raoul Bova, who played Marcello in *Under the Tuscan Sun*. Marcello takes Diane Lane's character, Frances, on a romantic jaunt, only to disappoint her in the end. It was one of the reasons Frankie had been insecure in the beginning. Giovanni was almost too handsome. She finally had to separate the men's similar looks of black wavy hair and steel blue eyes from the character in the movie. But when she was on the cruise, she discovered Giovanni had a fiancée in Italy. The two of them had never even dated, but the idea that Giovanni hadn't mentioned his girlfriend took Frankie by surprise when she found out. Not that it was any of her business at the time, either, but her secret crush was temporarily crushed until Giovanni broke off the engagement and explained it had been one of those "arrangements" that he never really approved of; he had just wanted to make his mother and father happy. But Giovanni wasn't happy, and neither was his fiancée, and as two modern adults, they went their separate ways rather than spend a lifetime with someone they didn't love. When Frankie returned after her cruise, with her lovelorn emotions slightly bruised, Giovanni surprised her with flowers and an invitation to dinner at the restaurant. At first Frankie thought it was simply a friendly gesture, until Giovanni made it clear that it was a date when he appeared immaculately dressed and seated himself next to her.

Granted, like in most new relationships, Frankie and Giovanni had their missteps when they first dated, but Giovanni was patient. And kind.

When Frankie went missing while the girls were in Tahoe, Giovanni went to great lengths to get to the other side of the country to help find her. He immediately enlisted the help of Richard and Peter, with Mateo providing the necessary transportation to get them there. Mateo was traveling across the country doing charity work for Share a Meal and had access to a private plane. When he got the call from Giovanni that Frankie was missing, he offered to have the plane fly the men out west. That was when Frankie was certain Giovanni loved her. She already knew she was in love with him.

Before they had become an item, Giovanni looked after her cat Bandit when Frankie traveled for business. Giovanni would also leave a dish in the refrigerator so Frankie would have something to eat when she got home. And that was all before the first date. But it was his affection for Bandit that sealed the deal for Frankie. *Love me, love my cat.*

Giovanni finished his shower, shaved, and splashed on Creed Aventus cologne. Then he put on one of his pressed white shirts and a pair of jeans. He slicked back his hair, the way Frankie liked it, and slipped into his Mauri loafers, without socks. Frankie would tease that it was his "uniform." Giovanni would joke back and say it saved time; it required no thinking or planning ahead. But when it came to special occasions, his wardrobe was a completely different story. His suits were tailored from fine fabric. It was an unspoken expectation in his family to be impeccably dressed.

He stopped at a local greengrocer market on his way over to Frankie's and picked up a bouquet of fresh flowers. That was one of the many things you could count on in New York: a deli or greengrocer within walking distance, and open twenty-four-seven.

Bandit's ears perked up. Just like he did with Frankie, the cat knew when Giovanni was entering the building. Frankie smiled at her furry security guard. "Daddy's home." She had no hesitation referring to Giovanni as Bandit's daddy. Sweet P. was still a little dubious of her new parent and sat at attention, waiting for the sound of keys in the lock. Frankie walked to the door and greeted Giovanni with a big kiss and nuzzled his neck. "You smell so good," she murmured. Giovanni pulled her close and kissed her on the top of her head.

"*Cara*, how did your phone call go?"

"Fan-tas-tic!" Frankie happily answered. "Everyone is on-board. We just have to get the schedules together." She grabbed his hand and walked him over to the sofa. "Can I get you anything?"

"Me? No." He took a seat and pulled her on his lap. "Tell me everything."

Frankie ticked off the names and approximate dates. She looked up at him. "Are you sure it's going to be alright if you and I share a room at your mother's house?"

"Of course. Why?" Giovanni questioned, holding her at arm's length.

"Tradition. We're not married."

"*Cara*, I broke tradition when I ended my engagement. Everyone must live the life they choose. And sometimes comes consequences. But no one is going to tell me who to love. *Questo è tutto*."

Frankie snorted. "That's exactly what I said to the girls."

"*Sì*? In Italiano?"

"*Sì*! I have to practice! But seriously, if it's going to be an issue, I can sleep on the sofa."

"Let's not worry about it now." Giovanni ran his fingers through her hair.

Frankie pulled Giovanni closer and nuzzled his neck again. "You smell delicious."

"What? Better than my bolognese?" Giovanni feigned an insult.

"Sorry, pal, but yes. Although I do love your bucatini all'Amatriciana." She giggled.

Chapter 2

Boston
Amy

Amy was all atwitter. She really didn't care where they went. It was always a magical and exciting experience being with the girls. Except for the little brouhaha on the ship two years ago . . .

At the beginning of the cruise, an elegant woman named Marilyn had been seated with them during dinner. She was several years older, refined, and exquisitely dressed. After a few days on the high seas, Marilyn hinted that she had met a nice gentleman but said very little else. The foursome was concerned that a woman of Marilyn's means might be an easy target for a gold-digging lothario. Marilyn was too nice to be taken advantage of, so the girls felt compelled to find out who this Romeo might be.

One evening, Amy and Nina stealthily followed Marilyn to one of the promenades and hid behind a stack of lounge chairs. When the mystery man arrived on the deck, Amy was shocked. Stunned. She had been having "Dad sightings" for the entire trip, but she thought it was just her conscience menacing her for leaving her father alone for the holidays. Now, here he was in the flesh! As she tried to reposition herself to get a better look, she tripped and sent the stack of lounge chairs crashing onto the deck. After the gasps of surprise subsided, Amy confronted her father.

"What are you doing here?"

William Blanchard, just as shocked to see his daughter, explained his golf outing in Palm Beach was cancelled, and since he was already in South Florida, he decided to go on a cruise. The explanation was followed by apologies to Marilyn from Amy and Nina. "We wanted to be sure you were safe." The apology was accepted, and the ruckus was now a favorite joke among the group, especially at Marilyn and William's wedding a year later.

Amy was looking through her scrapbook. Scrapbooking was one of her hobbies. She liked taking pictures, but felt putting them in an album evoked a stronger memory sensation than looking at an electronic image on your phone. There was something about the tactile nature of the photo, turning the pages of a book. It was a physical record of the experience. You were using more than one of your senses. A finger swipe on a screen did not convey the same sensation. She knew that to be true, or at least that was one of the things she was working on at MIT. The more senses you use, the more vibrant the experience. *Well, duh. That's why so many people are willing to plunk down over a thousand dollars for virtual reality glasses.* Her concern was that people were getting further and further away from reality, and it was causing so much angst, depression, and anxiety. She sighed and picked up her cat, Gimpy. "I'd rather snuggle with you any day." Blinky looked up from his perch as if to say, "My turn!"

"Yes, you too." She placed Gimpy on the floor and gave Blinky some mush. "So what do you think about me going to see the Hadron Collider?" she asked her kitty. He just stared blankly at her. "Alright. How about Italy?" His ears perked up at the word *Italy*. "That got your attention! Maybe it's all the pizza we eat," Amy giggled.

Peter was on his way home. It occurred to Amy that she agreed to go to Europe without conferring with him. She shrugged and looked down at her fur family. "Well, I'm going anyway. What was it that Frankie said? *Questo è tutto*?" If they could, Blinky and Gimpy would have shrugged their shoulders. Italian wasn't part of their human lexicon. They didn't even like pizza. Just the anchovies.

Amy remembered the banter Peter had with Giovanni about who made the best pizza. Giovanni was horrified at Peter's suggestion and told him he was crazy.

"Boston? Pizza? Pazzo!" Giovanni made the familiar gesture of his thumb touching his pointer and middle fingers and shaking his wrist. "Napoli! It's-a where they invented the pizza!"

Recalling that conversation gave Amy an idea as to how she was going to present the trip to Peter: *Giovanni wants us to be his guest at a villa in Salerno, and he will take you to the best pizzeria in all of Southern Italy.* It wasn't the complete truth, but she was sure she and Frankie could convince Giovanni that it was his idea and Peter would go for it. None would be the wiser. She leaned over and whispered to her whiskered friends, "Don't tell Peter." Blinky looked at her wide-eyed, and Amy pretended that he was reacting to her plan. "What do you mean, what's in it for you?"

Peter's keys clanged against the door. "What's in it for who? Or should I say whom?" he smiled.

"Oh, just a little convo I was having with the kids." She walked over and gave him a hug.

"Want to clue me in?" Peter asked, as he set his briefcase down on the bench in the entryway.

"I do, but in a bit. Let's decide on supper first." She paused. "How about pizza?"

"Sure. With a Caesar salad on the side?"

"Absolutely." Amy's wheels were turning. She'd remind Peter of his conversation with Giovanni and then segue into the trip. Brilliant. And, for all intents and purposes, she was.

"I'll go wash off the dust. Be right back," Peter said, as he headed up the stairs to the bedroom.

"Still under construction?" Amy called out.

"Yes. It's taking forever. I hope they're finished before the end of the year. Tax season will be a bear if we have to work under those conditions."

Peter was a crackerjack accountant and was making boatloads of money for his firm, but when he asked to be made a partner, his bosses decided to "keep it in the family." That was when he considered starting his own firm with the legal advice of Richard.

"Do not sign a non-compete clause. That's rule number one," Richard had told him.

Peter didn't think they would ask such a thing. "How would they expect me to make a living?" Peter reasoned.

"They don't care what happens to you after you leave the firm. It's an ugly truth," Richard stated.

"That doesn't seem fair." Peter was used to things being fair and exact. Numbers were exact. A nine was a nine was a nine, unless you cheated, but that was not Peter's way of conducting business.

"Fair? Where have you been living?" Richard chuckled. "Don't take it personally."

"But I brought a lot of business into the company."

"And they don't care about that, either, unless you take those accounts with you," Richard warned. "It can get very tricky."

Peter trusted Richard's counsel. Peter was a numbers guy. His only experience with legal matters was if a client was being audited by the IRS, which was rare—he was accurate, thorough, and careful.

"What do you suggest I do?" Peter asked.

"Can you go without a salary for a year?"

"Probably, but why would I want to do that?" Peter asked innocently.

"Then you can sign a one-year non-compete clause and then steal your clients," Richard chuckled.

"Can I do that?" Peter asked in wonderment.

"You can if the exit contract is worded correctly."

"Can *you* do that?" Peter inquired.

"I'll do my best to advise you," Richard reassured him. "Another idea would be to try to buy your way into the partnership. They may want to keep it in the family, but lots of families can be encouraged with a chunk of change," Richard continued. "I assume you have a good idea as to what the firm is worth in annual billing."

"Yes."

"Can you offer them a twenty percent buy-in?"

Peter considered. "Maybe fifteen."

"Mull it over. You have some options," Richard suggested.

As per Richard's advice, Peter approached the senior member of the family and offered a ten percent buy-in. *Start low. Aim high.* The patriarch of the family was quite impressed with Peter's confident proposal and made the deal with him, much to his sons' dismay. Peter would own ten percent of the business. Truth be told, Peter was the one doing all the heavy lifting at the company. The only heavy lifting the sons were doing was hoisting their Baccarat crystal tumblers filled with single malt scotch.

Richard stepped in to help reorganize the LLC, making sure Peter was protected should things go south. He would not be liable for any legal fees should someone bring a suit against the company if it wasn't one of his direct customers. Everyone was responsible for their own client list.

With the infusion of Peter's investment, the firm needed to

remodel their existing offices. Peter would now have a bigger office and a bigger space for his assistant. Hence the construction.

Amy heard the shower running and sent a quick text to Frankie:

Having pizza tonight. Will call. Tell Gio I'll be calling and he can invite Peter to do a pizza tour.

Frankie responded immediately:

You are brilliant, my friend.

Amy phoned the local pizzeria and placed the order. Amy looked down at her whiskered friend and saw Blinky licking his lips. "Of course, I'll get anchovies on the side!"

The woman on the other end of the call asked, "Excuse me? I didn't quite get that."

Amy giggled. "Sorry. I was talking to my cat. He loves anchovies."

"Yeah, okay, whatever. You wanted them on the side?"

"Yes, please," Amy answered in her normal perky tone. The woman gave Amy the total and said it would be about forty minutes.

A short while later, Peter hopped down the stairs, freshly showered and wearing a tracksuit.

"Going for a run?" Amy asked. "Pizza will be here in about a half hour."

"Nah. Just wanted to get into something less restrictive. As you would say, 'comfy.'" Peter let out a long, relaxed sigh and headed toward the fridge. He pulled out a Molson, and then poured it into a frosted glass from the freezer. "Would you like beer or wine with your pizza?"

Amy glanced at the crisp, chilled beverage in Peter's hand. "That looks refreshing. I think I'll have one of those."

Peter repeated the steps. Beer, glass, pour.

"You okay?" Peter sensed Amy was a little more wiggly than usual.

"Me? Yes! Why?" Amy knew she was starting to blush. She could feel the heat moving up her cheeks.

"You may no longer have purple hair, but I know when something is going on in that head of yours." Peter grinned.

"Just thinking about pizza." She batted her eyes innocently. "Oh, hey, I have an idea! When the pizza gets here, let's FaceTime Frankie and Gio. You can show him the best pizza in Boston!"

"You can be very amusing," Peter laughed, tussling her chestnut-brown hair streaked with golden highlights. "It's funny. When I first met you, I never thought you could be my type. Purple hair, black horn-rimmed glasses, and goofy clothes."

"Goofy?" Amy put her hands on her hips, pretending to be annoyed. "I'll have you know that I was considered one of the more fashionable people at Stanford."

Peter cleared his throat and smirked. He leaned against the kitchen counter. "Do you really think that's an accolade worth mentioning?" He knew he was getting her goat. "Stanford isn't exactly known for its couture." He cringed, expecting her to give him a friendly smack on the arm.

"Precisely. Ergo I went through an entire makeover." She curtsied in her palazzo pants.

Peter looked down at her feet. "But you couldn't give up the combat boots." This time he raised both his arms in jest to shield his face.

"These are Tory Burch, Mr. Smarty Pants." She lifted her right heel, revealing the double-T, crocodile-embossed pattern.

Peter placed his thumb and forefinger under her chin. "You know I'm teasing, right?" He kissed her on the nose.

"Of course." Amy blushed.

The doorbell interrupted their banter, and Gimpy and Blinky sat at attention. They could smell the anchovies from several yards away.

Peter paid the delivery guy while Amy got plates, forks, knives, and napkins. She stifled a giggle. She knew Giovanni would bust Peter's chops about eating pizza with a knife and fork. She could hear Giovanni instructing Peter, "You fold-a the pizza down-a the middle, like-a so." Amy thought it was cute that Giovanni would slip back into a noticeable heavy accent when he was excited.

Peter pulled out a chair for Amy as Gimpy and Blinky looked on, their heads bobbing left and right as Peter passed the anchovies. Amy took one of the small fish and cut it up into several pieces, put them on a plate, and placed it on the floor. If cats could applaud, they would have.

Amy and Peter clinked glasses. *"Cent'anni!"* Amy proclaimed. It was an Italian toast, when translated meant *One hundred years!*

"Oh! Let's call Frankie and Giovanni, and you can show him how good our pizza is. Looks. Whatever." Amy was animated.

Peter gave her an odd look. "Okay. If you say so, but we can't do a taste test over the phone."

"Well, duh." Amy twisted her mouth. "Come on. You can taunt him."

"Me? Taunt?" Peter gave her another odd look. He wasn't the taunting type.

"Oh, Peter." Amy cocked her head. "Don't you want to at least tease Giovanni about pizza?"

"Not really, but you seem to be keen on it." Peter looked at her suspiciously.

"If you must know, I spoke with Frankie today, and she reminded me about your ongoing pizza feud."

"Oh, I see." He closed one eye and examined her with the other. "Are the two of you up to something?"

"Me?" Amy placed both her hands on her heart. She was a terrible liar.

"Alright, professor. I'll get to the bottom of this deep-dish pizza challenge." He held out his hand for Amy to give him her phone.

Amy bit her lip in anticipation. Their plan was working. He opened the FaceTime app and hit the button that said *Frankie*.

Frankie answered. "Peter! Is everything alright?" She figured it was, but played along just in case there was a misfire in their scheme.

"Everything is just fine, thanks." Peter was giving Amy a suspicious look. "And you?"

"Couldn't be better. What's up?" Frankie kept her cool.

"Amy suggested we have a pizza smackdown, but obviously we can't do that over the phone." Peter smirked.

"I have just the person you need to speak to." Frankie turned the phone over to Giovanni.

"Pietro! *Come stai?*" Giovanni's big smile filled the screen.

"*Molto bono*," Peter answered, which made Giovanni laugh.

"*Molto bene*! But at least-a you try," Giovanni said. "What's-a this about pizza?"

"I have no idea, except Amy insisted I call you so I could show you what the best pizza looks like." Peter grinned.

Giovanni laughed again. "This is-a no contest. I'll make a deal with you. You come to Italy, and I bring you to the best pizzeria in all of Campania."

"And how do you suppose we do that?" Peter asked innocently.

"You and Amy come to Salerno for New Year's. I have a house you can stay at-a no charge."

"Seriously?" Peter asked.

"*Sì*. Very seriously. I am exchanging my apartment for a house in Baronissi for all my friends to visit with me."

"Sounds interesting," Peter replied.

"*Sì*. They are friends of my cousin in Salerno. They work at the university with him. They wanna spend New Year's at-a Times-a Square. So I offer them my apartment and they offer their house."

Amy could barely hold it together. She leaned her head toward the phone so she could see Giovanni's face. "A house? In Baronissi?"

"*Sì*. A few kilometers from my family. It's very convenient to Sorrento, Amalfi, Positano." He paused, waiting for it to sink in. "So, you come?"

Peter turned to Amy and chuckled. "Did you know about this?"

Once again, Amy could not fib. "Kinda. Sorta."

"That's a very generous offer. I am going to have to talk it over with Amy." He shook his head. "As if she would say no."

Amy crossed her fingers on both hands and looked up with those big round eyes. "Pretty please?" Amy was going, whether Peter said yes or no. She simply wanted him to decide whether or not *he* wanted to go. She just wasn't telling him.

"Sounds like a wonderful opportunity." Peter grinned.

Amy considered mentioning her side trip to Geneva, but thought it would be better if she had the visitor's permit in hand first. This way, it would be very difficult for Peter to object. Meanwhile, she was bouncing up and down. "Real pizza!" Blinky and Gimpy had already made haste away from the action. When Amy got excited, she could throw off seismic-type tremors across the floor.

"I need to bring Amy back down to earth. So, I guess we'll be spending New Year's Eve together, again," Peter chuckled. "But please promise we won't have to cook dinner for sixty people this time."

"Absolutely not. Only fifty!" Giovanni teased.

"Funny. I guess I'll leave the rest of the planning up to you, Frankie, and Amy." He grinned as Amy danced in circles around him.

"*Molto bene*! See you in a couple of months. *Ciao*, Pietro!"

"*Ciao!*" Peter replied, and ended the call. He turned to Amy. "How long have you been planning this coup?"

Amy stopped dancing and shuffled her feet. "Not long." Then she jumped up and gave Peter a big hug. "This is going to be fantastic!"

"I am going to leave all the travel arrangements up to you." He poked her nose with his finger.

"There is not a problem I cannot solve." Amy was exaggerating slightly, but Peter knew she was close to the truth. "I think we're going to have to reheat this." She pointed to the cold pizza.

"Thinking about real, authentic pizza makes me *not* want to eat this." Peter frowned.

"Don't let Giovanni hear you say that!" Amy blurted out. She gave him another squeeze, hoping it would keep her away from the subject of Geneva. At least for now.

Chapter 3

Upper Montclair
Nina

Nina was rummaging through her basket of bits of paper, business cards, and receipts. Winston, her big Bernese mountain dog, sat with his snout on top of his big puffy paws, his eyes following every move Nina made. Every so often he would let out a doggie sigh. "What's up, Win?" Nina looked down at him. "Yeah, I know. I should go through the basket at least once a month." She pulled out a grocery receipt from the year before. "Geez. At least once a year!" Winston agreed with another groaning sigh. "No comment from the peanut gallery." Nina stroked the soft fur on the top of his head.

At that point, she decided to get a large trash bag and clean out the basket once and for all. "I know Jordan's info is somewhere in here." She dumped the year-old scraps of paper on the floor, sat down next to Winston, and began combing through the mess, separating cards from receipts and various miscellaneous notes, unsure what most of them were. There was a cocktail napkin with the name *James* and a phone number. "Who do you suppose James is?" she asked her pooch.

"Someone I met in a bar?" Winston yapped in response. "Must not have been very impressive, huh?" Another short yap from her pal.

She was almost finished separating the scraps when she found the business card she had been searching for. "Ta-da!" Nina gave Winston another pat. The card read:

Jordan Pleasance
Producer
Mobile: 39-02-555-100
Email: RP@Rproductions.com
Milano, Italy

She checked the time. It was almost four in the morning in Milan. She got up from the floor, opened her laptop, and fired up her email.

Ten years ago, Nina worked with Jordan on an indie film called *A Distant Memory*. It was the story about a woman who had been in a coma for a decade. Much to everyone's surprise, the woman woke out of her deep sleep but had no memory of who she was. Part of the woman's treatment was hypnotherapy and regression therapy. Nina played the younger version of the woman, seen during a series of flashbacks. The movie was critically acclaimed but not a box office smash. Jordan appreciated Nina's notes during the filming and made her promise to keep in touch. They exchanged holiday cards every year and occasional emails, but Jordan had moved to Italy, and Nina moved back to the New York Metro area. Even though they hadn't seen each other in years, Jordan always ended his correspondence with "When are you coming to Italy?"

Nina scrolled through her deleted emails, looking for one of Jordan's previous invitations asking her that same question. The file folder was brimming with over two thousand discarded emails. "Remind me to clear this out regularly, as well," she said, looking down at the pooch. "At least I use a basket. From what Amy told me, she just throws everything into a brown paper bag. No wonder we get along so well. But don't you dare tell anyone I'm disorganized when it comes to personal stuff."

Winston yapped a response.

Nina got up and went into the kitchen to fetch him a treat. "Will this help keep my secret?" She tossed it at him, and he caught it in his mouth. She returned to her voluminous email folder and sorted the messages by *From*. Several from Jordan popped up. She opened the most recent one that begged the question again. It was from six months prior. "I really need to stay on top of these things," she muttered to herself. She hit *Reply*:

> Hey Jordan! I am going to take you up on your offer if you're around December 26th. LMK. XOXO Nina

She hit *Send* and crossed her fingers that she'd get a positive response. Her next move was to tell Richard in a way that made it sound like she was asking him if he wanted to go. Like Amy, she was heading to Italy with or without him. Over the past three years, Nina understood what the meaning of friendship was, and she was resolute in maintaining her relationships with her gal-pals. Granted, they were different in many ways, but they were glued together when it came to generosity, integrity, loyalty, kindness, and talking to their pets as if they were people, because as far as these women are concerned, pets are people, too! The wacky fun was just a bonus.

It was almost ten o'clock when her phone rang. It was Richard. They usually checked in with each other around the same time, unless one of them was out and about.

"Good evening, Mr. Cooper." Nina smiled into the phone.

"Good evening to you, Ms. Hunter. What trouble have you managed to avoid today?"

"Now that you mention it, I have some trouble lined up."

"Uh-oh. Will you need bail money?" he joked.

"I'm not sure yet, but if I do, it will have to be in euros."

"Euros?" Richard asked curiously.

"Yep! If you recall, we all agreed to get together again for New Year's, correct?"

"Correct. Let me guess. It's Europe," Richard chuckled.

"Wow. I can't get anything past you, can I?" Nina said playfully.

"I'm afraid not," Richard replied. "So, tell me. What have you fine women devised to levy on us unsuspecting men?"

"Well, since you asked, it was actually Giovanni's suggestion. He and Marco are going to close the restaurant for ten days and spend it with their mother in Italy."

"Christmas in Italy must be quite festive," Richard acknowledged.

"Especially if Marco and Giovanni have anything to do with it," Nina laughed. "But this is what I would like to propose: I would like to meet up with Jordan Pleasance, a producer I worked with years ago. He lives in Milan and keeps asking me to visit. I thought I'd go there first and then meet up with everyone in Salerno."

"Am I included in the 'everyone' part?" Richard asked.

"Of course you are!" Nina exclaimed. "You can come with me to Milan if you want to, if Jordan is available."

"Are you sure I wouldn't be horning in on any business, monkey or otherwise?" Richard joked.

"Ha! No monkey business, but I think the podcast thing is getting a little stale. At least for me."

"Really?" Richard was surprised. "I thought you enjoyed it. Plus, it's incredibly popular."

"I do enjoy it, but my creative soul is wanting something

more. Hashing out topics is stimulating, but I'd like to create something new."

"So, is this a job interview?" Richard asked.

"No, but Jordan always has something on the back burner. Maybe we can collaborate. I dunno. I just want to see how far I can stretch my imagination should there be another opportunity."

"You miss writing, don't you?" Richard was referring to the sitcom she and her colleague Owen Masters wrote together for two years. The network cancelled it due to a turnover in executive management, which led to Nina developing a podcast.

"Well . . . it's been a while since I got the juices flowing. I'm beginning to feel like I may be falling into a rut."

"You? Hardly." Richard knew Nina to be a person who pushed and pulled every ounce of inspiration from her fertile mind. "If I recall, you and Frankie talked about writing a book about the scenes beyond the camera."

"There is nothing I can say that hasn't been said before. Plus, I don't want to come off as an out-of-work, bitter actress."

"I am certain you wouldn't come off that way," Richard reassured her.

"Let me tell you, it would be very hard for me *not* to sound that way."

"I never thought you were bitter," Richard remarked.

"I'm not. Really. I had a great run. But the truth can be ugly."

"Perhaps you could be an inspiration to other actors?"

"My advice would be: Go to law school and become an entertainment lawyer."

Richard hooted. "That happens to be a very good idea. Law school isn't fun, or easy by any means, and there is no guarantee that you'll be successful. However, there are a lot of opportunities in the field of entertainment, and a lot of money to be made."

"Exactly!" Nina whooped. "I wish I had done it when it was a fleeting thought in my head."

"Was it really?" Richard sounded surprised again.

"Actually, yes. After being bounced around, I began looking into law schools in L.A. Then I had a chat with my lawyer about it, and he told me I'd hate law school and should find a rich husband instead."

"That's a little narrow-minded," Richard said.

"Ya think? Not to mention a few other adjectives," Nina huffed.

"I hope you fired him after that," Richard stated.

"No. I started dating him," Nina chortled.

"You're not serious, are you?"

"No, but I responded with 'Oh, you mean someone like you?' I think I shocked him. I was being facetious, but he was too dense to get the joke. He was short, fat, and bald, and I wouldn't have gone out with him if he held a gun to my head."

"A dense lawyer?" Richard mused.

"You must know a few," Nina volleyed.

"Dense? More like uptight."

"Same thing."

"What do you mean, 'same thing'?"

"People who are uptight have difficulty hearing what other people are saying. They shut down."

"Ah. I think I get where you're coming from. But let's get back to the trip. When do you want to go?" Richard asked.

"I sent Jordan an email, so I hope to hear from him in a day or so. If he's good with it, I'll fly over on the twenty-sixth, spend two days, maybe three, and then take the train to Naples."

"You mentioned this was Giovanni's idea?" Richard asked.

"Yes, and he has a house for us to stay in for free. As in F.R.E.E. He's arranging for a swap with two professors at the Baronissi campus of the University of Salerno. It's a few kilometers from his family's house, and it's a great location for day trips to Amalfi, Sorrento, Positano, and Capri."

"It's not far from Pompeii, if I'm recalling my geography correctly," Richard mused.

"Funny. I thought you might be interested in going there."

"Hmmm. You know me too well," Richard said.

"A lucky guess," Nina added.

"I think this sounds like a superb way to spend part of the holidays," Richard said in agreement.

"Oh, goodie! I was hoping you'd want to go. You know I had to commit to the girls."

"Of course you did. It's become a tradition." Richard cleared his throat. "We won't have to do any kind of cooking?"

Nina laughed. "I'm sure Giovanni's family will be doing most of that. Plus, we'll want to go on a few tours. Olive farms. Mozzarella factories. Pizza."

"Let's not forget the wine," Richard added.

"Never!" Nina shouted, startling Winston. He jerked his head and then realized it was Nina being enthusiastic.

"Alright, Nina Hunter. I expect to hear from you as soon as you know what the plan is."

"You shall," Nina cooed. "Thanks for being such a good boyfriend."

Richard laughed. "Boyfriend? Do people still refer to their significant other in such a way?"

"Now you're sounding like a lawyer and *not* my boyfriend," Nina chuckled. "I gotta go let Winston out. We'll talk more about this tomorrow. Love you!"

"Love you, too!" Richard signed off.

Chapter 4

Rachael paced the floor. Her son Ryan was at his father's house for a few days. Ryan was in high school now and wanted to spend more time with his dad and playing sports. Rachael had no issues with it, as long as Vickie, the newest Mrs. Newmark, was treating Ryan well. Like most split families with visitation, there was a lot of tension in the beginning, not to mention Rachael's rage over her now-ex-husband's extramarital affair. In retrospect, it was a blessing. She and Greg fought constantly, which is what he blamed his infidelity on. Too much conflict. But that was no justification as far as Rachael was concerned. When you have an issue with your mate, you deal with it together. But Greg decided it was easier to cheat than to face Rachael with his concerns. Rachael could be quite volatile, but it was still no excuse.

There had been rumors of Greg's indiscretions, but Rachael did not want to believe them, until she decided to follow him one late afternoon. She waited in the parking lot of the "No-Tell Motel"—a euphemism for a cheap place for lovers to meet. After Rachael sat patiently in the dark for two hours, Greg appeared with another woman. She couldn't deny the truth when she saw it with her own eyes, and then she exploded. As Greg walked the woman to her car, Rachael revved the engine of her SUV. She slowly inched her way toward him until he could see who was behind the wheel. The stunned look on his face screamed *Guilty!* mixed with fear as Rachael came closer, picking up speed. She swerved at the last minute, but not before Greg jumped out of the way and landed in a tangle of shrubbery.

"You are dead meat!" Rachael screamed at him. "Dead!" The sound of the squealing tires and her screeches brought people to their windows, and some opened their doors.

"He's a lying, cheating, piece of scum!" Rachael continued her rant. Much to her surprise, most of the onlookers hooted and applauded. One person shouted, "Take him for all he's got!"

Unfortunately, Greg had mangled Rachael's finances, but that didn't stop her from soaping his car with:

> Tell your girlfriend I cleaned out what was left in the bank. Now you're really broke.

But she wasn't finished with him. She put a sign on her lawn that said:

CHEATING HUSBAND YARD SALE
EVERYTHING MUST GO, ESPECIALLY HIM.

The divorce proceedings went quickly. Greg tried to use the excuse that she tried to kill him, but there was no proof and no witnesses except for the girlfriend, and she wasn't about to admit that she was with him at a motel. Greg then tried to squelch the monetary judgment claiming Rachael wiped out their bank account, but that didn't stop a judge from issuing a hefty alimony and child support payment every month. There was no wiggle room for Greg. No negotiations. Done. Over. Bye-Bye.

But not long after the final divorce decree, Rachael went on a mission seeking validation, something many women do when they've been cheated on. She visited dating sites and mixers, but the losers she met only drove her further into believing she wasn't worthy of a good partner. Many men were simply looking for a one-night stand, maybe two, and she was constantly disappointed, so she was excited when her friends decided to do the unthinkable and go on a singles' cruise. At least there would be a lot to do besides looking for Mr. Perfect, Prince Charming, or a Knight in Shining Armor. (*Psst . . . he doesn't exist.*)

During the cruise, Rachael met a famous dancer and instructor named Henry Dugan, who was at least a decade her senior. They bonded when Rachael took a few of his classes on the ship. Henry was involved in a foundation called Let's Dance that provided therapeutic dancing to children with special needs. They became lovers, and Rachael became part of the foundation, but things got a little murky between them, and Henry ended the relationship. However, for the first time in her life, Rachael did not place the blame on herself or whatever she thought her failings were. They had an amicable breakup. She was content. She had friends. She had a successful dance instructor business. She no longer had to prove herself to anybody, especially herself.

She glided her way into her home office and picked up her business phone and made a call.

"Randy Wheeler at your service. Just ask!"

"You don't always answer your phone like that, do you?" Rachael asked.

"It all depends on who is on the other line, dearie," he fussed. "And to what do I owe the pleasure?"

"Do you have holiday plans?" Rachael asked.

"That would be contingent upon whether or not they

sound like fun. What is going on in that tricky little head of yours?"

"My crew is planning our annual holiday trip. This year, it's Italy."

"*Molto bene*!" Randy cried.

"Is that the extent of your Italian or do you know more?"

"*Un pochino*," he answered.

"How little?" Rachael inquired.

"*Molto pochino*."

"So that *is* the extent of it, correct?" Rachael asked.

"*Correctomundo*."

"I don't think that's really Italian," Rachael huffed.

"Oh, so, whatev. But does that mean you're inviting me?" Randy perked up.

"Giovanni secured a house in Baronissi, just outside of Salerno. They're going to spend the holidays with his family, and he is exchanging his apartment in the city with some professor's house in Baronissi."

"Sounds divine," Randy cooed. "Where is Baronissi, anyway?"

"Just northwest of the city of Salerno. According to Giovanni, it's a great location for day trips to the Amalfi Coast."

"Now you're talking, sister!" Randy cheered.

"I thought we could fly into Rome first or maybe Florence for a day or so, then head down to the villa."

"Oh, darling, that's a marvelous plan. Where should we go first?"

"I've never been to Florence," Rachael answered.

"Me neither. What do you think? Two days in Florence and then two days in Rome?"

"We should plan to get to Salerno on the thirtieth." She was counting backwards. "That means we'd have to leave on the twenty-sixth. But I'm sure Frankie has a few things in mind, so we'll have to play it by ear."

"That's perfect. I like being flexible. My folks are coming

to New York to see the tree, and we planned on doing all the touristy things."

"I don't want you to cut your visit with your family short," Rachael replied.

"Believe me, we'll all need a break after a week of holiday cheer," Randy sighed.

"I thought you made amends with them," Rachael said.

"Yes. They've finally accepted my lifestyle, so the holidays are actually enjoyable now. I just can't take all the tourists and the crowds."

"Me neither. Although I don't think we'll be able to avoid them in Italy."

"At least it will be a different crowd in a different place."

"Good point! So, you're on?" Rachael asked rhetorically. She knew Randy would be up for almost anything she devised.

"Darling, you know I am! I have one more show on Christmas Eve. I got tickets for my parents, so they'll be able to see me in action."

"I don't know if watching you in action is the best plan," Rachael mocked.

"Aren't you funny. You oughta be in showbiz."

"I am kinda funny," Rachael defended herself.

"True. You always put on a good show. On or off stage!" Randy quipped back.

"Well then we should take our show on the road!" Rachael exclaimed. "Let me know when you want to fly out and where you want to go first, and I'll make the rez."

"Sounds fabulous!" Randy was thrilled to be invited to the reunion. It was hard to believe it had been almost a year since he first met all of them when they visited Lake Tahoe. He and Rachael became fast friends when she needed a cohort in her mischief of planting mistletoe and reindeer outside of the other women's rooms. She hadn't committed to joining them at first, but then showed up unannounced. Kinda. She kept leaving hints until she discovered Frankie had gone missing and Rachael went full force on a mission to help find her.

The annual girls' trip was more than just a reunion. It was the reuniting of a long, deep friendship that had temporarily gone off the rails. Misunderstandings can be damaging. It took a little time for Rachael to realize that in order for people to know what's going on in your life, you had to tell them. You couldn't expect them to miraculously figure it out. There's no such thing as "magic thinking." Perhaps there is when you want to try to "make a wish," but not when it comes to expressing your feelings. It's not fair to be angry with someone who hasn't been able to read your mind. Rachael had come to that realization with the help of Randy, who had never met any of them prior to their trip. He offered a fresh new perspective, which Rachael was grateful for. She was also grateful she found a fellow mischief-maker and was thrilled he agreed to go to Italy.

Chapter 5

Preparations Underway

The big trip was now only a month away. The first item on Frankie's agenda was to find a kitty sitter. Anita filled in the year before when Giovanni made an emergency trip to Tahoe, but everyone would be in Italy.

As much as people were in close proximity in New York, most didn't know their neighbors who lived down the hall—unless you were in a rent-controlled or rent-stabilized building, where everyone stayed in the same apartment forever. If you were able to find an affordable apartment, you held on to it. Frankie scoffed at sitcoms where the characters lived in New York and had massive apartments but did not have jobs to afford them. With the exception of *Seinfeld,* where Jerry originally lived in a small studio, there were few others that resembled reality for anyone looking to be fiscally solvent living in the Big Apple.

Frankie started with three roommates, then moved to a smaller place with two roommates, and then another apartment where she shared it with only one. She was thirty-five before she was able to afford her own studio, which was over twenty-five hundred dollars a month—a steal for the neighborhood. "Rent poor" was a common situation among most people under forty. She could have commuted from her folks' house, but she wasn't about to be one of those adult children still living with their parents. There were many reasons to take that route, but Frankie wanted to prove to herself, more than anyone, that she could make it on her own. Most of the time, she was living paycheck to paycheck, occasionally scrounging in coat pockets for change to take the subway, but Frankie was capable of managing her funds. She always put a few dollars away for her annual vacations, and a dribble into her retirement account, especially since her company matched it. But whoever said you should have at least six months' worth of savings never started at the bottom and lived in New York City.

Oftentimes her cynicism would get the better of her, and she would have to stop, take a breath, count her blessings, and remind herself that she was exactly where she's supposed to be, even if it might be painful or scary. The challenges of living in the big city were ever present with traffic jams, subway issues, and cramped, crumbling sidewalks. There are a few choice neighborhoods that are pristine, but those come at a very high price. As in *very*. A two-bedroom apartment on the Upper East Side could start at eight thousand dollars a month, and that wasn't even the luxury buildings. Being a New Yorker requires grit, determination, and optimism. Yes, optimism that things would improve from year to year.

In Frankie's case, they had, but not without a lot of angst, heartbreak, and disappointment. What doesn't kill you makes you stronger, and Frankie was as much a heroine at this stage of her life. She recognized talent, nurtured it, and was given the opportunity to develop her own line of cookbooks in a very competitive market. The salary wasn't what most people outside of publishing would expect, but it's not an industry you get into for the money; you do it because of your love of books.

Television glamorized the publishing industry with narratives of unknown authors making a fabulous living writing in their chalets on a mountainside. Frankie would laugh out loud when the storyline also featured some other unrealistic publishing myth, like an author who turned in a manuscript and the book was on sale two weeks later. "Like that would ever happen!" she'd bark, sending Bandit scurrying to his hiding place in the closet. Most people were not aware that books are turned in to the publisher a year before they go to press. It is a seemingly never-ending process of editing, copyediting, cover treatments, jacket copy, and the long line of production requirements. They say you don't want to know how the sausage is made, and Frankie suspected that applied to most things, including books. Occasionally she would try to explain the intricacies of book publishing, but people's eyes would glaze over.

Frankie had been living in the city for over ten years. It didn't take long for her to realize her ideals and principles would be constantly challenged, and life is filled with many lessons. Frankie made it her mission to learn them, and hopefully not repeat them if they were bad.

When it came to men, however, she wasn't very good at figuring it out until Giovanni entered her life. Even in the beginning of their relationship, she was dubious. And scared witless. She didn't want her heart to be broken again. Ever. It was always surprising when people discovered Frankie could be insecure. Her sense of humor and gung-ho approach to everything exuded confidence, and she *was* confident that whatever the situation, it could go one way or the other. Good or bad. Most people would use extreme odds to evaluate the possibility of success. Frankie used the fifty-fifty quotient. Perhaps that was why she tackled assignments, ideas, and life with enthusiasm. She figured she had a fifty percent chance of succeeding.

Now she was facing a fifty-fifty chance of upsetting Giovanni's family. Even though Giovanni insisted they could share a room at his mother's house, Frankie had misgivings. It would be her first visit to the Lombardis, and she didn't want to offend anyone by coming across as a floozie. So, there were two things on her agenda: find a kitty sitter, and talk to Giovanni about sleeping arrangements.

Frankie phoned her veterinarian and asked if they could recommend someone who could come to her apartment twice a day to feed the cats and change the litter. She was happy to hear that one of the technicians was up to the task, and she lived just a few blocks away. One issue solved.

She kept going back and forth in her head about the sleeping arrangements. Giovanni was adamant, but Frankie knew in her gut that there could be trouble when it came to Aunt Lucia. Frankie had never met her but heard stories. Giovanni showed Frankie a recent photo of her and his mother together. The photo looked like it had been taken a hundred years ago, with Aunt Lucia wearing all black from head to toe, down to the big, ugly, clunky shoes. Frankie wondered about Aunt Lucia's footwear. *Wasn't Italy known for their beautiful shoemaking?* She chuckled and told Giovanni that Aunt Lucia reminded her of Strega Nona, a character in children's book about an old woman who uses magic to help the villagers. In some places, the book had been banned because of the use of magic, but it had a moral story about authority, punishment befitting the crime, and most of all, trust. But it wasn't the storyline that Frankie recalled as much as it was how Strega Nona looked. True, her attire was more colorful than Aunt Lucia's, but they wore the same long dress, apron, and babushka. But it was the shoes that really stood out. Frankie couldn't get past the shoes. She told Giovanni that she may not be able to contain her laughter, but Giovanni assured her that everyone was aware that Frankie likes to laugh. A lot. She was sure she'd be hysterical the entire trip. But in a good way.

The next hurdle was what to pack. Salerno could be chilly at night, with temperatures in the mid-fifties during the day. Sweaters, slacks, and light jackets were probably a good bet, plus something dressy for church.

After the opulent dinner of the seven fishes, everyone was expected to go to church. Midnight mass at Duomo di Salerno—the Cathedral of Salerno, which was dedicated to the Saints Matthew and Gregory the Great—was a requirement. Considered one of the most spectacular cathedrals, it dates back to the eleventh century, built by the Normans, and then finished in the Baroque design in the 1600s. The spectacular Christmas service emphasized brotherhood, sisterhood, kindness, compassion, and generosity, remembering the gifts from the Magi. It was about sharing.

Frankie took it as "a good sign" that Matthew translated to Mateo, her friend and author. Frankie always looked for signs as her inner compass. She even kept track of those funny coincidences in a journal and discovered she had almost one per day. She truly believed that it was a higher power validating her existence.

She pulled the closet doors open and inspected her wardrobe. At least she didn't have to dig out her summer clothes. The temperature wouldn't be too different than winter in New York. They would be away for almost two weeks, so she decided to pack five pairs of leggings, five sweaters, two blazers, two casual dresses, and two fancy-ish outfits. Boots, sneakers, and an ankle bootie with a two-inch heel would cover the footwear. She assumed she could do a load of laundry at Mrs. Lombardi's, but she wanted to be sure she wouldn't be imposing. She phoned Giovanni to get the all-clear.

"Frankie, *cara*, you will not be allowed to do laundry."

"Oh." Frankie didn't know what else to say, but then Giovanni continued.

"Mama would never let guests do their own laundry. She will do it for you."

"Absolutely not!" Frankie protested. She didn't want Giovanni's mother dealing with her underwear.

"Please, Frankie. Not to worry about it."

"If you say so." Frankie envisioned washing her undergarments in the sink. But then what? Hang them where? She sighed. It was something she'd deal with when the time came. She didn't know Mrs. Lombardi very well. By the time Frankie and Giovanni were considered a couple, Rosevita had moved back to Italy. She would visit, but spent most of the time with the grandchildren, and Frankie was always working. This would be a fine opportunity for the two women to get to know each other better. Another reason to consider sleeping on the sofa. Make a good impression.

Frankie began the process of organizing her clothes in piles on the floor. She wanted to make sure she wasn't taking too much. She didn't want to overpack, which was an easy thing for most people to do. At least women. Men? They could pack one pair of underwear and think they've got it covered. Frankie chuckled. Not Giovanni. He was a little different than most. His suitcase would most likely be bigger than hers!

Speaking of suitcases, they decided to use one suitcase just for gifts and then leave it in Salerno. On the other hand, if the girls had their way, they'd need it for all their own shopping procurements. You don't go to Italy and return home empty-handed.

Frankie was taking inventory of her clothes when Bandit decided the pile of sweaters would make a nice cozy bed and curled up on the navy-blue cashmere tunic. "Hey! That's mine!" Frankie said to her furry friend. He stretched, yawned, got up, turned himself around, and settled back down on the soft batch of clothes. Frankie knew that was a signal that he wasn't about to move, and she was sure to pack a lint brush.

Frankie was perusing her *Lonely Planet Guide to Naples and the Amalfi Coast* and began making a list of day trips. Lists. Frankie was obsessed with them. She had stacks of four-by-six file cards in wooden boxes or trays in almost every room, including her office at work. Every morning or the night before, she would make a to-do list and carry the card in her pocket or in the folds of her tote where she packed her cell phone. She would make lists for her staff, her friends, her family. It was a running joke among her friends when they were on vacation: "Did you get your list today from Bossy Pants?" they'd ask each other. She never heard anyone from work call her that, but she was sure there were whispers behind her back. She didn't mind. She was a good boss. A fair boss. When push came to shove, her group knew she always had their backs, and they could go to her with any issues.

She ripped a page from one of her many wall calendars and started to plot her ideal trip. Naturally she would check with Giovanni, but having a wish list was always a good idea. The first few days would be spent helping Rosevita and Aunt Lucia shop and cook. Once the rest of the crew arrived, she could be more flexible, and Giovanni had no expectations of being with her twenty-four-seven. As long as everyone was together for New Year's Eve, Frankie and her gang could run rampant in Southern Italy. The trip was a month away, and she was already all over-the-top excited. This would be her first real vacation with Giovanni. The escapade in Tahoe didn't count, considering her band of friends was on a rescue mission, she ended up on crutches, and they happily volunteered to save New Year's Eve for the hotel guests. No, that was definitely not a vacation.

She pulled out an index card and wrote down her ideas:

- Pizza tour for Peter
- Mozzarella tour for Frankie
- Pompeii for Richard

It wasn't a lot, but it was a good start. Plus, Giovanni had a special place he wanted to bring everyone to watch the sunset with a bottle of prosecco. Maybe two bottles.

Frankie checked the time. It was past eight o'clock. No wonder her stomach was growling. She picked up her phone and called Giovanni and asked him to bring her something to eat. She always left it up to him, since he knew what the best dish of the night was. Bandit was still snoozing on her sweater, and Sweet P. was sitting on the back of the sofa, watching her with a keen eye. Frankie realized this was going to be the first time she was going to be away from her. "Oh, sweetie. Mommy is going to go on a trip with Giovanni. We'll be gone for"—Frankie counted on her fingers—"twelve darks. You know what that means?" She picked up the kitty and snuggled her face against Sweet P.'s neck. "You and Bandit will have the place all to yourselves." Sweet P. still wasn't convinced this was a good idea. She sprung from Frankie's arms and went back to the sofa. "Oh, don't be like that. You'll make Mommy sad." Frankie sat on the sofa and began to stroke the kitty. "It's going to be alright. I promise. Becky from . . ." Frankie stopped. She didn't want to mention the animal hospital. "Becky, a very nice lady, is going to feed you and check on you twice a day." She attempted another snuggle with the black feline. This time, Sweet P. acquiesced and rubbed her head against Frankie's chin. Progress! Frankie was surprised when the veterinarian told her that cats born in the wild, especially from feral mother cats, may never become completely domesticated, even if you adopt them at a very young age. Sweet P. was only six weeks old when she showed up at the cabin in Lake Tahoe, but even after a year, she was still wary of humans. Frankie let Sweet P. decide when she wanted to be petted, and when she did, Frankie stopped everything to oblige. It had been a long time coming, but Sweet P. found a comfortable place on the top of the back of the sofa.

After several minutes of bonding, Frankie decided to give Nina a call and see what she was up to and what ideas she had for the trip. Frankie had been doing a lot of research, and she was excited to share what she learned with her friends.

Frankie began, "I've been reading a ton of travel books. The Amalfi Coast sounds absolutely amazing! All the guidebooks say it is one of the most scenic stretches of coastline in Italy. Villages are built along the sides of steep cliffs, overlooking the Tyrrhenian Sea. The area is known for ornate villas, lemon groves, and domed churches. The coast is about thirty miles long, and this one twisting highway connects thirteen towns. Of course, there's Amalfi, and you've probably heard of Positano. But there is also Praiano, Conca dei Marini, Atrani, Minori, Maiori, Cetara, and Vietri sul Mare, all along the water. Then up in the hills. there's Ravello, Tramonti, Furore, and Agerola." Frankie was out of breath.

"You should have been a librarian," Nina joked. "What about Sorrento?"

"Sorrento isn't actually on the Amalfi Coast, but it's on the northern part of the peninsula, facing the Bay of Naples. And it's all within an hour."

"You are the best travel agent, honey bunch," Nina said.

"And I made a list of things . . ."

"Of course you did!" Nina snorted. "Sorry . . . continue, please."

"I know you said you thought Richard might enjoy going to Pompeii, although I don't know how enjoyable looking at ruins from a volcano could be, but hey, that's why there's chocolate and vanilla ice cream. Anywho, I wrote that down, as well as a mozzarella tour, and pizza tour."

"Are we going to have enough time to fit everything in?" Nina asked.

"That's why I make lists, honey pie," Frankie chuckled. "I figure I'll run all of this past Giovanni and see what he suggests. He also wants us to watch the sunset from the hillside. Not sure if that's part of the New Year's plan. We haven't gotten that far yet. I'm still trying to figure out what to get his mother and Aunt Lucia for Christmas."

"I do not envy you with that task," Nina noted.

"What did you get Richard's mother your first Christmas together?"

"A scarf from Saks. Who doesn't like to open a box from Saks, or Bloomie's? Too bad Bendel's closed. They used to have the coolest stuff."

"Yeah. But something from Saks would be nice, even though she lived here for twenty years. I'm sure she went there once or twice, ya think? Maybe?"

"The few times I saw her, she was always beautifully dressed."

"Yeah, but remember, she was also a seamstress."

"Good point. I'm still voting for a scarf from Saks," Nina added. "At least for Aunt Lucia."

"She covers herself in black. Head to toe, including some downright ugly shoes."

Nina laughed.

"Or maybe a pair of leather gloves," Frankie mused.

"That's too generic," Nina countered.

"Maybe."

"What about a shawl for Aunt Lucia? I'm sure you can find a black one!"

"That's a great idea! I'll run it past Giovanni. By the time I finish grilling him, he may be sorry he suggested this trip," Frankie laughed.

"I am sure he is enjoying every minute of the planning."

"I'm sure you're right," Frankie added. "Okay, so recap your plans for me."

"I'm waiting to hear back from Jordan. Ideally, I would fly to Milan on the twenty-sixth, spend two days with Jordan, and then take the train on the twenty-eighth. Its ETA into

Naples is around six o'clock. Richard is going to meet me there. We'll spend the night and then go to Pompeii the next day and meet up with you late afternoon, early evening of the twenty-ninth."

"Oh, goodie. I'm glad you and Richard are going to Pompeii. That was a day trip I really didn't want to do. Creeps me out too much," Frankie said.

"Me too, but I figured if Richard was game to follow us to Italy, the least I could do was accommodate his one request," Nina chuckled.

"Atta girl!" Frankie chirped. "So, I'm going over the ferry schedule from Salerno to Capri, and it looks like they only run from April to October. We could catch a ferry from Naples. Let me put on my thinking cap. We're flying out from Naples, so maybe we can go the day before and spend the last night in Naples."

"That could work. Heck, I have no idea what the rest of the trip is going to be like, so just count me in whatever you decide," Nina said cheerfully.

"I'll work on it." Frankie scribbled a few more notes on her white file cards.

"What are you planning on packing?" Nina asked.

"The weather is in the upper fifties, so a few sweaters, boots, jackets, and a couple of nice outfits for church and New Year's."

"I guess I'll have to do a little shopping. My granny skirts may not be ideal for walking around cliffs and all."

"Honey, that is why I wear leggings, low-heel high-shaft boots, and tunic sweaters. Throw on a pair of earrings, and you're good to go!"

"Excellent advice. Ya know, doing a podcast does not require any sort of dress code, so my attire has been, shall we say, casual?"

"As in wearing your pajamas all day?" Frankie teased.

"I'll have you know I wear a hoodie with my pajama bottoms!" Nina howled. "And my signature bandana."

"Naturally. We wouldn't recognize you without it," Frankie chuckled. "I gotta get going. Giovanni will be home soon, and I want to run a few scenarios past him. Gotta get my lists together." She chortled.

"You go, girl! I am really looking forward to this. I haven't seen Jordan in years, and I am delighted we'll be in Campania to ring in the new year. Hey, I heard they shoot confetti popper cannons all over. Is that true?"

"There's a whole list of things that happen."

"You and your lists!" Nina joked.

"Ha. I don't mean *my* lists, but I shall make one, because there are some things we need to be prepared for."

"Like what?" Nina asked.

"Like, make sure you bring a pair of red underwear. So, when you go shopping, put that on *your* list!"

"Seriously? Red underwear? Why?" Nina groaned.

"It doesn't have to be a thong, honey pie. Any red pair will do. I think. The list wasn't that specific, just that wearing red underwear on New Year's Eve will bring you good luck."

"Red undies, here I come!" Nina laughed. "Okay, toots, I shall let you get back to your lists. We should probably Zoom everyone in at some point."

"Yes. As soon as I run my lists past Giovanni."

"Okay, girlfriend. Talk soon. Love ya!"

"Love ya back!" Frankie smiled and ended the call.

Frankie looked down at the rug she was sitting on. Almost a dozen file cards were strewn about. Bandit sauntered in, stretched, yawned, and looked down at the mess of notes on the floor. Frankie could have sworn he shook his head. Sweet P. hadn't moved from her perch.

Chapter 6

Making Plans

"**S**weetcakes!" Nina's moniker for Frankie flowed over the airwaves.

"Hello, dahling," Frankie responded.

"What's shakin'?" This time, it was Nina's turn to ask.

"Just going through my lists." Frankie chuckled.

"A-ha! And how many lists do you have?"

"Uh, several. One for each day trip," Frankie admitted.

"Oh good. I like having a pushy-planner-person. Tell me."

"First, you tell me. Is everything set up with you and Jordan?"

"Yes! His family will be in Milan for Christmas, and I'll fly out the day after. I'll get to spend Christmas Day with my family, and they can haul my derriere to the airport."

"Perfect. Or should I say perfetto?"

"How are you doing with your Italian lessons?" Nina asked.

"Not as well as I had hoped. This time of year is gonzo, so I'm going to be depending on Giovanni."

"What are we going to do when we're on our own?" Nina chuckled.

"What we always do. Wing it!" Frankie laughed. Frankie wasn't always keen on winging it, but there was often a time and place for it, and this trip was bound to become a winging-it adventure.

Amy opened her email and whooped when she saw the message from the head of the department of physics. She was granted an extremely rare and limited tour of the experiment cavern at the CERN Science Gateway. She was going to see the Hadron Collider! She downloaded and printed the attached file that contained information about CERN and began to read it out loud. "There is a laboratory in Switzerland called CERN. It leads the world in particle physics." She looked over at her cat, who seemed genuinely interested in his owner's enthusiasm. "Oh Blinky, this is so exciting."

She continued to scroll through the document and read the salient pieces to her kitty. "Back in 1954, it was founded by the *Conseil Européen pour la Recherche Nucléaire*. Over a hundred countries collaborated to utilize complex instruments to study subatomic particles. They hope to be able to further understand the universe and how it works. So, this big thing called the Hadron Collider shoots a bunch of particles to see how they react. But I already knew that." She giggled. "They hope to continue research in physics in a sustainable way, and push technology forward and train new physicists. Like me!" She grinned.

Amy was so engrossed in her reading material that she hadn't heard Peter come through the door.

"Hey there."

Amy looked up. "Oh, Peter! I got permission to visit the CERN Science Gateway!"

"In Geneva?" Peter set his briefcase down on the bench.

"Yes! Can you believe it?" Amy was so red-cheeked, she looked like someone hit her in the face with a fuchsia paintball. She was bouncing up and down.

"That's great! When?" Peter walked over to give her a peck on her flushed skin.

"December twenty-seventh."

"Aren't we supposed to be going to Italy around that time?"

"Yes! But we can fly into Geneva first and then head down to Naples the next day."

"So, we'd get to Campania on the twenty-ninth?"

"Correct. I'll have to check the airlines, but I think it's less than a two-hour flight."

"I'm surprised you haven't bought the tickets yet!" Peter teased.

"I literally got this a few minutes ago." Amy grinned. "I was reading it to Blinky. Gimpy didn't seem all that interested. The only thing is, it's a pass for one person."

"So, what are you going to be doing while I take the tour?" Peter joked.

"Oh, aren't you the funny man?"

"I'm sure I'll find something to keep myself occupied. How long is your tour?"

"Two hours."

"Maybe I'll rent a motorcycle and do a tour around the area, or maybe a boat ride on Lake Geneva. But don't worry that brainiac head of yours. I'm a big boy, and I'll figure it out."

Amy did a little hop and gave Peter a big bear hug. "You're the best!"

"You're not so bad yourself!"

Rachael and Randy were debating where they should fly into. Neither had any interest in Venice. At least not this trip. It was a toss-up between Paris, Florence, and Rome. "If we fly directly to Florence, it will take over eleven hours and we have to stop in Geneva. If we fly to Rome, then it's only an eight-hour flight. We could start in Rome, take a ninety-minute train ride to Florence, and then take a train to Naples. The train is three hours."

"Is there a bar car on the train?" Randy asked innocently.

"For heaven's sake, Randy. Bring a flask," Rachael laughed.

"Well, that sounds like an excellent itinerary."

"Good. Let's start with that, and I'll check in with Frankie."

"Sounds good. Toodles!" Randy signed off.

Randy was a character, but a good soul. They had never traveled together, and Rachael had no idea what he might come up with, but at the very least, it would be interesting.

Chapter 7

Jingle All the Way

Time flew by once Halloween hit the calendar. It felt as if someone stomped on the gas pedal, and before you knew it, Thanksgiving was just a gastronomic memory, and Christmas was staring you in the face.

Amy was usually the first one to arrive home at the end of the day. She was in a tizzy trying to get her holiday plans nailed down and her shopping finished when she realized, "Oh, geez . . . my passport expired!" She had exactly three weeks to get it together. According to the website, she could get it expedited within fourteen days of travel, which meant she needed to get on the stick, pronto.

Peter walked through the front door and could hear Amy stomping around upstairs.

"Honey, I'm home!" he called out. No answer. Still stomping. Peter looked down at the two felines that were staring at him. "I don't suppose you guys know what's going on." Blinky and Gimpy gave him the equivalent of a cat shrug. Peter set his briefcase down on the bench and then proceeded to climb the stairs. "Amy? Everything alright?" He stepped into the craft and puzzle room and spotted Amy sifting through

a pile of papers, files, and receipts. A large brown-paper grocery bag sat crumbled next to her.

"My passport. It expired." She wasn't quite on the verge
of tears, but close enough.

"Take it easy. You can go to the passport office tomorrow.
Bring your ticket, your expired passport, your driver's license, and your birth certificate."

"That's what I'm looking for."

"Which one?"

"Birth certificate." Amy's face was beet red.

"Okay. Don't panic."

"It's got to be here somewhere," Amy whined.

"Give it here." Peter reached out his arm so she could pass
one of the files to him. He slowly and carefully separated the
dozens of papers. "Does it say 'Certificate of Birth'?" He bit
his lip, trying to keep from smiling.

"Of course! What else would it say?" She was one second
away from hysteria.

"It could say, 'Proof of an Absent-Minded Professor'." He
handed the document to her.

Amy shrieked. "How? But . . . but I went through those already."

"Well, the last person who touched this had something
sticky on their fingers. See?" He showed her the smudge that
had glued her certificate to an appliance manual.

Amy's eyes fluttered. "Oh, fudge."

"It's okay, honey. It was easy enough to overlook."

"No, I meant it *was* fudge." She licked her thumb and
tried to rub the crusted sugary substance off the document.

"I'll tell you what. After we get back, you and I will go
through this mess and separate everything into folders that
will be appropriately marked and catalogued."

A tear ran down her cheek. Peter lifted her chin. "Everything else okay?"

Amy let out a big sigh. "Yes. I guess I'm just nervous about everything."

"The trip?"

"Yes, and Christmas, and all of it. I was going to do some holiday shopping for the girls tomorrow, and now I have to spend the day at the passport office."

Peter glanced at the mess on the floor. There was a small stack of photos lying in the corner. "What's that?"

"Pics of us from the reunion, cruise, and Tahoe," Amy said with an air of distraction.

"How about this?" Peter took her by the shoulders and helped her up. "I'll make copies of the photos, and you can make little scrapbooks for everyone. Julia is going to the office supply store tomorrow. I'll ask her to pick up four books. We can go to the website, and you can pick out what you want. Then we can put them together once you get your passport situation taken care of. This way, you won't have to stress out about shopping."

"What about my parents? Your parents?"

"Gift cards to their favorite restaurants. We shall give them an experience instead of a thing." He used air-quotes for *thing*.

"That's a great idea. Everyone has pretty much everything they need." She gave him a big hug.

"You are so smart."

"Well, you ain't no dummy, professor. Just a little . . ."

"I know," Amy interrupted. "Absent-minded. Sometimes I think brains and common sense are mutually exclusive," she said pensively.

"And that's why you have me," Peter chuckled.

"Who'd have thought I'd fall for a compulsive, organized, numbers geek?"

"You mean there's another man in your life?" Peter feigned a double take.

Amy rolled her eyes and then stared at the mess she had made. "Well, I know Nina is as disorganized as I am."

"Really?" Peter was skeptical. "But she's a writer."

"Her thoughts might be organized, but her office is usually a hot mess. At least from what I've seen during our Zoom calls."

"Interesting." Peter closed one eye and gave it some thought. "How do you suppose she keeps track?"

"She has what she calls her 'Murder Board.' It's actually a whiteboard, but it's how she plotted the sitcom she was working on. It's kind of genius, if you think about it."

"True. I suppose when you consider writing, it's either on paper or on a computer."

"But it's a process. Having visual cues is very important. I learned about it when we were in high school, and I was working on the school plays."

"Maybe that's why you and Nina bonded. You both needed direction. No pun intended."

Amy laughed. "I think we all need direction from time to time. And look, you gave me direction."

"How so?"

"The scrapbooks." Amy picked up the pile of photos. "Oh, dear me."

"What now?"

"Dear. Me. My purple hair, goofy glasses, and that outfit. How did anyone let me leave the house looking like that?"

"You were in Silicon Valley. You blended right in." Peter chuckled. "The real question is, how did I fall in love with someone who looked like that?"

Amy laughed. "I know. Right? Thank goodness for Marilyn. She peeled off those layers and outfitted me with new ones. It's uncanny how she knew intuitively what I would like."

"Marilyn is worldly and astute. She tuned into your spirit."

"Whoa. Are you waxing philosophical?"

"Am I? My mistake," Peter snickered.

Peter shuffled through the photos. "You are the only one who looks different. Frankie still has the long dark ponytail."

"And the big doe eyes," Amy added.

"Nina, with the headwrap, and Rachael with the pixie hair." Amy stared at one of the photos from the cruise. "Hmmm."

"What?"

"Someone else has changed a bit." She patted his stomach with the back of her hand.

"Are you saying I've gained weight?"

"Me? No." Amy crossed her fingers behind her back; a little fib wouldn't hurt.

"Huh," Peter snorted. "According to my doctor, I have not gained any weight in the past year."

"That may be true. But this photo"—she held it in front of his face—"was taken *two* years ago."

Peter put his hands over his ears, pretending he didn't hear her. "What do you say we leave this mess and order something to eat? And, no, not pizza. I want a clean palate for Italy."

"And by the looks of it, you don't need any more dough." She patted his stomach again and giggled.

After careful consideration, Rachael and Randy decided to fly out of New York on the twenty-sixth, arriving in Rome the morning of the twenty-seventh. They would spend two days visiting the usual tourist spots and then take a train to Naples, where they would meet up with Amy and Peter and Giovanni and Frankie. Giovanni arranged for a van so everyone could ride together, and they would pick up Nina and Richard in Pompeii and then head to Baronissi. Once everyone was settled, Giovanni would take them for the "best-a pizza in all the world!"

Chapter 8

And they're off!

When Frankie went to check in online, she discovered Giovanni bought them business-class tickets. She was floored. She was expecting premium economy. Business class was over seven thousand dollars! Each! She phoned him right away. "Gio! You got us business-class tickets?"

"*Cara*, I wanna buy first-a class but they no offer. I hope you not disappoint."

"You . . ." Then she stopped and reminded herself to be gracious and simply say, "Thank you."

"We gonna have to stop in Rome, so it's gonna be a long trip. I wanna you to be comfortable."

"You are the best!" Frankie gushed. "This is so exciting!"

"*Sì*. I, too, am excited." She could hear the smile in Giovanni's voice.

"I've wrapped all the gifts. We may need a bigger suitcase!" She chuckled. "I hope your mother likes the wrap and gloves."

"How could she not? It's from you. And it's *bellissimo*."

Frankie cleared her throat, still uncertain where she stood with Mrs. Lombardi, who insisted Frankie call her Rosevita.

There was never any tension between them, but with some mothers, you just never know what they are thinking.

Frankie had gone to great lengths to find something beautiful and functional that she knew Rosevita wouldn't buy for herself. She started at Saks, then to Bergdorf, then to Bloomingdale's, and then back to Saks. She was getting weary when she spotted a cream-colored silk and cashmere Gucci shawl and matching cashmere gloves. Nina's voice echoed in her head—"gloves are so generic"—but they looked exquisite together. She also found a lovely black and gray, silk and cashmere shawl with silver threads by Ferragamo for Aunt Lucia. She wondered if she should buy something else for Rosevita, but the total for the scarf and gloves was over seven hundred dollars. Even the shawl for Aunt Lucia rang up just under four hundred bucks. While she was shopping, she pondered if she should phone Giovanni and ask him, but decided to show him the gifts first before she blew another hole in her wallet. Much to her relief, he was pleased with her purchases and insisted, "*Basta*!" That's enough!

Giovanni had several cousins who were also on the gift list, but they were easy to shop for. Anything with an American football logo would be greatly appreciated. Of course, it had to be "official." Bootlegged jerseys were easy to come by. He stopped at the NFL store on Fifth Avenue and purchased an assortment of Giants, Jets, Dolphins, and Chiefs shirts, hats, and sweatshirts. It occurred to him that he should probably buy the extra suitcase so he could haul his loot back to his apartment, where he kept most of his clothes. Turned out he needed to buy two suitcases and settled on one silver hardcase with the Carolina Panthers logo, and a red one with the San Francisco 49ers. He figured they would be easy to spot at the baggage claim. Between him and Frankie, they would have four pieces of luggage. Good thing he booked business-class tickets. He wouldn't have to pay for an extra bag unless

Frankie had something else in mind. But Frankie was a seasoned traveler and knew what the limits were.

The day finally arrived for them to head to the airport for a new adventure. Marco and Anita left the night before upon Rosevita's insistence; she wanted to have more time with her grandchildren. Giovanni was secretly relieved. It was going to be enough navigating the airport with just him and Frankie. Having two other adults and two children was a recipe for chaos.

A car service picked up Giovanni and his luggage first, and then they fetched Frankie. They planned to leave three hours before their flight just in case there was traffic, or lines at security. Their flight departed at nine o'clock in the evening, so the traffic shouldn't be terrible, but this was New York, and they were going to JFK. Anything could happen.

Frankie scooped up Bandit and explained one more time about Becky and how long they would be away. Sweet P. was on her perch, observing the ritual. Frankie set Bandit on the sofa and leaned toward her female feline, who didn't look too pleased. Frankie used her high-pitched baby-talk voice. "Oh, cutie patootie, Bandit is going to take good care of you. Right Bandit?" He gave her a look of acceptance, and Sweet P. allowed Frankie to give her a rub on the head. "I love you guys. Be good. Mommy loves you!" Frankie thought she might cry. She had never been away from her fur babies for more than a week.

The buzzer rang, letting her know Giovanni had arrived. When he came upstairs, he entered her apartment and spotted the cats. "*Si buono per la tua mama. Mi prenderò cura di lei. Tornerà presto.*"

Much to Frankie's surprise, they acted as if they knew what he said; both jumped off the couch and rubbed against their ankles. "What did you say to them?"

"It's a secret." He winked and grabbed her luggage. "*Ciao, gattos!*"

When they got in the car, Frankie insisted Giovanni tell her what he said. "Francesca, you should learn your Italian better," he teased.

Frankie pouted. "I'm going to miss them."

Giovanni hated to see her sad. "Okay, okay, I will tell you. I told them to be good. That I would take care of you, and you will be back soon."

Frankie squeezed his hand. "You really are the best."

They arrived at the airport without incident and moved quickly through the check-in process and security. Both had TSA clearance, so it was much faster, and they didn't have to take off their shoes.

Frankie had a small carry-on that fit under the seat. It was chock full of her makeup and personal items that she could not possibly go without should her luggage end up in Bulgaria. Giovanni also had a small bag with his shaving gear, hair products, and Frankie's favorite cologne. She loved to nuzzle his neck and inhale the fragrance, which she attempted to do once they were seated on the plane, but there was a small partition between their seats, so she grabbed his hand and sniffed the back of it instead. The flight attendants began their safety check, and the video played on the small screens in their cozy, private space.

After eight hours in flight, the plane landed in Rome, where they had to change planes for Naples. Hopefully their luggage would be heading to Naples, too. Although, it wouldn't be the first time Frankie ended up in one city and her bag in another. They finally found it the day she was leaving to go home. Good thing she had all of her facial products in her carry-on. All she had to do was run to the nearest department store and buy two outfits. She thought about it and realized she never wore those clothes again. She had to put donating those clothes on her to-do list.

The flight was smooth, and service was excellent. They announced all the gates for connecting flights, which lessened the anxiety. When they arrived at the gate, Giovanni and Frankie were nearly the first to deplane, and they had just under an hour to make their way to the next flight, which was only a few gates away.

The atmosphere at the terminal was festive. Christmas kiosks lined the concourse, with carolers dressed as elves entertaining the bustling passengers. Giant sleds were filled with donated toys that were to be distributed to a children's hospital. Frankie's first instinct was to buy a teddy bear at one of the kiosks. She handed it to one of Santa's helpers, who gave her a huge smile and a bellowing *"Mille Grazie. Dio ti benedica."* Frankie knew it meant "Thank you very much. God bless you," but she couldn't say much in return. She was kicking herself for not learning as much Italian as she hoped, but she couldn't take the time to study between planning the trip and having so many balls in the air at work.

They made their way through the throng of holiday travelers. Frankie noticed the mood of the crowd. Everyone was smiling, greeting total strangers with happy holiday wishes in a multitude of languages. You may not have been able to understand the words, but you could feel the sentiment. She imagined what Grand Central Terminal would be like at that moment. She pursed her lips. It would be totally bonkers. Hundreds of thousands of individuals, most carrying bags— suitcases, backpacks, Bloomindgale's Big Brown Bag—squeezing their way through a sea of people. She reckoned it was like trying to thread a needle with a sausage. She snickered.

Giovanni looked at her. "What?"

"Just thinking about how differently people behave when they're not trying to shove themselves into a place where there is no place to go."

He gave her a quizzical look. "Like-a the subway?"

"Or the train station." She continued to scan the area. It wasn't any less crowded than any other transportation hub, but it was the feel. The vibe. People were happy they were going somewhere. Anywhere. Especially if they were going to visit family; the family they actually wanted to see. Frankie giggled again.

Giovanni looked at her again. "You make yourself laugh. What is so funny? Do you not want to share?"

"Just silly thoughts. People. Family. Framily." It was the word Frankie used for people who may not share your DNA but were like family nonetheless.

"Ah, yes. Framily. Important. Very important." He placed his hand at the small of her back and guided her toward the gate, where the attendant was greeting everyone as if she were genuinely happy to see them.

"I think I need to take more frequent trips to Italy. Though, not necessarily at the busiest time of year," she said when someone accidentally bumped into her. But no problem. Several apologies, smiles, and good wishes. "See? If we were in New York, there would have been a brawl."

"Oh, Frankie. You are too cynical. You need to turn on the lights."

"You mean lighten up?" Frankie cackled, bringing more attention to herself.

Giovanni noticed the people staring and smiled sheepishly at the looks. "Sorry. I'm excited."

"My first trip. Here, I mean," Frankie added. "We're both a little excited." Then she leaned into the woman standing close to her and whispered, "Meeting the future in-laws." Not that they were engaged; she just thought it would be something funny to say. Frankie often made witty comments to total strangers.

The woman chuckled. "Good luck."

See? Frankie thought to herself. *You made someone smile for no particular reason, just by making a human connection.*

As they were shuffling their way closer to the jetway, Giovanni asked, "Why she wish you luck?"

"I told her I was going to hike Mt. Vesuvius." A fib, but that too brought a laugh. This time from Giovanni.

"Ah, I don't think so," he whispered, and then nodded at the woman.

The gate attendant scanned their boarding passes and wished them "*Buon Natale*, Merry Christmas." Frankie was getting goosebumps. It reminded her of her childhood, when she would reach the bottom of the stairs on Christmas morning. The air was electrified with anticipation.

Or was it anxiety? She took a deep breath and exhaled slowly. This was the last leg of their travels. She would be in Salerno in about two hours. She looked up at Giovanni. The expression on his face was serene and confident. He was on his own turf. Frankie could sense the shift in him and found it rather appealing. Even more so than usual.

The pilot made the departure announcement in English: "Flight crew, arm doors and cross-check." Then came the safety video. Frankie may have flown over a hundred times, but she always paid attention, especially noting: "the nearest exit may be behind you." The flight attendant repeated the instructions in Italian. A few people turned their heads, Frankie included.

The flight took just under an hour, and once again, they were among the first off the plane. Naples Airport was as buoyant as the one in Rome. The sound of music, laughter, and sleigh bells filled the air. You could easily picture yourself in the middle of a holiday-themed snow globe. Tiny sparkles of lights woven into garland wrapped the walls and were draped from above. It was magical. Giovanni placed his hand on the small of her back again, guiding her down the escalator to immigration, then to the baggage claim area. There was plenty of excitement on that level, too, but not as jovial. Passengers scurried from one carousel to another as the information constantly changed. At one point, none of the carousels had any flight information. Groans and moans bested the popular tune of "Jingle Bells." The honking sound and flashing light of an alarm signaled the next arrival of luggage. The moans turned into questions, and a confusion of languages. Someone blew a whistle, and everyone halted in place. First in Italian, and then in English, a security guard calmly asked people to be patient and then announced a few flight numbers and where they could fetch their belongings. Frankie was relieved. The contrast from the winter wonderland to the baggage debacle unnerved her a bit. She knew she had been masking her anxiety during the week prior and during their trip. Soon. Soon she would be in the Lombardi family home. It was a big deal. Truly.

Giovanni sensed Frankie's trepidation and kept his hand on her back or shoulder at all times. Frankie realized how important Giovanni was to her. Not because he was being protective. Not because he planned everything down to the minutia of their itinerary. Not because he generously paid for her parents. Not because of any one of those wonderful things. It was all of it. All the love he gave to her, her family, and friends. All the love he gave to his family and their legacy. Yes, it was the whole package that made up Giovanni Lombardi.

He spotted the red 49ers suitcase. "Don't move," he said calmly to Frankie. He pulled it off the rotating machine and set it down next to where she was standing. Next was Frankie's suitcase, then the Panthers bag. The unclaimed bags went around the turn again. Still no bag for Giovanni. They waited. And waited. The crowd had thinned, and there were two lonely pieces of luggage left to claim, but neither were his. Giovanni took a deep breath and approached one of the attendants and spoke to him in Italian. The attendant referred them to a small office, where Giovanni was instructed to fill out a form. Frankie could feel small droplets of perspiration run down the back of her neck. *Whyohwhyohwhy was this happening?* She was just beginning to relax, and now they had to deal with a suitcase mishap. But Giovanni was cool, calm, and collected. He showed no sign of annoyance. He thanked the counter agent and escorted Frankie to the customs area, where they had nothing to declare, although Frankie wanted to declare she was about to have a nervous breakdown.

Giovanni sent a text to the driver who was meeting them to let him know they were slightly delayed. He turned to Frankie. "Not to worry, *cara*. I can borrow something from Marco. We have to come back tomorrow for your family. Maybe they will have my suitcase."

Frankie was mystified as to how composed Giovanni was. She knew he could be animated at times. Passionate. But at that moment, he was not disturbed in the least. "We have the suitcases with the gifts. You have yours. We will be fine." He put his arm around her shoulders and gave her a tug. "Come. Let's enjoy our holiday."

They rolled their bags to the sidewalk, where a man was standing with a sign that said LOMBARDI FAMILY. Again, it struck Frankie: family. She was part of it now. Or was she? At this point, she shouldn't have any doubt, but then again, why hadn't he asked her to marry him? She shook her head. She had to stop the noise in her head and made a promise to herself that she would follow her own advice and take each day as it would come. And on this particular day, she was going all-in to absorb the essence of Campania.

Frankie noticed the air was crisp but felt different. Not in a bad way. Just different. It was filled with thousands of years of people who traveled this land. She recalled reading an article that said in Italy, you would be breathing the same air as Julius Caesar. Molecules are constantly rearranged, so it was possible at the subatomic level, she guessed. She made a mental note to ask Amy about it. But standing there, at that moment, she believed it was true.

She looked up at the clear, blue sky. Even the color was different. It was vibrant. Rich. She wondered what it had observed through the millennia. Granted, there were thousands upon thousands of volumes of written history. But being an editor, Frankie knew it was the perspective of the writer that went on the page. She was fascinated with the idea that the sky witnessed many unspoken stories.

Giovanni glanced at Frankie. He could see the amazement in her eyes. *Bene,* he thought to himself.

The driver loaded the luggage into the trunk and opened the door for Frankie. He spoke impeccable English and pointed out some highlights as they drove along the E45 highway. Mt. Vesuvius was not to be ignored. It was massive. Powerful. Humbling. She asked the driver if people were concerned about it erupting. He echoed Amy's information that it is monitored twenty-four hours a day, and that they would know weeks ahead if there was any danger. Giovanni patted Frankie's hand. "We have tickets."

"To watch an eruption?" she said in jest.

"*Cara*, sometimes you are very funny." He patted her hand again.

There was a striking contrast between the roaming hills and farms to the north and the villages along the coast. Some of the roads were as bad as the Brooklyn-Queens Expressway, while others were pristine. She supposed road maintenance was the same everywhere. The richer the residents, the better the streets.

As they neared Salerno, the driver continued on E45, which ran north of the city. From there, he exited to a winding local highway that took them past the Castello di Arechi, a medieval fortress built on a mountain, three hundred meters above sea level. Frankie had read that from there, you could view the city below and the Mediterranean that stretched to the Amalfi Coast. It was breathtaking and rendered Frankie to monosyllabic sounds of "oh, my, wow, oh."

Chapter 9

Arriving Home

The forty-five-minute drive came to an end as they pulled into a gravel driveway. Ahead was a large, two-story cement, stone, and wood building. Baskets of flowers, vine-covered urns, lemon trees, and olive trees adorned the slate walkway to the front door that was adorned with a beautiful wreath. Short palms were scattered around. It was the quintessential aged but well-kept Italian villa. Not fancy, but beautiful. Not opulent, but cozy. One could easily see and feel the care put into the maintenance of the gardens. Frankie thought she had stepped foot into a movie set.

"Oh, Gio. This is beautiful," she said dreamily.

"Welcome to my family home." He put his arm around her and looked up at the façade. He noted there were a few things that could use some attention, but he wasn't going to mention it to anyone. Maybe in a few days, but not at the moment. There was too much to do, too many people to see, and he didn't want to give his mother something to be concerned about.

The sound of dogs barking brought two women to the front door. Giovanni was halted in his tracks. His mother was dressed exactly like her sister-in-law, Lucia. She looked as if she'd aged twenty years since he last saw her a year ago. He forced a smile on his face and threw his arms around her. "Mama!"

"Giovanni!" She made the sign of the cross and kissed him on both cheeks.

Frankie was also taken aback at Rosevita's appearance, but she, too, forced a smile and greeted her with the two-cheek kiss. Giovanni introduced her to his aunt. Frankie wasn't sure if she should kiss her, curtsy, or shake hands. Lucia smiled, held out her hand, and leaned in. Frankie figured it was a cue to give her a peck on each cheek. She wasn't sure how much English Lucia spoke, and Frankie apologized for not speaking Italian.

"It's-a no problem," Lucia said. "We try to speak both here. My son, Dominic, is a professor at Baronissi." Lucia always liked to brag about her children. "He says it's important for people to be bilingual."

"That would be a good lesson for me to learn," Frankie grinned. "I am trying. *Ma non così buono.*"

Lucia laughed at Frankie's explanation that she doesn't do it so good.

"Come!" Rosevita instructed, and escorted them to the foyer. The floors were tile. The walls were also tiled. Pretty much everything Frankie could see was covered in tile.

Giovanni placed the suitcases in the entry, wondering where they should go from there. He and Frankie decided to leave it up to Rosevita to instruct him. In the meantime, he had to explain that his suitcase was missing, and he'd have to borrow something from Marco. Rosevita had already said that his brother was currently running errands and Anita was visiting cousins with the children.

His mother shuttled the group through the kitchen and out to a tiled patio with a vine-covered pergola. In the distance, you could get glimpses of the sea beyond the rolling hills. The two older women directed Frankie to one of the chairs that faced the scenery, and a spread of food welcomed the travelers. It was antipasto heaven.

Stone steps led to the lower level with another patio, also covered in tile.

"It is quite beautiful," Frankie said in awe. "No wonder you wanted to come back." She turned to Rosevita, who in turn nodded to her sister. Frankie was still in shock over how both women were almost identically dressed all in black. When Rosevita lived in New York, she was always impeccably dressed in pantsuits or skirts and blouses. She was hard-pressed to recall Rosevita wearing anything that wasn't fashionable, or pretty, for that matter. This change in her was definitely a conversation for her and Giovanni to have later.

Within a few minutes, Giovanni joined them with a bottle of homemade wine. "Is this the poison Mr. Parisi gave you?" he joked.

Rosevita shook her head. "Not so funny. It's very good." She picked up Frankie's glass and handed it to Giovanni to pour the dark, ruby-red liquid. She handed it to Frankie. "Here. You try."

Frankie waited for everyone to have their filled glass in hand; then she raised hers. *"Cent'anni!"*

"Cent'anni! See, you speak good Italian!" Lucia smiled.

Frankie was getting the idea that despite Lucia's appearance, she didn't come across as a cranky old lady. More fodder for her conversation with Giovanni later.

Frankie took a sip of the wine and was pleasantly surprised that it didn't taste like lighter fluid or kerosene. Then she told them the story about her grandparents, who were also originally from Campania but moved to America. Her grandfather carried on the tradition of winemaking until one of his bottles exploded in her parents' garage. It was months before the smell of fermented grapes finally eased, bringing an end to a family tradition.

The two older women howled in amusement, recalling several instances when the very same thing happened in the shed that was set back from the house. Lucia pointed to a small building that was once inhabited by gallons of jugs fermenting homemade wine. She explained that after the third explosion, she put her foot down. It scared the animals.

Rosevita laughed. "I was here one summer, and I thought Vesuvius was erupting! I was used to loud noise in the city, but here"—she raised her eyebrows—"not so good. I was a scaredy cat. Now it's a potting shed."

"A much better idea," Frankie agreed.

About an hour into their meal, the sound of children laughing and screeching filled the hall. Anita was scurrying behind them, telling them to calm down, to no avail. Rafaella, Dominic Jr.'s wife, wasn't far behind, chasing after her three kids. Dominic and Rafaella were around Marco and Anita's age. Loud introductions carried over the squealing of the children as they ran to their grandmothers' laps, each one trying to climb up first.

Lucia pulled Gerardo, the youngest of her grandchildren, toward her and seated him on her lap and started bouncing him on her knee. She was singing a children's song about skipping up and down. Gerardo giggled and began to play with her necklace. "*Stai attento.* Be careful," she said softly.

Again, Frankie was impressed with the sweetness of this woman—a woman whose attire belied a softer side. She thought maybe Lucia would not be offended if she and Giovanni shared a room. But that idea quickly dissolved when Lucia instructed Giovanni to take Frankie's suitcase to the fourth bedroom, and when his suitcase arrived, he could bring it downstairs. Frankie crossed one issue off her mental list. If nothing else, Frankie was relieved. She really, truly, honestly did not want to step over any lines. She thanked Lucia and Rosevita for their hospitality and gave Giovanni a *Don't you dare say a word* expression.

"Speaking of suitcases," Frankie continued, "last year, my friends and I went to Lake Tahoe. I had a bit of an accident."

The other women's eyes went wide.

"Everything turned out fine, but Giovanni did not have any clothes with him." The other women inhaled sharply. Frankie chuckled. "No, you see, he had to leave without packing, and when he got to Tahoe, he had to go shopping. But . . . the weather was freezing cold, and there was snow on the ground, and Giovanni had no boots, just the loafers he always wears. He went to a sporting goods store and bought some sweats, you know, jogging stuff and changed at the store, but then had to go to the shoe store to get boots. Well, there was Giovanni wearing a tracksuit with Mauri loafers!" Frankie snickered.

Giovanni listened and slowly shook his head. "What else was I supposed to do? Walk barefoot on the street?"

"Of course not. But, according to Peter, you were getting some very strange looks from people."

"I am a fashion innovator." He shrugged.

Rosevita watched the two of them banter. She was impressed with the way Giovanni and Frankie interacted. Over the past two years, the two had developed a strong bond. Respect. Kindness. It was as if they had their own secret language. She was delighted her son was happy, and particularly proud that he stood up to his father and all the other relatives who disapproved of him breaking off his engagement. That was when Rosevita knew Giovanni had become a man. And now, he was a happy man.

Frankie suppressed a yawn. She wasn't sure if it was the eleven-plus hours of traveling, jet lag, or lack of sleep. Probably a bit of everything, including Giovanni's missing suitcase and her glass of Mr. Parisi's wine.

"Frankie, come. I'll show you to your room. I think maybe a nap," Giovanni suggested. He thought he heard Lucia gasp and bit his lip, knowing his aunt's imagination was taking a walk on the wild side. He turned to everyone at the table and said, "I will come back and finish my coffee." He could swear he heard long exhales coming from her nostrils. It hadn't occurred to him before, but seeing how she dressed, he realized that Aunt Lucia had parked herself in the past. And she was dragging his mother with her. He couldn't wait to have that discussion with Frankie. His mother was in her early sixties. She had many years ahead of her. He didn't want her to be stuck. Granted, it was just over a year since his father passed, but the old tradition of wearing black from head to toe forever was expecting too much. People grieve in their own way. Putting expectations and pressure on someone to behave in a particular way wasn't fair. He hoped Lucia wasn't putting that kind of pressure on his mother. The women got along well, but Lucia could be very bossy. He wanted to be sure his mother was okay and that she could go on because life goes on.

When they got to the bedroom, Giovanni pulled the door so it wasn't quite shut all the way, but enough so no one could hear them from the other side of the house. He sat on the edge of the bed and patted the quilt. "Please. Sit."

"Giovanni? Is everything alright?" Frankie sat next to him.

"It's Mama."

"What?" Frankie's eyes went wide, and her mouth dropped. Her fertile mind was on the high-speed track of *something terrible has or is about to happen.*

Giovanni took her hands into his. "No. Nothing's wrong. Well, not exactly. You see how Mama is dressed?"

Frankie nodded. "Of course. Duh."

"I mean, I never saw her like this."

"She lost her husband, Giovanni."

"I know. I know. But she was always positive."

"I think she still is. She seems very happy to see all of us."

"True. But the clothes. The clothes, Frankie. I don't remember so much black."

"She's a widow." As if Frankie had to remind him.

"I know. But it's supposed to be for a year, and it's-a been almost eighteen months."

"Oh, Gio, I noticed it, too, but I think you're overreacting. They were married for how many years? Forty?"

"*Sì*." Giovanni hung his head.

"That's a long time." She wrapped her arm around his waist. "Maybe we shouldn't rush her. I know you miss your father, too."

"Of course. I think I'm worried she will become *solitaria*. Alone."

"Your mother isn't the alone type. She lived in New York for over twenty years. She helped with the restaurant. She loves people."

"I thought she would move back to New York. Be with her sons and grandkids. But she says she likes the peace here."

"I don't blame her. It's stunning here." She rested her head on his shoulder and gave him a side hug. "She'll be okay."

Frankie wondered if she was employing wishful thinking. Maybe when her girlfriends arrived, they could somehow influence Rosevita. How? She had no idea, but with her strike force with her in the near future, they'd figure out something. Even if it meant hiding all of Rosevita's clothes. She'd leave that escapade up to Rachael if necessary. She chuckled to herself at the thought of it.

"What?" Giovanni asked.

"Nothing. Just thinking about the girls and the rest of the trip." She gave him a peck on the cheek. "Now scram. I need a nap."

She kicked off her shoes and got horizontal. Giovanni pulled the quilt up to her shoulders.

"Thanks, sweetie." She drifted off as soon as he kissed her on the top of her head.

Giovanni approached the patio slowly. He wanted to hear what they might be talking about. When he heard the words *calamari* and *scungilli*, he knew the conversation had taken a turn toward the Christmas Eve menu. So far, everything was flowing at a nice, natural pace. All except for his luggage. Maybe he should never travel with luggage. *Just a pair of sneakers and a tracksuit in a carry-on.* That would cover most bases until he could get to a store. He wondered if Amazon Prime had next-day delivery in Campania. Probably not.

He approached the table. "What do you need for me to do?"

Lucia reached into her black apron pocket and produced a sheet of paper with items that had to be picked up at the bakery. Rosevita and Lucia planned to make the stromboli, but the pastries had to be from Fiorucci's. The stromboli was served on Christmas Day as part of a buffet for visitors. A formal dinner with roasted veal and all the other trimmings of a feast was an option, but with so many relatives coming and going, Rosevita and Lucia opted for an open house instead. They would serve the roast on New Year's Day.

A casual Christmas Day was well-deserved and much appreciated. The doors would be open to greet people from one o'clock until six. That allowed visitors to stop by for a drink and something to eat without having to worry about coming by a specific time. It also gave the children the entire day to play, and the adults time to relax and enjoy everyone's company.

Big dinners were wonderful, but they required a lot of heavy lifting on the part of the hosts and hostesses. Christmas Eve dinner of seven fishes should satisfy everyone in need of a gastronomical experience, although the buffet they planned for Christmas Day was nothing to sneer at. Stromboli, antipasto, grilled vegetables, salads, and breads would sit on a long table under the pergola.

The weather would be crisp, but the sun would warm the patio to a comfortable sixty-plus degrees. Cool enough for a sweater, but warm enough to sit outside and enjoy the blessings of food, family, and fun. If it got too chilly, they could fire up the tall propane heater. The kids knew to stay away from it, and they could run around the large yard and gardens until they fell over from exhaustion. The grown-ups could eat, chat, and sample Mr. Parisi's wine, if they dared.

Giovanni spoke: "I think I should have a car service pick up Frankie's parents. I don't think I could get to the Naples airport and back without getting into too much traffic." He pulled out his phone and called the driver from earlier that day and gave him instructions to pick up Mr. and Mrs. Cappella. Then he sent a text with their flight information. The driver would drop them off at the Lombardi house, Giovanni would do a quick introduction to whoever was scurrying about, and then he would take them to the house a few blocks away.

Giovanni was thankful accommodations had gone smoothly. Now to find his suitcase. The rest of the week was going to be one thing after another. What kind of order was the question, and knowing Frankie's crew, it could be disorder, as well. He smiled to himself. Maybe he should take a nap as well, but there was still much to do.

For big family meals, they would place a large sheet of finished plywood on top of the existing table, making it big enough to accommodate twelve people comfortably. The kids would have their own table in the kitchen. He went to the lower level and pulled the wood from the storage area, took it outside, and carefully carried it upstairs to the second level patio and then through the kitchen. Rosevita was moving things around and placed several large pads on the existing classically styled table. He leaned the heavy piece of wood against the wall and would wait for Marco to help maneuver it onto the pads covering the beautiful sesame wood finish.

Giovanni watched his mother fuss with the pads. Her hair was grayer than usual. He shook his head. Maybe Frankie could coax Rosevita into a fresh start. Woman to woman. He knew he wouldn't be able to talk to his mother about her attire. She would just pat his cheek and tell him not to worry. He wondered if she was dressing like that to placate Lucia.

Rosevita pierced his contemplation. "Gio, why so pensive?"

"Huh? Nothing, Mama. Just thinking about all the holidays we had here when I was growing up."

"Yes. Then we moved to New York in two thousand. You were thirteen."

"Is that when Aunt Lucia and Uncle Dominic moved into this house?" Giovanni was trying to remember the course of events.

Rosevita raised her eyebrows. "*Sì*. And then when Uncle Dominic passed in two thousand and ten, Lucia decided to stay here. Dominic Junior and Sergio started their own families and moved."

"So, she's lived here for fourteen years alone?"

"*Sì*." More raised eyebrows.

Giovanni was getting the impression that Aunt Lucia might think she had squatters' rights. "Has there been any conversation about selling the house?"

"Sell? Never!" Rosevita was aghast at the suggestion.

"*Scusa*. Sorry, Mama. It's a big house."

"*Sì*, it's a big house, and it's the family house. You, your brother, and your cousins will own it one day. This is one of the reasons I came back here."

"I thought it was because of Aunt Lucia."

"Yes, in part. But also for the family legacy."

Giovanni had mixed feelings about that tidbit of information. It could be a blessing or a curse. Many families were devastated by wills and estates.

Rosevita patted him on the shoulder. "Not to worry. Everyone gets a piece."

Giovanni wasn't sure how all that would go down, but with any luck, it was years away.

"One more thing, Mama." He was thinking about the odds and ends that needed mending around the house. "Who helps take care of the place?"

"Sometimes Dominic." She paused. "Sometimes Mr. Parisi."

Giovanni stifled a grin. Mr. Parisi had a much bigger role than providing a friendly bottle of wine.

Chapter 10

Friendly Neighbors

Frankie awoke from a deep sleep. At first, she didn't know where she was, until she looked out the window. The leaves on the lemon tree were swaying to the breeze. She could smell the air. Definitely different. She reached for her phone to see what time it was. Five o'clock where she was, and eleven where her parents were. She noticed a group text from Giovanni that was directed to her parents. A driver named Stephano would meet them on the sidewalk outside of the baggage claim area, and he would have a sign. He included Stephano in the text so everyone would have their contact information should anything go awry. Frankie smiled. Giovanni would make a great travel agent. Even better than her! She knew Giovanni to be very organized, often more compulsive than she was, but this trip? Impressive.

She stretched and sprung up from the bed. She needed a shower and a fresh change of clothes. She padded down the hallway. Voices were coming from the kitchen.

"*Buona sera*!" Rosevita called out. "Nice nap?"

Frankie still had what she called "the grogs." "Yes. I think

I need more sleep." She took in a heavy breath through her nose, trying not to yawn in her hostesses' faces.

Giovanni was drying some pots. "*Bella! Come stai?*"

"*Molto bene! Grazie.*" That was pretty much the extent of her Italian. Again, she was silently embarrassed for not taking the time to learn more—especially after being with Giovanni for almost two years. But he rarely spoke Italian in front of her, so it never was an issue. Learning Italian was going to be her New Year's resolution, she determined.

Frankie picked up a towel and began helping Giovanni with the dishes when there was a knock at the back door.

Rosevita glanced out the window. It was Mr. Parisi. Frankie noticed Rosevita take a glimpse of herself in the reflection and smooth her hair. *Interesting.* She still cared how she presented herself. A good sign.

Rosevita opened the door and greeted the nice man who lived a few houses down the road. "*Buona sera!*"

He set the two plants he was carrying on the counter, removed his hat, and made a slight bow. Frankie figured him to be in his mid-sixties. He had a full, white head of hair, and steel blue eyes. *A lot of Italians have blue eyes,* she noted. Must be a lot of recessive genes in the pool. She knew it to be true from her own family. Her grandmother had strawberry-blond hair and green eyes, and she was from Caserta, only eighty kilometers northwest of where she was. It would take less than an hour by car.

Over the centuries, Italy was subjected to many rulers and regimes long before the Roman Empire, overrun by almost every country from the Middle East to the Northern African Coast, and as far north as Normandy and Ireland. Geographically it was a throughfare for international trade. Tunisia was a mere 284 kilometers, or 176 miles, to Sicily by sea. Egypt was approximately a thousand miles to Messina, at the lower left part of the boot of Italy. It wasn't until 1871 when the area became unified and became the official country called Italy. It was no wonder that Frankie's ancestry showed she had a small percentage of both sides of the Mediterranean Sea in her DNA.

Frankie wiped her hands and greeted Mr. Parisi. She could have sworn there was a twinkle in his eye when he spoke to Rosevita. And did she spy a little blush on Rosevita's cheeks? Maybe it wasn't romance, but it was good to see genuine caring between friends. He handed one of the large, white poinsettias to Lucia and one to Rosevita. *Good move,* Frankie thought.

With the exception of Frankie, everyone spoke in half-English, half-Italian, with Mr. Parisi apologizing for his "miserable English." There was something very charming about this man. Her wheels were turning. Frankie mentioned his wine and how much she enjoyed it. He was very humble, explaining the recipe was in his family for generations. That was when Giovanni took the opportunity to ask, "Is it a *secret* family recipe?"

"Not so much, really. The grapes can be different from one year to the next. Depends on the weather. You get good grapes, you should get good wine," he said with a smile.

Frankie sensed there was more to Giovanni's question than just wine. Add that to her list of things to discuss. *Where were her file cards when she needed them?*

Mr. Parisi told them he was on his way to pick up his brother and then go to his daughter's house in Rome. He wanted to be sure to wish everyone a *Buon Natale* before he left.

Rosevita casually asked when he was going to return.

"In three days."

"For New Year's Eve?" Frankie interjected.

"*Sì.* We have to throw the pots and pans outta the window," he laughed.

Frankie heard it was one of many traditions, but she had to ask, "Do you really throw them out the window?"

"*Sì*. You wanna send the bad luck away."

"But what do you do the next day? Do you have to buy new pots and pans?"

"You only throw away the old ones, *cara*," Giovanni chuckled.

"So, who cleans them up?"

"One of Santa's elves," Giovanni teased.

Frankie snapped the kitchen towel at him, and everyone laughed out loud.

"You can come and help us throw out the pots and pans, yes?" Frankie decided she was on a mission. Frankie was going to play makeover and matchmaker.

Little did she know that Giovanni was on one, as well. He was determined to get his mother's secret panettone recipe before he left.

Mr. Parisi was about to excuse himself when Rosevita asked him to wait just a minute. She went into the large pantry and returned with one of her famous panettone cakes wrapped in beautiful foil paper. She handed it to him. Her face was slightly flushed. "For your family."

"*Mille grazie*. Thank you very much." He might have been blushing, too.

"Mama, you made the panettone already?" Giovanni was disappointed. He anticipated he was going to help her and try to convince her to share her secret. Now he had to figure out a different plan.

"Of course, Gio," she said casually, and walked Mr. Parisi to the door. "*Buon Natale*! Drive safe! *Ciao*!"

Frankie noticed that Rosevita watched until Mr. Parisi pulled out of the driveway. Did Giovanni notice, too? Frankie gave him one of her sideways glances. He rolled his eyes in reply.

Chapter 11

A Family Feast

The sun was setting over the sea with shades of blue turning to shades of lavender and pink, while the clouds reflected bright colors of red and orange, creating an effect of cotton candy.

The children dragged themselves inside, having spent the afternoon running through the gardens and playing tag on the lawn. Marco promised he would teach them how to play bocce the next day. It was the first time the cousins had met in person, but one would think they had been pals since birth.

Anita and Rafaella marched the children to the laundry room and helped them wash up for dinner. Anita suggested they change their clothes, as well. Their grandmothers would not appreciate the dust and pieces of brush in the dining room. Rafaella had anticipated lots of rollicking and brought an extra set of clothes for Gerardo, age four, Eugenio, age six, and Celeste, age seven. Once Sophia and Lorenzo finished washing up, they ran to their room with Anita racing right behind them. She had painstakingly packed their suitcases and did not want to clean up a clothing explosion. As tired as they were, they seemed to have gotten a second wind from simply washing their hands and faces. But it was good to see the children enjoying every minute of their visit. It was the first time they were away from home, and Anita had wondered how they would react. She was happy that although it was somewhat chaotic, it was in a good way.

Marco arrived with bags of groceries and set them on the kitchen table. Giovanni immediately enlisted his help with the tabletop. When he was sure everyone was out of earshot, he told Marco that their mother had already made the panettone.

"Now what do we do?" Marco scratched his head.

"I have an idea." He halted his sentence as Rosevita entered, carrying linens for the table.

"An idea? For what?" she asked casually.

"What to cook for New Year's Eve. Marco and I are going to make dinner for everyone." He eyed Marco, hoping he would get the hint.

Rosevita turned to Marco. "*Sì*? You boys do that every day. You came here for vacation."

"Mama, you have been working very hard. We want to do something nice for you. We'll make the roast."

"But Mr. Parisi is having the New Year's party at his house this year."

"That's right." Marco replied.

"And we have plans for New Year's Day," Giovanni added.

"So, we'll make a nice dinner for you before we leave." Marco gave his mother a hug, and Giovanni gave him a thumbs-up.

Frankie was in the kitchen, helping Lucia put away the groceries. Lucia directed Frankie to place most of them in the pantry, which was the size of a small bedroom. Shelves lined the walls from floor to ceiling. It was truly a cook's pantry. There were baskets of onions, potatoes, and garlic. Canned tomatoes, canned tomato sauce, jars of roasted peppers from mild to molten lava. A row of pasta in every shape imaginable was on one side, and store-bought canned goods on the other, in case of an emergency. She spotted a half-dozen panettone breads wrapped in the same paper as Mr. Parisi's. She wasn't a fan of fruitcake, but Mrs. Lombardi made it a little different, and it was a secret she hadn't shared. Rosevita's was moist and spongy with raisins and only the slightest amount of candied fruit. It made wonderful French toast, or just regular toast to dunk in your morning coffee.

"Is there anything you need?" she called out to Lucia.

"Two packages of fettuccine. We'll make fresh pasta for Christmas Eve dinner. And a jar of the tomatoes. Not the sauce. Just tomatoes," Lucia replied.

Frankie returned to the kitchen with the pasta and freshly canned garden tomatoes. "What else can I do?"

Lucia pointed to the patio with her knife. "Parsley, oregano, and basil."

Lucia didn't specify how much of each, but Frankie had a pretty good idea—that is, if they cooked the same way Giovanni and Marco cooked. She spotted a small pair of shears near the window. "Shall I use these?"

"*Sì*," Lucia said over her shoulder. "You know how much to cut?"

"I think so." Frankie hoped so. She didn't want to remind Lucia that she was involved with a restaurateur, and she was the publisher of several best-selling cookbooks. That would be showing off. She returned with the appropriate amount of each of the herbs.

Lucia gave a nod of approval.

"What time your parents arrive tomorrow?" she asked.

"Their flight gets in around eleven in the morning."

"Who is going to pick them up? I need Giovanni and Marco." Lucia sounded a bit terse. "Dominic has something at the school."

"Giovanni already made arrangements for them to be picked up and brought here," Frankie called from the patio. She thought Lucia might be feeling overwhelmed. There were four additional adults, and two children underfoot. Plus, all the comings and goings including the two big Bergamasco shepherds. The dogs were known to be calm and patient, which was a plus with all the chaos. She walked over to Lucia, who was putting a big pot of water on the stove.

"I know the holidays can be stressful, and we will do anything you need to make it easier for you and Rosevita."

"*Grazie.*" Lucia let out a huff.

It occurred to Frankie that the visiting clan was on Rosevita's side of the family, and perhaps Lucia may have resented the imposition.

Rafaella entered the kitchen with three freshly dressed children who were on the verge of exhaustion. Sophia and Lorenzo were in a similar state: clean, but tired. Over-tired. She could understand if Lucia felt put-out, but everyone was there to lend a hand. Although at the moment, the volume and energy was at a very high pitch. Frankie thought Lucia would be used to children running around, but later found out that wasn't necessarily the case. Rafaella was also a professor at Baronissi, which took up a lot of her time. She was rarely at the house with the kids.

For Frankie, Lucia was a puzzle. *Was she a happy person?* she wondered.

Marco and Giovanni got the dining room table sorted while Frankie set the kitchen table for dinner. Dominic arrived just in time for the simple meal of sausage, pasta, and salad, and of course, Mr. Parisi's wine.

Rafaella called the children to come up from the lower level, where they were watching a movie. There were only five of them, but at that age and with their enthusiasm, it sounded like a dozen. She seated them at a small table in the corner, also known as the "kiddie table." On Christmas Eve, they would stand next to their parents as they said grace, and then be relegated to the kitchen, where they could make as much noise as they wanted. So could the adults in the dining room.

Everyone scrambled to the table while Rosevita and Lucia

filled the large pasta bowl that would be shared family-style. Giovanni tossed the salad, while Marco poured wine for the grown-ups and water for the children. Milk was not considered a beverage in Italy. You put a little in your coffee. But that was all. Serving it with food was considered a crime against Italian cuisine.

Dinner was usually served around eight-thirty. By the time they were on the salad portion, each person was trying valiantly to keep their eyes open.

Rafaella told the children to go downstairs to finish their movie, while Giovanni, Marco, and Dominic made haste at clearing the table, washing the dishes, and cleaning the kitchen. By the time they were finished, Rosevita and Lucia had already excused themselves. The children were fast asleep while *Rudolph the Red-Nosed Reindeer* played on the television. Rafaella carried each of her kids up the stairs one by one and put them in the car seats with the help of Anita and Frankie. It was after ten o'clock, and it was time for everyone to tuck themselves in.

Giovanni kissed Frankie goodnight at her bedroom door and padded to the lower level, where Rudolph was still hanging around. He tossed his jeans, socks, underwear, and blue pin-striped shirt in the washer. He was going to have to clean his outfit daily while he waited to hear from the airline. Meanwhile, he borrowed a pair of pajamas from his brother. It had been many years since they slept under the same roof, let alone in each other's clothes. There was something reassuring about it. What, exactly? Perhaps nostalgia.

The following morning, Frankie's parents sent a text that they were changing planes in Rome, the same route Frankie and Giovanni took. The kids were playing outside, and Rosevita handed Giovanni a list, and another one went to Marco. Frankie wondered what she was going to do with herself for the next few hours. Then she got an idea. "Rosevita, can you tell me what the menu is for tomorrow?"

"As usual. Seven fishes," Rosevita replied.

"Yes, but can you tell me in what order?"

"Ah. *Sì.*" Rosevita began to tick off the items on the menu:

Steamed mussels
Clams oreganato
Scungilli salad
Calamari marinara over linguini
Scallops oreganato
Baked stuffed cod
Shrimp scampi

"Then for dessert, we have cannoli, sfogliatella, and baba au rhum. Giovanni will pick up. Come. I'll show you." Rosevita walked into the dining room and showed her the sideboard, where two large serving dishes had struffoli and chiacchiere. Frankie knew what it took to make those desserts: lots of time and patience. The struffoli are small balls of dough, the size of an olive, deep fried and covered in honey and sprinkles, formed into the shape of a wreath or a dome. The chiacchiere was also fried dough, made in one-inch by four-inch ribbons and covered with powdered sugar.

"Wow. You've done so much, Rosevita. How can we ever thank you?" Frankie's eyes welled up. The hospitality was tremendous.

"You make my son happy." Rosevita took both of Frankie's hands into hers. Frankie couldn't resist flinging her arms around the woman and giving her a bear hug. That's when she noticed Rosevita also had tears in her eyes.

"He makes me very happy, too." Frankie gave her another squeeze.

When they broke their embrace, Rosevita stepped back and said, "We will have a nice lunch for your mama and papa. Just like yesterday."

"Oh, you don't have to go to the trouble." Then Frankie

remembered to be gracious. "What I mean is, I appreciate you making my parents feel at home." She looked around at the extended table. "Let me set the table for dinner tomorrow. That is, if you don't mind."

"That would be very nice. Thank you."

Rosevita turned to tend to the activity on the kitchen stove. "I have a couple of things to take care of. I'll be back in a few minutes."

Frankie trotted down the hallway. She unpacked her laptop, even though she promised herself she wouldn't, but this wasn't work-related. She pulled up a template for a menu and began to type:

The Lombardi Family
Christmas Eve Dinner

Steamed Mussels
Clams Oreganato
Scungilli Salad
Calamari Marinara Over Linguini
Scallops Oreganato
Baked Stuffed Cod
Shrimp Scampi

Dolci
Cannoli, Sfogliatella, & Baba al Rhum

Mangia Bene, Ridi Spesso, Ama Molto

She included one of her favorite phrases at the bottom of the menu: *Eat Well, Laugh Often, Love Much*. She added a border of garland as a final touch. Then she Googled for a printing shop in Salerno and began to call the first number on the list. Her first question was: "Do you speak English?" When she got an affirmative answer, she asked if they could do an overnight print job. "I would like to have twenty menus printed."

She listened carefully. "Bravo. Wonderful. I will email the artwork now. I know I'm pressing my luck, but is there any chance you can deliver them?"

She listened again. "Yes, I can pay for a messenger service. Do you also have a whiteboard? Markers?" She explained as best she could and she got an affirmative response. She gave them her contact information, a credit card, and the address.

"Mille grazie. Buon Natale!"

That would be her small, humble contribution. She could ask everyone to sign their names on the back of each one, and then they would have a memento of the evening. They didn't call her Bossy Pants for nothing!

Frankie returned to the kitchen, where the activity continued. Giovanni and Marco were back from their second round of errands. Both had their hands filled with pastry boxes and loaves of bread. Then the two brothers were out the door again.

The morning moved quickly. The sound of a car on the gravel driveway perked up the dogs' ears. Nunzio and Rocco were at the ready, slamming their tails against Rosevita's legs. Frankie sprinted to the door and followed the dogs to the approaching vehicle. Rosevita said something in Italian, and the dogs sat at attention.

The car stopped, and the driver got out, as did Frankie's parents. The driver retrieved their luggage from the trunk. Frankie's father tried to tip him, but he refused to take the money, saying that he appreciated it, but Mr. Lombardi had taken care of everything.

Frankie hugged her parents and linked arms with her mother. "Rosevita! So nice to see you!" Bianca beamed.

"Nice to see you again, too," Rosevita replied. "How was your trip?"

"Long, but good." They kissed each other on both cheeks.

"Guillermo! *Come stai?*" Rosevita asked Frankie's father.

"*Molto bene!*" He took his turn pecking cheeks, including Frankie's.

"My, aren't we very European!" Frankie laughed.

"And while I am here, I am pleased to be called Guillermo."

Both Frankie and Amy's fathers were named William, so when they wanted to refer to Frankie's father, they called him Guillermo. Partly as a tease, but mostly to differentiate the two.

Giovanni pulled into the driveway with a large Christmas tree tied to the roof. He got out and greeted the Cappellas. "I'll be right with you."

He returned to the car and cut the rope, freeing the tree. He rolled it off the top and leaned it against the car. "When Marco comes, we'll bring it inside."

Guillermo offered to help, but Giovanni politely refused.

Rosevita showed the Cappellas into the house, through the kitchen, and out to the patio, the same path Frankie had taken when she first arrived. Bianca was stunned by the view, and Guillermo was amazed at the food set before him. He should have realized he was walking into the home of a family who fed people for a living. To the Lombardis, it was an art form.

"Please. Sit. What would you like to drink?" Rosevita asked.

"Oh, you must try Mr. Parisi's wine!" Frankie suggested. "Unless I polished all of it off last night." She pretended to shudder.

Rosevita smiled. "Mr. Parisi brings four, five bottles all the time."

"How much does he make?" Frankie was interested in this local vintner.

"Sometimes fifty cases per year," Rosevita said casually.

"Fifty? Holy moly! That's a lot of vino!"

"We drink a lot of vino!" Rosevita laughed. Then she explained that Mr. Parisi had a little over two acres of land.

"Exactly how many grapes does it take to make fifty cases?"

"I think maybe nine hundred kilos," Rosevita replied. "If there's time, I am sure he would like to show you his vineyard. It's petite, but he is very proud of it."

"So, he can make fifty cases from a ton of grapes?" Guillermo asked as he scanned the liquid in his goblet.

"He says so." Rosevita lifted her glass and made a toast: *"Cin cin!"*

It was pushing past three o'clock. After two hours of conversation and specialty meats, cheese, olives, and roasted artichokes, it was time to take the Cappella family to their Airbnb.

"I'm going to need a nap." Frankie's father grunted.

"I did the same thing yesterday," Frankie said, laughing.

"Come." Giovanni got up and gallantly helped Bianca from her seat. He walked them to the door, then turned to his mother. "When Marco comes back, do not let him leave. We must bring the tree inside."

This time, Giovanni accepted Guillermo's help moving the tree to the front porch.

"This is a beauty," Mr. Cappella remarked.

"I reserved from a farm a few kilometers away. They do a nice job," Giovanni said proudly. "Before you leave, you must go to see the Luci d'Artista Light Show. It's through the entire town. Walk along the main shopping street, Corso Vittorio

Emanuele, and then to the Piazza Portanova. It is where you will find a fantastic tree."

As they walked to the car, Giovanni continued, "Anita and Rafaella are bringing the children to see Santa Claus in the late afternoon. They must take two cars so you can go with them."

"That sounds like fun. Will we see the lights during the day?"

"You will be there until sunset, while dinner is being prepared, so yes, you will see the beautiful lights."

The three settled into the car when Bianca spoke. "Giovanni, I cannot express my gratitude for everything you've done for us."

"It's a pleasure. I am happy everyone can be together."

Giovanni drove the half mile to the Airbnb. "If you wanna, you can walk back to the house tomorrow morning for breakfast. I cannot promise you peace and quiet," he said, chuckling.

"This is wonderful," Bianca replied. She noted that it was truly only a handful blocks from the Lombardi home.

"You wanna come back for dinner later?" Giovanni asked. "We eat around eight."

"Oh, I think I've surpassed my caloric intake for today, but I appreciate the offer," Bianca said.

"If you get bored, you can call me. I'll come get you."

"Maybe we'll take a stroll later, but right now, I really do need a nap." Bianca chuckled. "My body clock is very confused."

Giovanni laughed. "I understand!"

He helped them with their suitcases and got the key from the owner. The Airbnb was a small guest house at the rear of another large, old villa.

"You come and go as you please. If you wanna breakfast, you go to the main house." He nodded toward the other building. "But we would like you to come to our house."

"Of course! We want to spend as much time as we can visiting," Bianca exclaimed.

"If not dinner later, and you are not too tired, you come for coffee? Dessert?"

"I'll give you a ring once we get settled and rest a bit," she said.

"*Molto bene!*" Giovanni got back into the car and waved.

Chapter 12

Family Secrets

Giovanni was relieved the Cappellas' trip was uneventful and they arrived with all their luggage. His thoughts were interrupted by the buzzing of his cell phone. It was as if the thought of his luggage made his phone ring. It was the airline informing him that they found his suitcase. It was in Milan. It would take at least two days before he could retrieve it in Naples. Giovanni was convinced the sneakers and a tracksuit in a carry-on was going to be his look for this trip.

But he needed a suit for mass, and Marco only had one with him. He checked his watch. It was four o'clock. He had a little time to run into town to see what he could purchase before he had to be back at the house. He phoned Frankie to let her know he was on a mission. For clothes. Again.

"Gio, what about one of your father's suits? Or did your mother give them away?"

"I dunno."

"Hang on a second." Frankie went through the house in search of Rosevita.

"Ah, Rosevita. Gio still does not have his suitcase. I don't know how to ask you, but do you still have any of Mr. Lombardi's suits?"

Rosevita blinked several times. "*Sì*. I was going to donate for the holidays but did not have time. There are a few beautiful pieces I think will fit Giovanni. Tell him to come home now, and we will see what we can do."

Giovanni could hear his mother on the other end. "Perfetto!" But he had mixed feelings. He was annoyed that his luggage was still days away; he was happy he didn't have to beat his way through last-minute shoppers, but he was also confused as to how he would feel wearing something that once belonged to his father. Worse, how would his mother feel about it? He supposed he was going to find out.

Within minutes, he was back at the house. The first thing he noticed was the Christmas tree leaning precariously to one side. He straightened it before he went in, wondering when his brother would return.

Frankie met him at the door. "You really need to find a better way to travel," she joked. "But your mother has two gorgeous suits that may fit you."

Giovanni was uneasy. Would they smell like mothballs?

His mother was at the top of the stairs of the second floor, where her and Lucia's bedrooms were situated.

"Gio! Come!" She was very animated.

Giovanni followed into her bedroom. On one side of the room was an armoire. The doors were open, exhibiting two impeccably tailored suits. One was dark gray and the other dark navy. She held the navy suit up against his chest. "I think this will work!"

Giovanni was slightly taller than his father, so the pants might be an issue, but the clock was ticking. At least he wouldn't look any more ridiculous than he did in the tracksuit and loafers. He took the suit into the bathroom and tried it on. The jacket fit perfectly, but as he suspected, the pants hit at his ankle. Perhaps a dark pair of socks could make everything blend in. Besides, who was looking at your shoes when you were in church? Probably everybody.

He walked over to where his mother and Frankie were standing. His mother's hands flew up to her face, but not in horror. It was delight.

"You remind me of your father. So handsome."

Frankie agreed. "That suit looks spectacular on you."

Giovanni looked down at the hem of the slacks. Frankie stooped to see if there was any wiggle room for dropping the length. She glanced up at Giovanni. "Better wear a dark pair of socks."

"Like I say before, I am a fashion innovator." He hugged his mother. "You sure you don't mind?"

"No! I am happy you can wear it." Rosevita was ver-klempt. "Okay, take it off now, and I'll hang it outside so it can be fresh for tomorrow."

Giovanni returned to the bathroom and changed back into his own clothes. "I am going to need a shirt and tie."

"I know Marco has a white shirt. I put it in the laundry this morning. I'll iron it for you."

"What about Marco?"

"You will have to live with short pants. He will have to live with a different shirt," Rosevita said firmly.

The dogs announced another vehicle. Rosevita looked out the window. "Speak of Marco. He is here."

"*Bene.* We can bring the tree inside," Giovanni said, with relief in his voice. Why did traveling and clothes become a problem for him? At least this problem was solved. Sorta.

Giovanni and Frankie hurried down the stairs while Rosevita hung the suit on the lamp on her balcony.

The furniture had been moved earlier that day in order to accommodate the large tree. Rosevita directed them through the archway as the brothers lugged the giant fir into the house. Traditional ornaments and strings of lights were stacked in boxes, ready to adorn the tree. In order to keep the chaos under control, the plan was to decorate it after the children went to bed.

There was no room in the kitchen to prepare a big meal that evening, so it would be an early dinner of soup, bread, cheese, and dried sausage. Rafaella agreed to let Sophia and Lorenzo have a sleepover at her house to be sure they were out of everyone's hair. Once the tree was secure, Marco drove the kids to his cousin's house and returned about forty minutes later.

It was past seven before the first strand of lights was placed on the tree, and it took another three hours to finish the job. Rosevita handed the tree topper to Frankie. It was an angel decorated with gold, holding a star in her hands.

"You can do this."

Frankie was flattered. It was an honor to place the star at the top. Giovanni helped her up the ladder and held on to her hips. He had no other option if he wanted her to remain steady. They were on one side of the tree, and the others were on the other side, making it easy for Giovanni to give her a pat on her hiney. Frankie tried to stifle a giggle, but to no avail, and almost lost her balance.

"Easy!" Rosevita exclaimed. "That angel has been in the family many years."

"Not to worry, Mama. Everything is under control," Giovanni reassured her.

"Sometimes you are worse than the children," Lucia muttered.

Frankie noticed Lucia was in a bit of a sour mood. Maybe she was tired?

"Lucia, come. Let me make you some tea," Frankie offered.

Lucia looked surprised.

"I have a recipe my grandfather would make when we decorated the tree. You have some brandy?"

"Of course." Suddenly Lucia's face brightened. "Come."

Giovanni gave Frankie a raised eyebrow, and she responded with a wink. The two women shuffled into the kitchen, and Frankie put the kettle on the stove while Lucia fetched the brandy from the pantry.

"We use this for cooking," she said as she handed the bottle to Frankie.

"We use it for drinking," Frankie said with a devilish grin.

Lucia laughed out loud, her mood shifting into something more pleasant. She pulled out a chair and sat at the table. Frankie reached into the tea canister and plucked a few bags. Then she went back into the pantry and found a bottle of honey and a fresh lemon. When the water started to boil, she removed the kettle from the heat and poured the water over the tea bags, added the honey, a squeeze of lemon, and then the brandy. She took the bags out quickly.

"You no let it steep?"

"Just enough for flavor." She stirred the concoction and handed a cup to Lucia.

Lucia looked skeptical but took a sip. She nodded. "This is not so bad."

Frankie purposely wanted to spend some time alone with Lucia. She was determined to find out what made her tick. She began by asking questions about living in Salerno, waiting for an opportunity to bring up her husband. Frankie sensed there was a lot of pain the woman was holding inside, but it had been years since he passed. What was she clinging to?

Before she could get down to the heart of the matter, the rest of the family entered the kitchen, asking if they could have some of Grandpa Cappella's special tonic. By that time, Lucia had loosened up and was more relaxed. Rosevita gave Frankie a nod of approval.

Frankie made more of the evening elixir, and everyone enjoyed a cup together before they returned to the living room one more time to admire their work. Lucia carried a tray of very small cordial glasses filled with brandy. Each took a glass, and they made a toast to the spectacular tree adorned with five hundred tiny white lights and over a hundred ornaments. They said their goodnights and retired to their rooms.

Frankie's body clock was still in flux, and she woke up around two in the morning. She figured she should make herself another cup of tea, or maybe just skip straight to the brandy. The kitchen was dark, with the exception of light coming from under the pantry door. She thought she heard voices and became uneasy. Her first instinct was to pick up the heavy cast-iron frying pan that was sitting on the stove. But then what?

She crept closer to the door and leaned against it, but it wasn't latched, and she stumbled. When she steadied herself, she was holding the frying pan over her head, with Marco and Giovanni crouched on the floor. Evidence of panettone crumbs were all over their faces.

"What are you doing?" she said in a hushed, nervous voice.

"What are *you* doing?" Giovanni retorted. "Shush. Close the door."

Frankie slid to the floor, now eye to eye with the brothers. She noticed that they were eating from the bottom of the bread.

"I repeat. What are you doing besides pilfering the panettone?"

Giovanni gave her another *shush* and wiped his hands on a towel.

"We are trying to find out Mama's recipe."

"Why don't you just ask her?" Frankie wondered.

"Because it's a secret," the brothers whispered in unison.

"And what are you doing with a frying pan?" Giovanni asked.

"I don't know. A weapon?" Frankie said awkwardly.

"You were gonna fight a burglar with a skillet?" Marco asked wryly.

"It was a reflex," Frankie defended herself.

"Like one of those stupid movies when the babysitter goes in the basement?" Marco joked.

"Ha. Ha. No, I was going to scream while I was beating them over the head. 'Stay away from our panettone!'"

Frankie stopped abruptly. She thought she heard footsteps coming down the stairs. "Shush."

She reached up, turned off the pantry light, and pulled the door tight.

They listened for more sounds. Someone stepped into the kitchen. "Hello?"

It was a woman's voice. Perhaps Rosevita. Whoever it was didn't say anything else, but turned off the kitchen lights and moved down the hall and back up the stairs.

When it was quiet, Frankie slowly opened the door and crawled out. She looked down the dimly lit hallway. The coast was clear, and she waved the brothers out.

"We have to wrap the bread," Giovanni whispered.

"As if no one is going to notice a half-eaten panettone?" Frankie asked.

"We only ruined the bottom of one of them."

"And did you accomplish your mission?" Frankie chided them.

"Not exactly. But I will fix this. I'll be sure this one is in the back, and I'll cut it up on Christmas." Giovanni cleaned up the crumbs, wrapped the bread, and placed it behind the others.

They finally tiptoed their way back to their sleeping quarters, hoping their scheme wasn't discovered by anyone else. Frankie shook her head. It was like being with the Little Rascals.

Chapter 13

Frankie got a text from her parents, asking if they could come over for breakfast. She replied they should absolutely come over.

It was almost ten, but things were already bustling in the large kitchen. Frankie didn't want to put anything else on Rosevita and Lucia's plate—no pun intended.

"My parents are on their way, but I don't want to get in *your* way."

"No worry," Rosevita assured her. "I put a platter together of breakfast pastries. They're in the pantry."

Frankie froze. Had they left any evidence of their chicanery?

Rosevita continued, "There is fresh fruit in the refrigerator. You can make a nice pot of espresso."

"You are amazing," Frankie gratefully responded.

She ducked into the scene of the crime and discovered everything was still in place. A platter containing brioche, croissants, and other sweet pastries was waiting. It was a typical Italian breakfast. No bacon and eggs, pancakes, or waffles. Just enough to kick-start the day. Frankie had warned her parents not to expect a Denny's meal, which was totally fine with them. They knew the major caloric intake was set for later in the evening.

Frankie carried everything out to the patio so they wouldn't be under everyone's feet. It was a clear, cool morning in the low sixties. Giovanni turned on the outdoor heater to take the chill out of the air.

With the children still at Rafaella's, the house was quiet, with the exception of Christmas music playing in the background. The plan was for Anita to pick up her children at Rafaella's, give them baths, a change of clothes, and get them ready for their jaunt into town to see Santa. With the crowds of locals and tourists, it had been advised to make an appointment if the children wanted to sit on Santa's lap. Fortunately, they were able to get one just under the wire. It would be the last one of the day; Santa had his work cut out for him for the rest of the evening.

Frankie's father was curious about Pompeii and wanted to do the two-hour tour that started at one o'clock. It was approximately a thirty-minute drive from the house to the ruins. Giovanni apologized that he could not accompany them and arranged for a driver to take them there and back.

By the time they finished their sweet breakfast and cappuccino, it was eleven-thirty, and their driver arrived. He wanted to be sure they got there in plenty of time. After their tour of the ruins, they would return to the house and meet up with Anita and Rafaella, and venture into town.

While the kids were with Santa, the Cappellas planned to navigate the decorated streets, visit the markets, and observe the vast amount of decorations, particularly the lights. It was going to be festive chaos.

Frankie gave her parents a peck on the cheek and ordered them to have fun, although looking at ruins from a horrific event, with bodies frozen in time, didn't sound like a good time to her. It gave her the shivers.

As the car pulled away, another one entered the driveway. A young man got out, carrying a box under one arm and what looked like her whiteboard in the other. She let out a long sigh of relief. She needed organization. Yes, it was one of her quirks. She claimed it saved her from herself. Surprisingly, she could be very scattered if she didn't have something to reel her in. Visual cues were always a plus.

She tipped the young man and scooted into the house. She didn't want anyone to ask her any questions. The menus were a surprise. The whiteboard identified her orderly eccentricity. But she felt it was justified, especially with the multitude of distractions.

When she got to her room, she opened the box that contained the menus. They were beautiful. Much more than she expected. She hoped everyone would be as pleased as she was. She removed the plastic covering on the board and set it up on the chair in the corner of the room. Eventually someone was going to notice it, but she'd explain if necessary. She pulled out a marker and began to make boxes like a calendar. Each box had dates, names, and places.

26th
Nina to Milan—Jordan Pleasance

27th
Amy and Peter—Geneva
Randy and Rachael—Rome

28th
Nina meets Richard—Naples
Randy and Rachael—Rome
Amy and Peter—Geneva

29th
Randy and Rachael—Naples
Nina and Richard—Naples
Amy and Peter—Naples
Meet up with everyone in Pompeii
Giovanni to rent van
Pizza tour

30th
Positano & Amalfi Coast
Dinner in Sorrento

31st
Everyone on their own until evening
Mr. Parisi Party?

Jan 1
Brunch at Baronissi house
Giovanni and Frankie to bring food

Jan 2
Battipaglia—Mozzarella farm and store

Jan 3
Return

Frankie stood back from her slate of activities. A sense of calm flooded her body. She felt so much better having a visual of the agenda. The only thing that was still loosey-goosey were the final plans for New Year's Eve. Giovanni wanted to show everyone a typical Salerno celebration. Mr. Parisi was planning a party at his house to open the latest wine production. The idea was to go there for a short visit and then go back to the house while Rosevita and Lucia continued at Mr. Parisi's. The children were going to sleep over at Dominic's and Rafaella's, who hired a babysitter in so they could attend a party with some of their professors and colleagues. Giovanni and Marco told the crew they could watch fireworks from the second-floor balcony, a tradition they held before they moved to New York.

Frankie turned when she heard footsteps getting closer. It was Giovanni, wearing a big smile.

"I knew you couldn't go on without something in front of your face."

Frankie sighed. "I know. I know. I tried to keep it together on my laptop, but it wasn't doing it for me. I needed a large chart to keep everything in focus."

Giovanni put his arm around her. "You are a very funny person."

"Funny? I'm organized." She pouted.

"That's why I love you, *cara.*" He kissed her on the top of her head, something he did frequently. At first Frankie thought it was weird. Now she kinda liked that particular gesture of affection.

The two of them left her room to see how they could help with all the preparations. It was past noon, and the kitchen was bursting with the aromas and promises of gastronomic delight. Frankie asked if she could start setting the table and noticed there wasn't a centerpiece.

"Rosevita, what do you put in the center of the table?"

Rosevita's hands flew up to her face. "Madonna mia! I forgot to order the flowers! So much going on!"

Frankie placed her hands on Rosevita's shoulders. "No problem. I shall come up with something."

Frankie went to the side of the house where Marco left some of the tree clippings. There was enough to get started. She returned to the dining room with an armful of fir cuttings and rummaged around in the sideboard for candles. She knew there had to be a few in the house, and found several boxes in a variety of sizes, glass votive holders, and candlestick holders. *Perfect!* She began to lay the branches down the middle of the table and set the candles in groupings of tall, medium, short. Then she went into the living room and pulled several ornaments from the back of the tree. She interspersed the ornaments among the branches. Simple. Elegant.

The dishes were stacked on the sideboard in order of the courses served. Frankie placed twelve charger plates on the table. Rosevita invited her two neighbors every year. They weren't Catholic. In fact, Rosevita had no idea what religion they practiced. But as far as Rosevita was concerned, as long as you believed there was something greater than all of us, you were okay in her book. Peace and harmony was the theme.

It took almost two hours for Frankie to complete the table setting, taking special care to fold the napkins so the menus would stand upright on the plates when she later placed them there. Crystal glasses finished it off. She dimmed the chandelier to get an idea how everything would look once the candles were lit.

She let out a satisfactory murmur, "Uh, huh."

Frankie returned to the kitchen, which was at fever pitch. Marco was cleaning the cod that had been soaking for a few days, and Giovanni was cleaning the mussels and the clams. He was glad he talked his mother into letting the fishmonger clean the scungilli and calamari. Scungilli, the meat from a conch shell, is sliced, then marinated in lemon juice, zest, celery, olive oil, olives, and garlic for several hours. The calamari, also known as squid, also had to be sliced and pounded. Giovanni prepared the marinara sauce in advance. The calamari takes about forty-five minutes to cook to be sure it is tender.

Lucia was cutting the pasta dough into long thin strips and laid them on a board. The calamari was going to be served over the fresh linguine.

Everyone was busy with their tasks while Andrea Boccelli's voice crooned Christmas carols over the speakers. The mood was festive and intense at the same time. This was the biggest dinner event of the entire year. Everything had to be perfect.

Around four o'clock, the Cappellas returned from their history lesson, and the children were wound up in anticipation of Santa. Anita and Rafaella strapped the kids into their respective car seats, with Bianca riding in the front passenger seat of Anita's vehicle, and Guillermo in the front passenger seat in Rafaella's. Each of the kids had a small gift they would give to Santa to bring to the children at the hospital. The two cars were chock full of merriment as everyone sang Christmas carols in English and Italian.

As they approached the town center, Bianca gasped in awe. "This is like nothing I have ever seen before."

Giant ornaments made completely of lights were suspended above the streets. It didn't matter that it was still daylight. It was magical. No wonder Salerno was considered a stage of lights at Christmas; the Luci d'Artista exhibits were like no other. Bianca wasn't sure who was more impressed, her or the kids, each pointing to the next fantastic display.

When they reached their destination, Anita and Rafaella corralled the kids to make their way to Santa, and the Cappellas would walk around town. They agreed on a meeting time and place to return to the house.

After walking for two hours, the sun was setting and the lights were brighter, a phantasmagoria of illuminations. Bianca noted there was joy in every nook and cranny on the streets, in the windows, and on the face of each passerby. If you couldn't get into a holiday mood there, then you were not paying attention.

"I can understand why Giovanni wanted to spend the holidays here. It's like being in a wonderland," Bianca sighed dreamily.

Guillermo agreed and threaded Bianca's arm through the crook of his. He felt like a kid again.

When they returned to their meeting place, each of the

children had a candy cane either in their hand, stuck to their mitten, or crumbled on their jacket. The two mothers knew it wasn't going to be difficult to get the kids into bed later. "Wear them out" was the plan. After dinner, Rafaella would take their children home, where they would be put to bed by a babysitter. It was the same plan for Sophia and Lorenzo. Even though the children were getting along like peas in pods, the parents wanted to have time with their children on Christmas Day. They would be able to bounce off the walls together, later in the day. But for tonight, they had to change into holiday dress.

Chapter 14

Christmas Eve

Dinner was to start around seven-thirty. At six-thirty, there was a knock on the door. Rosevita answered the door. There stood two young women and a young man dressed in waitstaff attire. *"Buon Natale!"*

Rosevita looked puzzled, so they explained that they had been hired for the evening.

"Giovanni? Marco?" Rosevita called out to her sons. They came to the front entry and smiled.

"Buon Natale," Marco greeted them. He let the trio in and pointed them toward the kitchen, while Giovanni explained to his mother that they were students from the college he'd hired to help serve dinner. He and Marco wanted the same thing for their mother and aunt as they had at the restaurant the previous year: dinner with family where nobody worked, at least not for the rest of the evening.

"Oh Giovanni. Marco. You boys didn't have to do this."

"Consider it a thank-you for everything you've done for us," Marco said. "Now go get dressed. Giovanni and I will explain everything to them."

Lucia had joined them when she saw the three strangers

enter the kitchen. She had heard Giovanni's explanation and was speechless. Such a kind gesture. She wondered if her Dominic was in on this, as well, but she didn't dare ask.

Everyone excused themselves to finish dressing for dinner.

Frankie was in her room, just finishing up. She was wearing an embroidered purple jacket over black slacks and knee-high boots. Her long, black hair was pulled back in a high ponytail, revealing amethyst earrings. The effect was stunning.

She grabbed the box of menus and dashed into the dining room before anyone else had a chance to see what she was up to. She lit all the candles and dimmed the chandelier and the wall sconces. The room had a warm, beautiful glow.

Lucia was the first to enter the dining room. She halted at the doorway. "*Bellissimo!*" she exclaimed. "And what is this?" She gingerly fingered a menu.

"A little keepsake to remind people of this wonderful dinner you and Rosevita prepared."

Lucia's eyes welled. "So beautiful. So nice."

Rosevita entered the room and had a similar reaction. The spectacular table and the hired staff was more than either of them anticipated or imagined.

Giovanni entered next, wearing his father's suit.

Now Rosevita gasped. "You remind me of your father."

Giovanni was concerned he upset her. "Mama, if you wanna, I can change."

"No. Please. You look so handsome." She sniffled and pulled a handkerchief from her sleeve. Her *black* sleeve on her *black* dress. Frankie wondered what she was going to think about the cream cashmere wrap and gloves that she bought her. Could be a major faux pas. *Oh well.* She had good intentions when she bought them.

The doorbell rang; the dogs barked. It was the spinster neighbors, Adelaide and Evie. Both were in attire similar to what Lucia and Rosevita wore. It was then that Frankie saw that Rosevita was wearing a beautiful gold brooch. *A little glam*, Frankie noted. Maybe there was hope of a wardrobe renewal.

Marco, Giovanni, and Dominic pulled out the chairs for the women, and the children stood between their parents. Dominic was the oldest, so he said grace.

"Heavenly father, and all the saints above, bless this food, our family, and all the souls of the world. May we all live in peace. Amen."

A loud "Amen" response reverberated through the room, with the children scampering off to the kitchen, where their special table awaited. Frankie had made sure she put a small centerpiece together for them from a few pinecones she found in the yard under the stone pine trees.

Once the children were settled, the adults could relax and enjoy the evening. Dominic opened a bottle of prosecco and poured. Lucia made a toast: "*Mangia bene, ridi spesso, ama molto*"—the same words that were on the menu. Frankie was pleased. She took it as an acknowledgment of her efforts.

The waitstaff began to serve the first course, then the second, and each one that followed, clearing the dishes in between. With each course, words and utterances of delight went around the table. Chatter and laughter increased as the evening went on. It was almost ten o'clock when the last dish of scampi was removed from the table. Everyone agreed to save dessert for after mass. By Frankie's calculations, that would be somewhere around two in the morning. No wonder Christmas Day was a little more laid-back.

The sitter for Dominic and Rafaella's children arrived to bring them back to their house, and the sitter for Sophia and Lorenzo was not far behind. The kids gave their nonnas very tired kisses goodnight, wished them a *Buon Natale*, and yawned their way to their respective vehicles.

Due to the popularity of the Christmas mass at the Duomo di Salerno, reservations were necessary if you wanted to get in the door and sit in a pew. When Giovanni first approached Frankie with the suggestion of going to Salerno, he asked Dominic if he could make the arrangements, which were well in advance.

The closer they got to the cathedral, the larger the crowds. Giovanni was happy he hired two cars; otherwise, they might not find parking within miles of the church. It was a special night, and his family deserved to be treated with special care.

The church was adorned with thousands of lights inside and out. The domed interior was covered with carvings, tile, and paintings in the Baroque style. Every square inch was covered with a work of art. It was almost overwhelming.

The usher took their tickets and showed them to their pews. It was an extravaganza, from the opulent dinner to the opulent church. It was a night that would be remembered.

The hour-and-a-half service consisted of prayers and music. You didn't have to know Latin to feel the importance of the Cardinal's words. He spoke of peace. Kindness. Tolerance. Patience. Gratitude. It was a beautiful service, especially the part when everyone turned to the person next to and behind them to wish each other Peace on Earth.

The ride home was rather quiet. Perhaps everyone was deep in reflection. There was a lot to reflect on. A lot to be thankful for.

Chapter 15

Christmas Day

By the time they got home from mass, it was way beyond two in the morning, and everyone voted to save dessert for breakfast. Eating something sweet was the usual breakfast fare anyway. The only thing left was to put the children's gifts under the tree.

Sophia had asked Santa Claus for a bicycle, but there was no place for her to ride it in the city, which brought up an important conversation between Marco and Anita. It was time to move to a neighborhood with trees, a yard, and a place to ride a bike. They decided to break the news to everyone on Christmas Day by giving Sophia a photo of her new bicycle and Lorenzo a photo of his bouncy house. Naturally everyone would ask where she would ride it and where would they put the bouncy house? That's when Marco and Anita were going to announce they put a deposit on a house in Ridgewood, just a few blocks from Frankie's family. It was time to move on, but not far away. They were nervous about telling everyone, especially Giovanni, but his life was evolving, as well.

By seven a.m., the kids were awake and eager to see if

Babbo Natale—Santa Claus—had visited. Groggy-eyed grown-ups in loungewear gathered in the living room, happy to dive into the pastries and cappuccino. The kids were served hot chocolate. Marco and Anita decided to go first. Marco handed a very large box to Sophia. She thought it would be heavier, and she shook it to hear what might be inside. Nothing but paper rattling. She tore off the decorations and lifted the lid. Inside was a photo of a turquoise and white bicycle. She looked confused and held it up for everyone to see.

Anita laughed. "You wanted a bicycle, yes?"

"Yes, but a real one. Not a picture." Sophia was about to burst into tears when her father interrupted and explained.

"Sweetheart, it is a photo of your new bicycle that is waiting for you at home. Santa left it there so we wouldn't have to take it on the plane back to America."

Sophia started jumping up and down. "I got a bike! I got a bike!"

Lorenzo was already ripping his packaging apart. He, too, had a perplexed expression. "This?"

This time, Anita explained. "You will have your bouncy house when we go back to New York."

"But where?" Lorenzo may have been four years old, but he knew there was no place for it in the apartment.

Marco got up from his chair and stood behind Anita. He put his hands on her shoulders. "We have an announcement." Before anyone would guess that it was another baby, he quickly described their plans.

"It's time we lived in a place where the children could go out in their own backyard and not wait for someone to take them to the park."

Everyone nodded in agreement. When he explained the location, cheers and applause followed.

"That's wonderful!" Rosevita stood and hugged her son and then her daughter-in-law. "I was wondering if you would move. You spent a lot of time in that apartment."

"True. But we were teenagers. We didn't need constant supervision when we went outside." He eyed his brother.

Giovanni smiled. "Not always."

Frankie was especially pleased. She would be able to visit Marco, Anita, and the kids every time she visited her parents. She looked at Giovanni to see his reaction.

"I'm happy for you, Marco . . . as long as you show up for work on time," he jested.

"Oh, I will make sure of that!" Anita chuckled. "I'll want him out of the house, pronto! And I also got a job in Ridgewood." She was a special education teacher, and they were in high demand. "It's at the elementary school where Sophia will attend, and then Lorenzo." She hesitated. "That is, if everything goes as planned."

"Did you already buy the house?" Lucia asked.

"We put a deposit on it. We got approved for the mortgage. We're just waiting to have the closing," Marco replied.

"And you were doing this behind my back?" Giovanni grinned again, teasing his brother one more time.

"We didn't want to say anything until everything was final. No jinx," Anita said. Superstitions ran deep in the Italian culture.

"This calls for a toast!" Rosevita announced. She got up and headed toward the kitchen. Frankie followed.

"So, what do you think?" Frankie was anxious to hear Rosevita's opinion.

"It's wonderful. Marco is right. He and Giovanni were teenagers. They had their playtime when we lived here. Now it's time for Marco's children to have the same advantage." She handed a bottle of prosecco to Frankie to open.

Once the cork popped, Frankie said, "And there will be lots of room for you to visit."

Rosevita smiled. "I must confess. I miss the children, so yes, I will visit more often."

She gathered several champagne glasses and two small

glasses that she filled with ginger ale and a dash of cherry juice. "For the children!"

Frankie carried the tray back to the living room, where the kids were unwrapping gifts from their nonna and zia, Aunt Lucia. It was a combination of pajamas, mittens, Legos, and several learning toys.

Frankie decided it was time to hand over her gifts. First to Lucia, who proceeded to carefully remove the tape and made every effort not to tear the beautiful wrapping paper. Then she removed the lid, separated the tissue, and lifted the shimmery shawl from the box. From the expression on her face, Lucia was pleased and surprised. *"Bellissimo!"*

Frankie thought she glimpsed a tear in Lucia's eye.

"Mille grazie." She stood and kissed Frankie on the cheek.

"Prego!" Frankie used one of the five words she knew. Then she handed Rosevita her gift. This was the one that was creating a great deal of angst.

Like Lucia, Rosevita carefully opened the present so as not to disturb the paper. "We'll use for next year's panettone."

Giovanni and Marco gave each other a conspiratorial glance. One of them was going to have to rescue the mangled bread before anyone noticed.

Rosevita removed the wrap from the box and rubbed it against her face. "So soft! Beautiful!" Then she held up the gloves. "Perfetto!"

Frankie breathed a sigh of relief. "I'm so glad you like it."

She took no time to place the wrap around her shoulders. "Yes. I love!"

Giovanni took that moment to excuse himself and hurried into the pantry. He grabbed the panettone in the back. He realized he hadn't done such a terrific job rewrapping it and was glad he got his hands on it before someone else discovered it. He quickly removed the wrapping, brought the bread to the kitchen, and surgically removed the evidence of the assaulted bread. He sliced the bread and placed it on a platter.

His thought was to make French toast when the gift-giving came to a halt. "Perfetto!" he assured himself.

When he returned to the living room, he nodded at his brother. All was well.

Giovanni reached under the tree and pulled out a small box. Frankie held her breath. She really didn't know what to expect. Surprise was the theme of the morning. *Was there one in the box?* Her hands were shaking. She ripped off the paper, revealing a blue Tiffany box. She opened it slowly, and inside was a gorgeous pair of princess-cut diamond stud earrings. At least a karat each.

"Oh, Gio. These are exquisite." Her hands continued to tremble. She wasn't disappointed that it wasn't a ring. In one way, she was relieved. Not that she didn't hope they would get married one day, but the subject hadn't come up, and it would have been way too much to deliver that kind of intimate message in front of everyone. She held the box so everyone could see the dazzling gems.

"Let me help you." Giovanni took the box from Frankie and attempted to remove the earrings, but his hands were too big.

Rosevita decided this was a job for a woman. *"Dammelo, per favore."* She gestured for him to hand it over. Rosevita gingerly removed Frankie's amethyst earrings and helped her put the new dazzlers in her ears.

Frankie's hair was pulled back with a wide, white faux-fur band. The square cut of the diamonds accentuated her high cheekbones.

"Bellissimo!" Rosevita exclaimed. "Gio. You do good work!"

He blushed. "Anita helped me."

"Anita, *you* do good work!" Frankie announced and threw her arms around Giovanni. "Thank you so much." She went over to the large ornate framed mirror. "Oh, my. They're stunning."

Then it was time to give Giovanni his gift. He had worn the same watch since she knew him. It was a nice, simple, functional Movado, but she thought he could use something dressier and bought him a Baume & Mercier tank watch with a black leather strap. She almost felt guilty that she spent much less on his watch than he had on the earrings. Plus, all the money he shelled out for this trip? For everyone? She could have kicked herself, but a thousand dollars for a watch wasn't chump change, either. Besides, she couldn't afford the ten-thousand-dollar Cartier. But she could tell by the expression on his face, she could have given him a ten-dollar wind-up, and it would have made him happy.

"Frankie. You know I always wanted a watch like this, no?"

"No, I did not. Lucky guess." She grinned.

The exchange of gifts was winding down, and it was time to get the food ready for the comings and goings of friends and family.

Giovanni was taking no chances with the panettone and announced he was going to make French toast for anyone who was interested. Marco followed him into the kitchen and examined his brother's handiwork.

"You could be a criminal."

Giovanni looked around to see if anyone was in earshot. "We have to find the recipe. Go look in the box."

"You think she's going to keep it with everything else?"

"Why not?"

"Because it's a secret!" Marco hissed.

"What's a secret?" Rosevita appeared out of nowhere.

Now it was Marco's turn to cover their tracks. "Mama, we wanted to surprise you."

"Oh? With what?" she asked innocently.

"With tickets."

"For what?"

"Andrea Boccelli."

"Oh my! When?" she asked with excitement.

"When he comes to New York."

"But when?" she pressed.

"I'm not sure. April. May. I have to look." Marco could feel his nose growing like Pinocchio's.

Giovanni bit the inside of his lip to keep from laughing. This was going to be interesting. For one thing, no one knew if Boccelli was even going on tour.

"This is wonderful!" Rosevita exclaimed, and returned to the living room.

Marco knew he was going to have to find Boccelli, wherever he might be performing in the coming year. He went into the pantry and pulled out his phone, searching for concert dates. Lucky for him, one was scheduled at Madison Square Garden the following fall. He silently thanked Santa for watching over him and delivering his wild promise, even though tickets were three hundred dollars each. And he had to buy at least two! *Maybe it was a lesson in fibbing,* he thought, smiling to himself.

Bianca and Guillermo arrived in time for Giovanni's French toast. They also had a few gifts that were appreciated and unexpected. Rosevita and Lucia were given silver photo frames, and Sophia and Lorenzo each got a twenty-dollar bill. Everyone agreed ahead of time that they would not buy gifts for the rest of the adults with the exception of their hostesses and the children.

Back in the kitchen, Giovanni whipped up the French toast, plated it, and covered it in powdered sugar—hiding all evidence of their late-night nibbling.

The two brothers set up a long table on the lower patio for the buffet. A second table was set to accommodate the pastries and the reconstructed panettone.

The sun was bright, and the temperature was around sixty degrees. The outdoor heater was at the ready, as was the downstairs kitchen to heat up the stromboli and the stuffed mushrooms when guests arrived. Several bottles of Mr. Parisi's wine sat on another table that served as a bar. The food was sumptuous and plenty, as friends, neighbors, and cousins arrived and left at their leisure.

As promised, Marco brought out the bocce balls and taught the children how to play. It was as simple as lawn bowling, and the kids took to it easily.

When all that remained was the immediate family, they gathered around the warmth of the heater and decided it was truly a lovely way to spend the afternoon.

PART II

Chapter 16

December 26th
Milan

Nina heaved her suitcase into the back of her father's BMW. She went down her checklist: Ticket. Passport. Phone. Then she remembered what Frankie said about wearing red underwear for New Year's Eve. Neither of them had any idea where that tradition came from and decided it was probably a man. Nonetheless, why tempt fate? She checked her carry-on bag one more time: makeup, haircare, contact lens solution, bandanas, and yes, the red undies. She deliberately put them in her carry-on just in case her suitcase went to parts unknown. When she heard Giovanni's luggage was sidetracked to Milan, she offered to try to fetch it for him, but it was too late. It was already on its way to Naples. Or so they were told.

When she arrived at the airport, she checked her large suitcase, went through security, and waited at the gate. The only flights to Milan left around midnight so she opted to leave late Christmas night to arrive the following morning, giving her almost two full days in Milan before she moved on to Naples.

The airport was relatively quiet. She assumed most people were where they were planning to be. People-watching was one of her favorite pastimes. It was grist for her writing mill. People were smiling. *In an airport in New Jersey?* She snickered. *Miracles happen.* It was still Christmas, after all.

Everything seemed to be running smoothly. Too smoothly? Not that Nina was a negative person; she was just wary when things were going well. Her experience with Hollywood was one big example after another. You're on a hit TV show, and it gets cancelled. You're hired to write a sitcom, and even though the ratings were good, new executive management decided to "make some changes in programming." There was always the opportunity to have the rug pulled out from under you.

At the moment, she was secure with her podcast. It was successful, and she was basically the boss. But life is filled with "you never knows." Frankie was often on her case about keeping a positive attitude, reminding her that the "you never know" can lead to something good. She knew Frankie was right. Even though Nina had been through several huge disappointments, she always managed to land on her feet. *So far.*

She was excited to see Jordan again. He was a Brit with a keen sense of humor. He had several well-made and successful films under his belt, and Nina knew that one does not necessarily include the other. You could have a great film, but if nobody watches it, then it's not deemed a success. Conversely, you could have a financial blockbuster with a mediocre script and talent. So much of Hollywood was hype, which was another reason she was happy to meet up with Jordan. British filmmakers were focused on the script and good actors. Celebrity wasn't necessarily the driving force.

She remembered an interview with Helen Mirren when the host had asked her how often people bother her when she is out to dinner with friends. Nina couldn't remember the exact quote, but it was something to the effect that the royal family was the country's celebrities, and the rest were commoners.

The gate attendant announced they would begin boarding soon. Nina had decided to try a boutique airline that featured only business class for the eight-hour flight. She heard that some of the smaller airlines do not get priority when it came to takeoff and landing, but that was a rumor. She couldn't imagine adding one more thing for an air traffic controller to think about. The only people who were getting priority treatment were those flying first or business class. ATC prioritized flights if there were delays. At any given moment, there can be up to five thousand planes traversing the friendly skies. She didn't want to think about that.

Boarding went quickly, as there were only seventy-six seats on the plane. So far, so good. She reminded herself to stay positive in spite of the fact she hated to fly. Most people did these days, but it was often a necessity.

Once they reached cruising altitude, the flight attendants brough warm finger towels before they served dinner, and she had choices. A real menu! The food was remarkably good, the seats reclined, and the TV screen in front of her was substantial.

About two hours into the flight, she noticed that she wasn't feeling claustrophobic. She took it as a good sign.

Nina pulled a fashion magazine from the side pocket of her seat. She never considered herself a fashion maven, not even close, but she appreciated interesting and unique designs. She read that Italy was kicking the pants off Paris when it came to the fashion scene. No pun intended. Gucci appeared to be fueling the fashion renaissance, with Moschino mixing bizarre elements such as fringed hems on everything. Armani was still classic, while Prada featured whimsical accessories. *Fun* seemed to be an ongoing theme.

She chuckled, remembering Amy's garb from two years ago. She better not see the article Nina was reading, or she'd go back to her mismatched outfits, purple hair, and clunky boots. Wait. Amy *hadn't* given up the clunky boots, but at least now they were designer! Ha!

An announcement came over the PA informing the passengers they were beginning their descent into the Milan area, and they would be landing in approximately thirty minutes. Nina wondered what time it was; then the pilot announced it was eleven-thirty in the morning, and the flight was due to arrive at noon.

Once the plane landed, it took little time to get off. She easily found her way to the baggage claim, passing rows and rows of holiday trees and decorations. Global Entry also went smoothly, as did getting her luggage. She made her way to a line of taxis. Jordan had given her his address, which she handed to a cab driver who spoke fluent English. She asked him about the Gothic Duomo that housed da Vinci's famous mural, *The Last Supper*. He explained that it took six hundred years to complete the building. It was no wonder it was one of the largest cathedrals in the world. He went on to explain the word *duomo* signified the principal church of the town, and not necessarily a cathedral.

"There must be over a thousand churches in Italy, no?" Nina asked.

"Yes. And there are nine hundred in Rome alone," he shared, glancing at her in the rearview mirror. "To be honest, I do not believe anyone knows the total number, because there are many small chapels in villages all over the country. But did you know that only one-third of the country actively participates in religion?"

"Seriously?" Nina was surprised.

"Depends on what part of the country you live in. There are a lot of old traditions that are mixed into their beliefs."

"That makes sense. I know there are a lot of superstitions associated with the culture."

"Very true," he replied. "We are going to pass the Duomo;

it's in the Brera section of the city and about a five-minute walk from where you are staying. But if you want to go, I recommend you get tickets in advance."

"Noted." Nina wasn't sure how much time she would have to be a tourist. She was going to follow Jordan's lead.

The driver added one more fun fact. "More visitors go to churches here than the people who live here."

"Get out! Seriously?"

"It's true. Almost every tourist goes to at least one cathedral. See, you will go to one too, I am sure."

He had a very good point. Everyone she knew who had traveled to Italy went to at least one or more.

"Almost there." He turned into the Brera District of Milan. It was a quaint neighborhood with three-story buildings that flanked the narrow cobblestone streets. It exuded history with its architecture, cafés, museums, and galleries. There were window boxes filled with seasonal greens hanging from many of the buildings. Nina understood why Jordan would want to live there. It was a balance of industry and art.

The cab pulled in front of a nondescript building on a quiet street. The driver rolled her suitcase up to the door and rang the buzzer. She was surprised when it opened to what appeared to be a freight elevator. She paid the driver, thanked him, and gingerly entered the caged lift.

"*Grazie*. Thank you. Enjoy!"

"*Ciao*!" Nina called out.

She pushed the button that said PLEASANCE. It was the top floor. When the elevator creaked and jangled to a stop, the door opened directly into Jordan's apartment.

"Nina! *Bella*!" He threw his arms around her and rocked her side to side. "I am so happy to see you! Come."

He ushered her to the large living space with an open floor plan. The modern interior was in vast contrast to the historical exterior. On one end was a wall of windows and doors that opened to a roof terrace. The two bedrooms were on opposite sides of the living area.

"This is gorgeous," Nina exclaimed. "It's deceiving on the outside. I was expecting, well, I really don't know what I was expecting." She laughed.

"Let me show you to your room. You must be exhausted."

Nina followed him past the large sectional sofa, then past the long island kitchen counter. There was a bathroom and then a modest-sized room that obviously served both as a guest room and his office.

"Am I going to be in your way?

"Not at all. I am on holiday. No work for me this week."

"Great!"

"Are you hungry? Tired? What would you like to do first?"

"Take a shower and change into a fresh set of clothes."

"Coming right up." He unfolded a small stand and plopped her suitcase on top. "There are fresh towels in the bathroom."

"Wonderful." Nina knew she was running out of steam, but masked her exhaustion as best she could.

"I'll make us a cuppa." He was referring to the British slang for a cup of tea.

"Fab. Thanks," Nina said. "I'll be right back."

"No rush, darling."

Nina opened her suitcase and chuckled. Frankie was right about her wardrobe. Good thing she bought a couple of new tracksuits, a pair of jeans, and a blazer. She refused to wear anything but her hiking boots while she was traveling. She knew she would be doing a lot of walking. She had brought one nice pair of flats for dinners and the New Year's Eve party.

She pulled her locks into a tight bun and donned a shower cap. When she turned on the shower, she noticed that it wasn't as hot as she was accustomed to. Jordan had told her it was considered "instant heat," but it wasn't really all that hot. Warm, yes. Hot, nope. *Some things you take for granted.*

She finished quickly, toweled off, and jumped into a fresh pair of fleece pants and a matching hoodie. She wrapped her hair in a bandana and swiped on some lipstick. If they were going somewhere special, she would up her outfit to fit the circumstances. For now, comfort was key.

"Ah, there she is." Jordan handed her a warm mug. "Honey, correct?"

"Yes. You have quite a memory." Nina was impressed.

"Isn't it odd the things that one remembers?" Jordan replied.

"I totally get that. There are days when I can remember what I wore the first day of class when I was in the fifth grade, but don't ask me what I wore to a party last month."

"Exactly. Selective memory, I suppose."

"Isn't that what they say when people choose what they want to remember?"

"Yes, that too," he snickered. "So, my darling, what would you like to do today?"

"I have no idea. I've never been to Milan before."

"Ah, well, we have a fabulous museum just a few blocks away. You up for some culture?"

"I suppose it couldn't hurt." Nina chuckled.

"Are you hungry?"

"Not right now. But I am sure I could go for some veal Milanese later!" Nina was referring to the way a certain dish was prepared. The veal was pounded into thin cutlets, dredged in egg mixture and breadcrumbs, fried, and served with arugula, sliced cherry tomatoes, and shaved Grana Padano cheese on top.

"When in Milano . . ." Jordan joked.

He pulled out one of the stools at the counter and patted the cushion. "Sit. Tell me all about your life."

Nina laughed. "I was an actress. Then a writer for television. Now I do a podcast. That's it."

"All of it?" He gave her a quizzical look.

"You know the rest. You're in the biz."

"Somewhat. Good thing for residuals."

"Are you working on anything now?" she asked idly.

"I have a few ideas floating around." He raised his eyebrows. "But, as you said, you know the rest."

"I am sure you wouldn't have a hard time finding the production money," Nina said confidently.

"You'd be surprised what the expectations are. Guarantees. Who can guarantee anything today?"

"You mean besides politicians making fools of themselves?"

"Sweetheart, they've been doing that for well over a thousand years."

"My point, exactly," she retorted.

"Touché."

"So, tell me what's going on in that creative mind of yours?" she asked.

"*When Harry Met Sally* on *The Orient Express*."

"Huh?" Nina asked with bewilderment.

"Six episodes. Murder, mayhem, and romance. Each episode from the point of view of one of six different people. Do you remember *Murder 101*? It was a Hallmark series. She was a professor of crime writing, and the hero was a police officer. Sexual tension. Banter. A murder to solve."

"Sounds like it's been done before."

"Yes, but not necessarily the mash-up I have in mind."

"Continue," Nina probed.

"Each episode shifts perspective, so you keep guessing until the end. And of course, you don't know if the romance is real or if it's a guise to hide the real murderer."

"Sounds a bit like *Knives Out*. Please don't compare it to *Glass Onion*. That was horrible."

"I agree. I think it was the usual bunch of celebs sitting in a room figuring out how to make a few extra million dollars. The star power of the movie was the draw, plus the success of the first movie to entice viewers."

"Gotcha. I understand why you don't want to deal with Hollywood."

"Precisely. I have some serious connections with producers whose shows have been picked up by BritBox and Acorn, two excellent digital streaming services."

"Would you be the producer?"

"Yes, but I also want to write it."

"Ah. Tell me more." Nina rested her elbow on the counter, chin on her fist.

"I thought it was rather serendipitous that you contacted me."

"Oh?" Nina's eyes went wide.

"Yes, because I thought of you as a co-writer."

"Me?" Nina was stunned. "I wrote a sitcom. I've never written a film."

"Oh, darling, a script is a script. It's how it's developed that counts."

"This is very intriguing, Jordan." Nina smiled. "Do you have an outline?"

"Indeed I do. Wait right here. You don't mind if I go into your room, do you?"

"My room? Ha! It's your office." Nina chuckled at Jordan's polite inquiry.

"I want to make certain you don't have anything you don't want me to see."

"Like what? Another pair of sweatpants?"

"A-hem. Speaking of sweatpants, that jogging suit is perfect for hiking, but when you are in Milan, well, darling, you should up your game a bit. No offense."

Nina laughed out loud. "None taken! You sound like Frankie. But remember, I've been sequestered at home for a

couple of years. First was writing the show, and now the podcast. No one cares what I look like."

"Well, *you* should care." He patted her on the knee. "Be
right back."

Nina pondered what he said. Had she become lazy? Sloppy?
Wouldn't Richard have mentioned something? She contem-
plated how she dressed when they were together. Not shabby,
but not glamorous, either. Perhaps Jordan had a point.

Jordan went into the room that was his office, now Nina's
guest room. He plucked a folder from his desk and brought it
out to the kitchen counter and handed it to Nina. She
scanned through the pages.

"Interesting. But how can I help?"

"Dialogue. You have a knack for it."

"Why, thank you, Jordan. I really appreciate you saying
that."

"I remember when we worked on that movie, and you had
a suggestion for your character, and it worked beautifully."

"Thank you again. Coming from you, that is very high
praise." Nina put the pages back into the folder. "So where
do we go from here?"

"Are you available? Are you willing? I can't pay you anything right now, but if it gets optioned, we'll split the option
money, and we can draw up a contract for when it goes into
production."

"You mean *if* it goes into production?" Nina corrected him.

"My dear girl. Positive thinking." Jordan grinned.

"Again, you sound like Frankie."

"Frankie sounds like a very interesting person."

"Yes, she is. And she is half the reason I'm here. Her boyfriend's family lives in Salerno, and he invited us to share a
house in Baronissi. His cousin is a professor and has friends
who are swapping their house for Giovanni's apartment in
New York. They wanted to spend New Year's Eve in the Big
Apple."

"Brilliant."

"And generous. We are only responsible for our airfare and meals."

"Now that is one fine Christmas gift."

"You're right. Which reminds me, I need to find a gift for him."

"Any ideas?"

"Well, the airline sent his luggage here, and last I heard, it was slowly making its way to Naples, but nothing yet."

"Sounds like he might need a shirt. Sweater, perhaps?" Jordan suggested.

"Excellent idea!"

"I have a few from time to time." Jordan smiled. "Are you up for a stroll, or do you need a nap?"

"I'm good. Let's take a stroll and sit at a café and pretend we're European," Nina joked.

"Do not joke. European? Hardly. I'm a Brit!"

"But you live in Europe."

"Details. Details. Now go put on a pair of slacks. You do have a pair, I trust?"

"I think comedy may be in your future, because it ain't in the here and now," Nina volleyed back.

"But first you must tell me why you reached out, or did you simply want the charm of my company?"

"Because I'm getting bored." Nina sighed. "Podcasting is fun and topical, but that's just it. There's little room for creativity. Besides, there are a zillion podcasts now, and I doubt if I'll be relevant in a year. You know how fast technology changes and how everyone needs to be part of the latest annoying social media."

"Do I ever. You do have a good point. So what do you want to do about your boredom?"

"I think you may have solved that riddle." Nina winked and got up from the stool. "Pardon me while I slip into something more appropriate for the fashion capital of the world."

"Brilliant!" Jordan called out after her.

Nina rummaged through her suitcase. *Slacks? Yes. Whew. White shirt? Yes. Slightly wrinkled, but the blazer will cover the creases. Shoes? Done. Now what about this hair?* She remembered the black felt floppy hat she stowed in the pocket of the suitcase. *Hello, friend.* Within a few minutes, Nina transformed into a respectable tourist. Not runway material, but also not lying on the sofa eating bonbons, either. She returned to where Jordan was looking over his notes.

"Ta-da!"

"Much better, darling. Now I won't have to explain that you're a waif if I run into any of my friends."

"When did you turn into such a snob?" Nina joked.

"I've always been a snob; haven't you been paying attention?" Jordan quipped.

"As if." As she looked around his immaculate digs, she could see how it was possible. His taste was flawless. Several pieces of fine art graced the walls. The furniture was sleek, modern Italian, featuring a three-seater Dante sofa, and the lighting complimented every item on the concrete wall unit. "Do you think having good taste makes one a snob?"

"No, but it helps," he snickered. "Come. Let me show you my slice of heaven."

He donned a Dolce & Gabbana bomber jacket and wrapped a bright yellow cashmere scarf around his neck. He pressed a button for the lift.

"Aren't you worried that someone can just walk right in here?" Nina questioned.

"No, you need a key."

"Duh." Nina smacked herself in the head.

When they got to the street level, they walked few blocks to Emporio Armani. She immediately spotted a great-looking lightweight blazer with a detachable inner panel with a hood. It had a hang tag that said, Travel Essential. Nina laughed.

"As long as the airline doesn't lose it." Then she grabbed a classic-collar shirt with a chevron design in medium blue.

Jordan nodded his approval. "I don't know what kind of taste your friend has, but you can't go wrong with either of those."

"I'll take both," she said to the finely dressed sales associate. She turned to Jordan. "Giovanni deserves it. Not only did he arrange for a place for us to stay, but he is also hosting a New Year's Eve party for all of us."

Nina handed the sales associate her credit card. She didn't even flinch at the total of $875.

"Sounds like a good chap."

"He is." Nina took the shopping bag from the clerk. "Now, where to?"

"Shall we stop at the Pinacoteca di Brera? It's a Medieval and Renaissance museum, once used by Napoleon."

"Sounds interesting." She linked her arm through his. "Tell me, do you think he was a hero or tyrant?"

"I suppose it depends on who you ask."

"I'm asking you," she said, squeezing his arm.

"I suppose you have to have a streak of tyranny in order to become a leader. But even the French can't seem to agree. And of course, France and England have never been BFFs. But if you want my honest opinion, I think he was a megalomaniac. British naval strategy kept him from invading England. He tried to conquer through economic means, but the Continental Blockade, or the Continental System, as some call it, failed, and England survived the Napoleonic Wars."

"Impressive. I mean, your knowledge of history."

"Darling, I was born and raised in England. It's in our DNA."

Nina laughed out loud. "All of history?"

"Don't be daft."

They continued to walk to the museum. When they entered, Nina let out a cheeky, "Ooh. Very museum-ish."

"Oh, shush. New York is not the only place with incredible art."

"Did I say it was?"

Nina was taken aback by the enormity of the galleries. Masterpieces by Caravaggio and Modigliani graced the walls, but her favorite was *The Kiss*, or *Il Bacio*, by Francesco Hayez.

Jordan could tell Nina was moved by that painting. "They say it conveys the main feature of Italian Romanticism."

"I can see why. You can almost feel it."

"That's the point of art, darling."

They spent another hour admiring the vast collection and then decided it was time for a coffee. Nina ordered a decaf cappuccino and got an odd look from the server. Nina leaned in and whispered, "This is Starbucks, correct?"

Jordan laughed. "It's an Italian Starbucks! Get with the program, toots. Decaf? And cappuccino in the afternoon? That's only for the morning."

"Really? No after-dinner cappuccinos here? And I don't want caffeine because I need to take a nap."

Jordan checked the time. It was almost four o'clock. "Perfect. You'll nap, I'll tighten up the outline, and then we'll have dinner."

"Sounds like an excellent plan." They finished their beverages, wiped the crumbs from their faces, and headed back to Jordan's flat.

When they got back, Nina realized she left her phone on "Do Not Disturb," and there were a half-dozen calls and texts from Richard. She called him immediately. "So sorry. I was having phone issues."

"Oh?" He sounded a bit annoyed. "I thought you were going to call me when you landed."

"Sorry. Things were hectic at the airport, and when I got here, I . . ." She didn't want to say she forgot to call. "I couldn't find my charger, and the battery was dead."

She really hated to lie, but she didn't want to hurt his feelings, either. It was an honest oversight. *Oversight*. Not a good word for your boyfriend.

"So, are you all charged up now?" He sounded sarcastic.

"Yes." Nina waited.

"How was your flight?" Richard asked coolly.

"It was great. Interesting airline. It's French, and they fly from Newark to Milan, Paris, and Nice. All the seats are business class."

"Sounds interesting." Still annoyed.

"Richard, is everything alright?"

"Fine, Nina. It's just, well, you're on the other side of the Atlantic with a man I've never met. You were supposed to call when you arrived, and you didn't. Excuse me if I'm a bit miffed."

"*Miffed*? Is that a legal term?" Nina was trying to lighten the mood, but it wasn't working.

"Look, if you want to be with someone else, just tell me now."

"Richard, you have got to be kidding." Nina was stunned. He was not the jealous type. At least not up until now.

"How would you feel if the shoe was on the other foot?"

"My hiking boots?" Another attempt at levity.

"Can you be serious for a minute?" Richard's patience was growing thin.

"Okay. Okay. I'm sorry I didn't call as soon as I landed. I had phone issues." She cringed at her half-truth. She did have issues, but not the kind she said she had. *Oh, well.*

Richard exhaled sharply. "So how are things going with Jeremy?"

"It's Jordan. Now who's trying to be funny?" Nina squawked and then realized Jordan might hear her. "Can we just let this drop? Please?"

"Yes. So how are things with Jordan?" He sounded more like himself.

"Good. He has a project he wants me to consider."

"Well, that *is* good. What kind of project?"

"A rom-com-whodunit. If *Harry Met Sally* on *The Orient Express.*"

"I don't understand."

"*Sleepless in Seattle* with *Columbo*?"

Richard snorted. "Oh, I get it now. Romantic comedy with a murder to investigate."

"Bingo!" Nina responded. "Could be fun, but it's just in the infancy stage. He's still working out the plot and wants me to work on the dialogue."

"Is this a paying gig?"

"Not yet, but it will keep my creative juices flowing while I dismantle more cultural clutter."

"I'm happy to hear it." Richard was relieved. He had been concerned about Nina's state of mind. She wasn't depressed, but she was definitely indifferent. Blasé.

"So, what have you been up to today?" Nina decided to change the subject.

"Errands. Packing," Richard replied.

"Oh, I picked up a shirt and jacket for Giovanni as a Christmas gift."

"Good thinking," Richard said. "I was thinking of buying him a nice bottle of brandy, but he can get any kind of brandy at the restaurant."

"Well, my choice was twofold. We needed a gift, and the airline lost his luggage."

"You're kidding."

"I kid you not, sir. Ironically, his luggage landed in Milan and is now on its way to Naples. Or so they've been told."

"It's become a thing: Giovanni and traveling with no clothes."

Nina snorted. "That can be interpreted in many ways, depending on punctuation."

"Very true."

"Listen, I really need to take a nap. My body clock is running on a different time zone from where I am." She was overstating the obvious, but it needed to be said. *Men can be so thick sometimes.*

"Okay. I shall see you day after tomorrow. Oh, I decided to fly to Naples so we can meet at the airport. Too many moving parts, as Frankie would say."

"Excellent idea. What time does your flight get in?"

"Around ten-thirty in the morning."

"Great. Mine gets in around the same time. I have to change planes in Rome."

"We should have planned this better. You could have flown to Milan non-stop, and then we could fly to Naples together. And to think, we both have college degrees." He punctuated it with a *tsk-tsk.*

"We can't be geniuses all the time," Nina said brightly. "Look at Amy. She's a brainiac, but she could get lost on an airplane."

Richard chuckled. "Good thing she's flying with Peter."

"Amy and Peter will arrive in Naples on the twenty-ninth. As far as I know, so will Rachael and Randy, but I'm not sure if they're flying from Rome, driving, or taking the train. Rachael wasn't very organized about that part of the trip." Nina paused. "I think she was going to leave it up to Randy."

"Oh, boy. The two of them in Rome. And without supervision."

"My thoughts exactly. Okay, so I'll text you all my flight info. Giovanni said he will meet all of us at four o'clock at the entrance at Piazza Immacolata."

"Has Bossy Pants handed out the itinerary yet?" Richard joked.

"Not all of it, Mr. Funny Man. But I think the plan is for Giovanni to show Peter what real pizza looks and tastes like."

"I am really looking forward to this, Nina. Sorry I was a bit of a grouch before."

"No problem. If I was having an affair with Jordan, do you think I'd tell you about him?" Nina teased.

"Trying to throw me off the scent."

"Don't equate yourself to a dog. They are far superior."

"Hey! Not nice."

"But true. I gotta go take a nap. If you don't hear from me, that's because Jordan and I are taking a bath together."

"Now who's being funny?" Richard smirked.

"Moi!" Nina said in French. She made a kissing sound and ended the call. She was exhausted.

About two hours later, there was a soft knock on the door.

"Hello, darling. Are you awake enough for dinner? It's past seven."

Nina rubbed her eyes. "Whoa. Where am I?" she said half-jokingly.

"Milano, darling." Jordan slowly increased the lighting with the dimmer switch.

Nina pulled the pillow over her head. "But I don't want to go to school today!"

"The only lesson we have in store is how to eat veal Milanese like a true Milanese." He grabbed the pillow from her face. "Come on! Up and at 'em, missy."

Nina rolled over and slowly sat up. "Wardrobe suggestion?" She had changed from her previous outfit back into her sweatpants before her nap.

He wiggled a finger at her. "Certainly not what you have on now." He shuddered. "Put the clothes you had on earlier. I promise we won't run into anyone who will remember."

"Such a sport." Nina threw the pillow at him.

He turned and pulled the door closed behind him in order for her to make herself presentable. Again.

"And ditch the hat," he called out from the other side of the door.

Nina stuck her tongue out at no one.

While she was shifting back into acceptable attire, her phone rang. It was Frankie.

"Sweetcakes!" Nina chirped.

"Honey pie! We're finally in the same time zone!" Frankie chuckled. "How's it goin'?"

"Really good. Jordan has a project rolling around in his head and wants me to work on it with him."

"Film?"

"Miniseries. It's in the rough outline stages, but he wants me to work on the dialogue."

"Sounds exciting!" Frankie cheered.

"Yes, but it's still a work-in-progress, and there is no infusion of finances at the moment. That being said, I still have the podcast, and this will keep me on a creative track."

"Excellent. So glad to hear it," Frankie replied.

"Has Giovanni nailed down any plans yet for New Year's Eve?"

"Party at his family's house. His mom and aunt are going to Mr. Parisi's, but we're invited also. We were thinking about stopping there for an hour or so and then heading back to the house with our crew."

"I like the sound of that. Who's cooking?" Nina chuckled.

"Ha! Not me," Frankie chortled.

"Me either!"

"Did you bring your red underwear?" Frankie asked.

"I most certainly did. I even brought them on the plane with me just in case my luggage went by way of Giovanni's."

"Good thinkin'. Speaking of luggage, they still haven't been able to locate it. Unbelievable."

"What is he doing for clothes?" Nina asked, not sure if she should divulge her surprise.

"He's been washing his jeans every night, borrowed pajamas from Marco, and finally was able to get to a store to buy another pair of slacks."

"What did he do about Christmas Eve?"

"Oh, my, his mother loaned him one of his father's suits. I have to say, he looked rather natty in it."

"Wasn't it kinda weird?" Nina asked.

"Surprisingly, no. His mother seemed pleased. The only issue was the length of the pants. They were about two inches too short."

Nina cracked up laughing. "I can only imagine Mr. Impeccable with short pants!"

"He was a very good sport about it," Frankie added.

"Isn't he always?"

"Most of the time." Frankie chuckled. "What's on the agenda for tonight?"

"Veal Milanese, what else?"

"Yum!"

"We went to a museum today and strolled through the piazza. Jordan's place is in an historic part of the city. Narrow cobblestone streets. Low buildings. Cafés. Quite charming."

"I'm finding most things so far have been charming. Except for the lost luggage, but in the scheme of things, no biggie. People have been awesome. Food, awesome. Wine, awesome. That's one of the reasons why we want to go to Mr. Parisi's. He makes incredible wine."

"I'm game if he doesn't mind a few extra people invading his vineyard."

"It's an open house. They do that a lot this time of year."

"I actually like that idea. Less stress."

"We did it for Christmas, and it was perfect. Lots of people coming and going at different times of the day."

"No big dinner?" Nina asked.

"That was the night before. Oh. My. Goodness. Feast of the Seven Fishes."

"Why is it called that, besides the obvious?"

"Seven sacraments, so they say."

"Makes sense for a Catholic country, but the cab driver told me that less than a third of Italians go to church," Nina informed her friend.

"Well, we never did unless it was a holiday," Frankie replied. "But I thought that was us being American. Or lapsed Catholics."

"What about your grandmothers? Did they go to church?"

Frankie thought for a moment. "No. They had their own little altars set up in their bedrooms. Nonna on my father's side had a statue of the Madonna, a statue of St. Francis, a green plant, and a candle. She said that the village where they came from had a small chapel, but a priest would only visit once a month. If you wanted to pray, you prayed. You didn't need a ceremony to do it."

"At least you're praying because you want to and not because people are watching you," Nina mused.

"Exactly! Good people are good people. That's all that matters."

"So true." Nina suppressed a yawn. "Get this: I forgot to call Richard when I landed. Jet lag, time difference, travel, blah, blah. Well, boy, was he annoyed! He actually asked me if I was having an affair!"

"Get out!" Frankie snorted. "Does Richard know Jordan plays for the other team?"

"No. I never mentioned it. It never occurred to me that his personal life choices were anybody's business."

"I agree with you. But you know how judgmental people can be," Frankie sighed.

"Yes, but it's not on my evaluation checklist. Brown eyes? Blue eyes? Boyfriend? Girlfriend? As long as they are good people."

"Yep. Back to my previous statement. Being a good person is really all that matters."

"And being a good person encompasses many qualities." Nina was in agreement.

"Indeed it does," Frankie remarked. "Do you want to invite Jordan to the New Year's Eve party?"

"Do you think Giovanni would mind?"

"Do *I* think Giovanni would mind? Really? Would I even suggest it if he did? You know how much he likes to entertain with food and wine."

"I know. Just trying to be polite, sweetcakes." Nina yawned again. "Sorry."

"Ooh, maybe he and Randy might hit it off!" Frankie said playfully.

"Then what will we do with Rachael?"

"She'll probably have a boyfriend by the time they get from Rome to Naples," Frankie joked.

"Aw, she's been pretty laid-back about that."

"True, but she hasn't been around gorgeous Italian men, either!" Frankie added and laughed.

"Good point."

"So are you going to tell Richard about Jordan's preferences?"

"Nope. I kinda liked the idea that he was a little jealous. Keep him on his toes."

"Where did he spend Christmas?"

"With his folks in Villanova. I'm glad he did. Between his commuting from Philly to New York and throwing me into the mix, he hadn't been spending much time with them. I encouraged him to do it. I don't want his parents resenting me."

"Resent you?" Frankie was surprised.

"You know how it can go. Mothers can be very protective of their sons."

"You mean possessive," Frankie corrected her.

"Well, yeah. I don't think she liked the idea he was involved with someone in showbiz."

"That's ridiculous. You are a successful and independent woman," Frankie bristled.

"I think she was hoping he'd marry a judge or someone more in line with his profession."

"Again, ridiculous."

"Listen, I gotta jump. I can hear Jordan pacing. We're going out to dinner."

"Okay, honey pie. See you day after tomorrow. Oh, wait! I almost forgot." She gently touched the sparkling diamond on one ear. "Wait 'til you see the fabulous earrings Giovanni got me. You might have to wear sunglasses!"

"Ha! I'll bet they are beauties."

"Incredible. Oh, just one more thing. How are you liking Italy so far?"

"I've been here exactly"—she counted on her fingers—"seven hours. But so far everyone has been *molto bello*."

"Ah, you know the difference between very good and very nice. *Molto Bene*!" Frankie giggled. "*Ciao bella*."

"*Ciao*!" Nina signed off, stretched, wrestled out of her baggy clothes, and made herself presentable. She went into the bathroom to survey her makeup. It was in desperate need of a fix. That part was easy. But what to do about her wild hair? A bandana would not go over well with Jordan. She surely didn't want to look like a pirate, unless . . . unless she could turn it into a cool-looking turban? Wrap? But what else could she do? Her hair was beyond its normal state of unruly. She rummaged through her suitcase and found a long black sash she planned on wearing on New Year's Eve with her black jumpsuit. She stared at it for a minute, then folded it in half, placed it under her hair, behind her head. She pulled the two ends up over her ears and tied it in a knot at the top. She looked at herself from a few angles. *Pretty chic*. She applied some foundation, blush, a smudge of eyeshadow, and plum-colored lipstick. She stared in the mirror. Maybe it was time *she* had a makeover. It did wonders for Amy. But Amy didn't have baloney curls. She had straight hair. Much easier to style. Maybe Jordan could make a suggestion.

One more inspection, and she was ready.

"Well, look at you! Love the head-thingy," he said, with a smile and his notorious finger wiggle he used as punctuation.

Nina took a little spin. "You approve?"

"Yes. I like it. But lose the hoop earrings. Too much going on." More finger wiggles. "Got anything close to the ear? Button-type?"

Nina gave him a sour look. "Button-type? Do I look like a button-type-earring wearing kind of girl?"

"I know you have a gypsy heart, lovie, but you look classic right now without all that dangling bits and bobs." More finger wagging.

"Okay. Okay," she huffed, and brought the earrings back into the bedroom. She had no others, so she would have naked lobes. She tugged the head wrap down a smidge and returned to the discerning eye of Jordan.

"Much better." He tossed his yellow scarf around his neck. "Shall we?" He gave her his arm as they walked to the lift.

As they were riding down to the street level, Nina asked if he had plans for New Year's Eve.

"Sadly, I do not. Paul and I broke up a few months ago, and I am not in a celebratory mood."

"Then I have just the right antidote for that. Come to the party in Salerno. Giovanni is hosting it at his family house. From the roof, we'll be able to see fireworks along the coast."

Jordan stopped short. "Hmmm. That could be fun. But where shall I stay?"

"According to Giovanni, it's a four-bedroom house. I am sure we can figure something out."

"So who else will be there?"

"Richard, Amy and Peter, Randy and Rachael."

"That's a lot of *R*s," he joked.

"Ha! I hadn't thought about that."

"So, are Rachael and Randy an item, too?"

"Not exactly." Nina wasn't sure if she should say anything else. Better let him figure it out when he got there. "They're good buddies, and neither of them had dates for New Year's Eve. That's how this whole thing started." She proceeded to tell Jordan about the reunion and the pact they made. She went on about the cruise and how she met Richard, and Amy met Peter.

"And Frankie and Giovanni?"

"She lives a few blocks away from the restaurant he shares with his brother. He would kitty-sit for her cat when she traveled. Then one thing led to another . . . yada, yada, yada."

Nina continued, "Last year, we went to Lake Tahoe, which was a madcap experience. If you come down, I am sure someone will fill you in."

"Okay. Count me in! I'll fly down around noon on the thirty-first and rent a car."

"Great! I think you'll enjoy our crew. We're a nutty bunch."

"I don't doubt it."

"Amy is a molecular physicist. She is going to Geneva first. She wrangled an invitation for a private tour of the Hadron Collider."

"That huge thing that blasts subatomic particles?"

"You know about it?" Nina was impressed.

"It's been in the news, dear."

They linked arms again and walked a few blocks, admiring all the holiday decorations.

"Everywhere you look is a winter wonderland."

"Wait until you see Naples and Salerno. I think they're tied for having the most displays. Both consider their city as the City of Lights."

"I thought it was Paris," Nina said.

"Don't say that to anyone from Campania," he chuckled.

"My lips are sealed."

The restaurant was small, with only fifteen tables. It reminded Nina of Marco's in New York. Christmas music played in the background, and the aromas of fine cooking filled the air.

"*Buona sera*, Signor Pleasance."

"*Buona sera*, Emilio. This is my friend, Nina Hunter."

Emilio nodded. "Your face. *Familiare*."

"She was on a television show in the States."

"Ah. *Sì*." He smiled. "*Benvenuta*."

"Thank you." Nina gave him one of her dazzling smiles.

Before Jordan could say anything, a waiter brought over a bottle of wine. Nina noticed it didn't have a label. He poured two glasses. "*Cin cin!*"

Jordan raised his. "To a new beginning. In life and love."

"Salute! Cheers!" Nina clinked glasses.

"Did you know that the reason they say 'cin cin' is because it is the sound of two glasses touching?"

"Ah. Learn something new every day."

Nina suggested that Jordan order for both of them, since he seemed to be a regular customer. He rattled off a few items that sounded familiar, especially the Milanese part. They would start with bruschetta; gorgonzola, in the blue-cheese family; then osso buco, cross-cut veal shanks cooked in herbs and wine; and a side of polenta, the Italian version of grits. Nina was convinced she was going to tip the scales when she got back to the States.

One of the things she appreciated about Italian cuisine was the pace in which the dishes are served. No one is rushed. You are expected to eat slowly. Savor. Enjoy. She thought she might be able to get used to this pace. Such a contrast from the New York metropolitan area.

"Tell me, what made you decide to move here instead of going back to England?"

"Have you ever tried the food there? Mean cuisine."

"Too much bangers and mash?"

"Exactly. Where else can you find such a variety of freshly prepared dishes? And people who love to cook and eat?"

She raised her glass. "And drink wine."

He clinked glasses with her again. "Milan is where industry meets artistry. It's a perfect place for me right now."

"I can understand that." Nina recalled Jordan's relationship with Paul had lasted for several years. Now Jordan was on his own, and in a friendly environment with great food, art, music, and fashion.

He smiled at her. "I'm rather keen on us working together. You always brighten my day."

Nina almost spit out her wine. "Me? Brighten?"

"Yes. Because you are so 'in-your-face'. You pluck all the nuggets and savor them."

Nina was surprised. "I do?"

"Darling, I don't think you fully appreciate yourself. Look what you've accomplished. You take a troubling situation and find a way to flip it."

"Huh. I guess I'm always in survivor mode."

"Well, it's working for you. And do not underestimate yourself." He became slightly animated. "Why on earth would someone of my stature consider working with you?" he joked, but then got serious. "It's because you are talented."

Nina sat in silence for a moment. She was blown away. Jordan was a mentor when they worked together. He was successful, and his words meant the world to her. She started to tear up.

"You're not going to cry, are you?" He handed her his handkerchief.

"Me? Never," she sniffled, and happily took the folded linen.

"Aside from going over the outline tomorrow, what else would you like to do?" he asked.

"I think I've been bitten by the Renaissance bug. Do you think we could go see da Vinci's *Last Supper*?"

"I would be delighted to take you there. I'll phone my friend at the Santa Maria della Grazie church, who will be able to get us a private tour."

"Aren't you fancy?" Nina gave him a sly smile.

"Always, darling."

Chapter 17

December 27th
Geneva, Switzerland

Amy could hardly control her excitement. For her, visiting the world-renowned science center was like a kid going to Disneyland. Unless you were a scientist, it was difficult to comprehend the importance of their work. Amy tried to describe the concept to Peter in layman's terms.

"It was built by the European Organization for Nuclear Research, CERN. It's only the world's biggest, highest-energy particle collider."

She looked at him. His eyes hadn't glazed over yet, so she continued.

"It took ten years—from 1998 to 2008—and more than ten thousand scientists from hundreds of universities across more than one hundred countries to build it!"

He was still following her explanation, so she went on, "It was built to discover why matter has mass, and that might advance our understanding of other dimensions."

That's when he gave her a sideways glance.

"Stay with me," Amy said. "It was very controversial because it operates by smashing particles together."

"That much I can understand," Peter finally spoke.

"In fact, the Italian physicist Francesco Calogero wrote an essay in 2000 claiming that it could destroy the earth and send it into a black hole."

"Oh, boy." The color seemed to have drained from Peter's face.

Amy patted him on the arm. "Well, we're still here."

"That's a relief. But for how long?"

"Does anybody know the answer to that question?"

"Are we having an existential conversation now?" Peter just wanted this part of the trip to be over.

"Only if you want to."

"Not really."

"Okay. I get it." Amy smiled. She knew she could be very tiring when she went on one of her academic tangents. She changed the subject to the mountain ranges below the aircraft.

"Wow. You can see Mont Blanc in the distance. Too bad we won't be here long enough to really see it."

"We *are* seeing it." Peter leaned across to peek out the window.

"Oh, you know what I mean." Amy smushed her face.

Peter chuckled. "I do. Just teasing."

Geneva sits at the southern tip of Lake Geneva, surrounded by the Alps and Jura Mountains. From the window of the plane, it looked exactly like a picture postcard.

"Have you decided what you're going to do while I'm at the center?"

"It will depend on the weather. I thought about hiking, but I think it might be just a little colder than I'm used to. Look at all that snow." He pointed to the white-capped scenery as the plane made its final approach.

"I'm sure you'll find something you'll enjoy."

"How long is the tour?"

"They told me to be prepared to spend at least three hours there. I am going to meet with a few of the scientists after the tour. Oh, and I will have to leave my phone with security, so I will be out of pocket for most of the time."

"Alright. We'll pick a meet-up time and place before you leave in the morning."

"Sounds good. I want you to know how much I appreciate you humoring me." Amy batted her eyelashes.

"What, and let you loose in a foreign country?" Peter chuckled. "You could end up who knows where."

"Oh, stop." Amy gently slapped his arm again.

"You keep that up, and I'll be wearing a sling."

She was just about to do it again and then stopped herself. "Sorry. It's just that I'm so excited."

"I hadn't noticed," he teased again.

She slapped him again, then said, "I'll buy the sling for you." Then she gasped. "Oh, geez! Did I pack the scrapbooks?"

"No, you didn't." He paused. "I did."

Amy let out a huge gush of air. "Thank you. Thank you."

"I knew you were in too much of a tizzy to think of everything."

"You are very kind," Amy said fondly.

"As are you. You were already out the door when I did a once-around the house to be sure everything was intact. Cat food. Litter. Basket for the mail. A list of emergency numbers. And there was your little pile sitting on the chair in the dining room, so I stuffed them in my suitcase."

"What would I do without you, Peter?" Amy was very sincere.

"Probably leave the house without your shoes."

"Well, *that* I haven't done," she said, and smirked.

"Not yet."

She gave him another light tap on the arm. She seemed to

dot almost every sentence with one. They had a playful relationship. An accountant and a scientist. A perfect example that stereotypes often do not apply.

The jet reached the gate, and they followed the crowd to immigration, then to baggage, and on to customs. They realized they were going to have to go through the same routine when they landed in Naples.

"Keep all your documents together. Better yet, give them to me," Peter instructed her.

"I'm going to need ID," Amy responded.

"Your driver's license should do. If you lose your passport, that would be a much bigger hassle."

"You're such a grown-up," Amy said.

"Good thing." He grabbed the tote bag from under Amy's seat, as she was about to forget it. "You may need this."

"Oops."

"Was that your quote in your yearbook?"

"Of course. What else would it be?" She grinned.

CERN was only fifteen minutes from the airport, with several nearby hotels, but they decided to stay at the Fairmont on the lake. They were too early to check in, so they asked the cab driver if he could take them on a short scenic tour. The man spoke with a French accent and said he was happy to oblige. He drove north, past the commune of Pregny-Chambésy, where there are a number of foreign missions due to the proximity to the United Nations. He then drove east toward the lake and stopped at Plage du Vengeron, a popular lakeshore swimming area in the summer, but also quite beautiful in the winter. From there, he drove south along the Rue de Lausanne, where parks and museums rested alongside the lake. As they approached the hotel, Jet d'Eau, the Geneva Fountain, was rising almost five hundred feet into the air. One of the largest fountains in Switzerland, it represents power, strength, and ambition. It was an unquestionable hub for banking and international politics.

Once they checked into the hotel, they took a quick stroll along the lake, but after fifteen minutes, they realized they really weren't equipped for the weather. They were going to be there for two days and didn't want to overpack with bulky clothes. They hurried back to the warmth of the hotel and then had an early dinner.

When they got back to their room, Amy was wired and bursting with excitement. Peter didn't know what to do to keep her from bouncing off the walls. Maybe cognac? Brandy? He phoned room service to see what was available. "What do you recommend to help relax?"

The voice on the other end had a French accent. "Monsieur, I recommend a hot cup of Caotina with a snifter of cognac on the side. You can add it as you wish."

"Perfect."

"Shall I send two servings?"

"Yes, thank you." Peter realized he, too, was running on adrenaline, just not at the same octane as Amy.

Several minutes later, there was a knock on the door. Peter opened the door to a very tall, stern-looking man wearing a white jacket, with a tray propped up to his shoulder. Peter asked him to place the tray on the café table near the window. The man nodded, placed the tray down as instructed, pivoted, and walked out the door without saying a word.

Amy and Peter shrugged. "Must be a Swiss thing."

"With a dash of French," Peter said.

"They seem to be very nice, polite people, but I'm not getting a warm and fuzzy feeling," Amy commented.

"Maybe it's the cold weather," Peter joked as he poured the entire snifter into Amy's hot chocolate. "Here you go. This should help you relax."

"Thank you, Peter. You are so good at looking after me." She took the warm cup and wrapped both hands around it. "Smells delicious."

"They say it's the best hot chocolate in Switzerland."

"I guess they ought to know." She raised her cup in a toast. "Here's to colliding subatomic particles."

Peter almost spilled his cocoa. "Let's not tempt the fates."

Amy finally dozed off after tossing and turning for about an hour. Peter pulled the blanket up to cover her shoulders. He really loved his absent-minded professor. She was smart, kind, and quirky. He considered asking her to marry him but didn't know when. They never discussed it. Their relationship had been organic in the sense that it moved at a natural pace. *So what was next?* Maybe he'd get some advice from Giovanni and Richard. Perhaps they were having similar ideas? All three couples were going on three years. All three couples seemed to be pleasantly ensconced with their significant other, unless someone was doing a good job of pretending. He figured he'd find out in a day or so.

The following morning, Amy was up at the crack of dawn in anticipation of her big day at the science center. But that wasn't for another five hours. What to do until then? Peter was fast asleep. She didn't see the need to wake him, so she decided to get breakfast and maybe take another walk. It was a bright, sunny day. Then she remembered she didn't have the right wardrobe for Alpine weather. Instead, she decided to bring the information she had about the LHC with her and review it one more time before her tour and catch up on some factoids about Switzerland.

She thought it was rather perplexing they built it so close to civilization should anything go awry. She snickered to herself; maybe she wasn't the only absent-minded scientist. But why would the government allow it? She read on, hoping to glean an answer to her query.

The Swiss government is very stable. People have a direct say on issues rather than having representatives make decisions for them. She continued to read more about the country. It was rich, as in the average person's net worth was just under seven hundred thousand dollars, compared to the U.S., at eighty-three thousand. Amy blinked several times and reread the sentence. Then she read on. They were neutral in world affairs. They had little or no crime, and four languages were spoken. They were also considered very reserved people. She remembered one of her graduate school classmates was from Switzerland, and yes, she was very reserved. *Maybe it was the climate.* Amy decided Switzerland was an enigma and left it at that.

She checked her watch for the tenth time. She had two more hours to go. She went back to the room, where Peter was sitting by the window having coffee.

"I thought you ran off with a ski instructor," Peter teased.

"No, thank you. After last year's escapade, I don't think I'll be doing much skiing again. Quite honestly, I don't love it. But the idea of an instructor might convince me to do it again."

"Are you trying to make me jealous?" Peter eyed her.

"Never! Just kidding."

" 'Just kidding,' never running off with an instructor, or never trying to make me jealous?"

"How about both?" She went over to him and gave him a side hug.

"Did you have breakfast?"

"If you call bread with butter and jam, yogurt, muesli, and orange juice breakfast, then yes. And coffee."

"Missing your blueberry muffin?" Peter teased.

"Kinda." Amy checked the time again. "Why is this morning moving so slowly?"

"Because you keep looking at the time every fifteen minutes."

Amy let out a huff. "I'm going to get changed. Maybe the clock will move a little faster."

A half hour later, Amy appeared wearing a burgundy, professional-looking pantsuit.

"You look very nice. Very professorial." Peter grinned.

"Thank you, sir. Can we go now?"

"Why not? We can take the scenic route again."

Peter finished his coffee and grabbed his jacket, and they made their way to the elevators, down to the lobby, and hailed a cab.

The drive along the lake was as beautiful in the morning as it had been in the afternoon, with the light coming from a different direction.

"It's really pretty here," Peter commented.

Amy was unusually quiet.

"You okay?" Peter noticed the sudden change in her mood.

"Yes. Just a little nervous, I suppose."

"Well, you're not going to have to do anything. You're not making a presentation, and it's not an interview. You will be a guest."

Amy grabbed his hand. "You're right, as always."

Peter asked the cab driver to wait as he escorted her to the entrance. As they approached the world-famous complex, they were greeted by Swiss agents. Amy showed them her ticket for a private tour, and they escorted her to an area opposite where the general public was heading. "Your private tour will consist of several other scientists, and a guide from the facility. I am going to have to ask you for your mobile phone, please. The area where you will be visiting does not allow for them." He spoke with a German accent.

She handed it to him without question.

"Please wait here," he said, then turned and left.

"Are you okay? Are you less nervous?" Peter asked, knowing that Amy was probably freaking out even more.

"Yeah, yeah, it's fine. I'll see you later." She gave Peter a quick kiss goodbye and squeezed his arm. It would be fine, she figured; she would be introduced to the others shortly. She smiled weakly as she watched Peter go back to the taxi.

Several minutes later, a half-dozen people arrived; all were speaking German. She didn't understand a word of it and wondered if the tour were going to be in German. She raised her hand but then quickly put it down. She felt like she was in grammar school. But she didn't have to worry. The guide spoke fluent English and German and instructed everyone to follow her.

As they moved through the center, she explained that the first accelerator was installed in 1957, long before home computers and digital cameras existed. She then showed them a 3D-video mapping of the first synchrocyclotron. As the group moved ahead, she explained the Higgs boson particle while they toured the control center of the ATLAS experiment. From there, they walked through an interactive exhibition.

For Amy, it was all the basic information that she already knew, but she was thrilled to be immersed in it.

She thought it was odd that the tour only lasted ninety minutes, instead of the two hours she was expecting. The guide led the group to an outside area, where they were met by a transport bus. Amy thought the bus would be taking them to another area of the facility but soon discovered the bus was leaving the complex! She got up from her seat to talk to the driver. He understood English but did not understand how she ended up as one of his passengers.

Meanwhile, the private tour guide was frantically looking for Amy within the visitors' waiting area. Where could she have gone? She alerted security that a visitor was unaccounted for. They located her cell phone in the security center, but no Amy. After an hour of searching the premises, it occurred to one of them that Amy may have gotten confused and ended up with the wrong group. But which one?

The transport driver phoned the security center. He wasn't sure if Amy was telling the truth that she probably got with the wrong group. It wasn't a normal occurrence. After few exchanges, he handed his phone to Amy.

"Hello?" There was a slight bit of panic in her voice. "I'm on a bus, and I don't know why."

The voice on the other end was calm and patient. "You will have to let the driver bring his passengers to their next tour or they will be late. Please bear with him, and he will return you to the facility in approximately three hours."

"Three hours?" Amy knew that Peter would be waiting long before that, and what about meeting with the scientists? She was trying to remain calm. "Can somebody get in touch with my boyfriend and let him know I took a wrong turn, and he should come fetch me at four o'clock?" Amy gulped. "He's on my speed dial. Peter Sullivan."

"We will need your PIN."

Amy gulped again and gave the person her password. At that point, she thought she was going to throw up her muesli.

"Just one moment," the woman said kindly. She could hear the angst in Amy's voice.

In the background, Amy could hear the woman speaking to Peter. The woman chuckled. Amy didn't think any of this was funny, but if it got her back to the complex unscathed, she would be ecstatic.

The woman turned her attention to Amy. "He will be here at four o'clock. Until then, I'm afraid you are going to have to go along for the ride."

Amy shook her head. How could she have joined the wrong group? She had to do something about her lack of focus outside the confines of the university where she taught and studied.

"Okay. Thank you."

Amy was deflated when she realized she missed her special private tour and got the usual visitor tour. Then, in typical Amy fashion, she realized half a loaf was better than none and put it in astrophysics speak: "Half a quark is better than none!"

She settled into her seat, resigned to the idea she was a hostage on a bus with a bunch of German tourists. The ride in the passenger van wasn't as horrible as she feared. She got to see the lake again from a different perspective, and once the other passengers understood her predicament, they were kind, and offered her candy bars and nuts.

Three hours later, she was deposited back at the facility, no worse for the wear, with the exception of embarrassment.

When she saw Peter, she ran toward him and jumped into his arms. "Am I ever so glad to see you!" She buried her face in his jacket.

"Same here. When I got that call, my first thought was that something terrible had happened to you. Maybe you fell into a black hole or something."

She gave him one of her affectionate taps on the arm. "Let's get out of here."

Chapter 18

December 28th
Rome

Rachael and Randy's non-stop flight arrived at the Leonardo da Vinci-Fiumicino Airport at eight o'clock in the morning. They were a bit foggy from the time change and the eight hours in the air. The airport was bustling with passengers, elves, and music.

"Frankie was right," Rachael announced. "Italy at Christmas has to be one of the best places to celebrate!"

Randy was in awe. "If this is how the rest of our trip is going to be, then I am over the moon, girlfriend."

"Giovanni has a lot of things planned for us once we get to Naples and Salerno."

"I'm longing for a real slice of pizza," Randy said, licking his lips.

"For sure! He has a bet with Peter about the best pizza in the world."

"Peter can't possibly think it's in Boston!" Randy sneered.

"Everyone who lives in Boston thinks Boston has the best of everything."

"Well, beans, for one. Baseball, for another," Randy mused,

then suddenly grabbed Rachael's sleeve. "I'm going to have to hang onto you. This place is crowded!"

Rachael picked up the pace. "Did you know almost thirty million people passed through this airport in 2022?"

"I think they're all here right now!" Randy exclaimed. "Let's grab a coffee before we wrestle through customs, immigration, and watch suitcases go around in a big circle."

Even though Randy had Rachael's sleeve as she steered them through the throngs of people, he could barely keep up with her. She pulled him into a café, where a young man greeted them.

"Buongiorno!"

Randy held up two fingers, and the young man nodded for them to follow him.

"This place is really busy for this hour, isn't it?" Randy posed it more as a statement than a question, but then the young man answered.

"Many flights from the U.S. arrive early in the morning." He nodded and glanced toward the packed concourse. "This airport is busy. Always."

Rachael and Randy understood the hordes of travelers. It was an international hub.

Once they finished their cappuccinos and brioche, they wiggled their way through the crowd, and completed the process of entering the country and retrieving their baggage.

They were lucky they booked their room months ahead at the Roma Hotel, in the heart of the historic section of the city. It was within walking distance of all the sights they planned to visit, and there were no hotels with vacancies during the holidays.

Having been friends for a few years, they decided to share a room with double beds, since most of the time they would be sightseeing. Plus, there wasn't going to be any hanky-panky going on between the two of them. There wasn't anything neither of them had seen before. When they were doing competitive dancing together, there were many costume changes behind someone holding up one sheet for both of them.

Once they got settled in their room, Rachael announced, "I think we should start at the very beginning where the city was founded, in Palatine. Then to the Colosseum."

"Okay, but I'm going to need a little snooze time before we walk two miles," Randy responded with a yawn.

"Not a bad idea," Rachael replied. She threw herself on top of one of the beds and immediately dozed off. Randy did the same, except he removed his neatly pressed blazer first, which had been carefully hung in a closet by the flight attendant on the trip. Randy couldn't help but flirt with the very handsome young man. And it paid off. By the time the plane was making their final descent, the attendant returned Randy's jacket unscathed.

Around noon, Rachael awoke with a start. It took a minute to get her bearings when she realized it was Randy snoring. Maybe sharing a room wasn't such a good idea. She threw one of her socks at him. It didn't wake him but made his nose twitch.

"Randall! Wakey-wakey!"

He batted his eyes several times and rubbed his nose.

Rachael laughed. "Welcome to Roma!"

"Oh, my. I was in la-la land." He sat up and looked around the room. "So here we are!"

"Yep! Now get up, and let's get busy!"

When they got to the lobby, they asked the concierge the best route to Palatine and where they could grab something for lunch.

The concierge explained they could purchase a standard ticket to visit the Colosseum, the Forum, and the Palatine Hill and Gardens.

"Sounds like a good idea to me!" Rachael said with enthusiasm. "What about the Trevi Fountain and the Pantheon?"

"I recommend you do that separately, and do not forget the Spanish Steps. Lots of walking."

"*Sì!*" Rachael answered. "*Grazie!*" She knew she could never pull off a good Italian accent, but at least she was giving it a try.

As they made their way to Palatine Hill, the sidewalks were filled with merrymakers. Street performers, Santas, musicians, and artists were scattered along the sidewalks. Rachael and Randy stopped for a few minutes to listen to a trio consisting of a stand-up bass, a guitar, and an accordion. Several blocks from there, a one-man band entertained dozens of onlookers. No matter what the entertainment, it was meant to make you smile.

Rachael was intrigued by one man who seemed to be levitating on the sidewalk. She even waved her hand under his suspended body!

When they reached the ancient ruins, Rachael overheard a tour guide explaining why legend has it that Palatine Hill is the birthplace of Rome. It is said that Romulus and Remus could not agree on how to build a city; therefore, Romulus killed Remus, and the city was born. In ancient times, it was the most desirable area to live in, with aristocrats and emperors occupying the elite hill. On one side is Circus Maximus, and on the other is the Roman Forum.

As they gazed upon the centuries-worn edifices, it gave them pause. So much had happened in the very place where they stood. This time it was Rachael's turn to grab onto Randy's jacket. It was almost overwhelming. After several minutes of silence, she turned to her companion. "You can actually feel a certain energy that is different from anywhere I have ever been."

"Ghosts, perhaps?" Randy wasn't being facetious.

"More like spirits," Rachael said solemnly. "But it's not creepy."

"Wait until we get to the Colosseum. You might get the creeps thinking about all the people that were killed for sport."

"Thanks for the history lesson."

They worked their way down to the Forum, where much of the Roman laws were made, processions occurred, elections, speeches, and day-to-day life observed. It's been referred to as the most important meeting place in history, perhaps the world.

Once they arrived at the Colosseum, Rachael wasn't sure she could endure any more ancient history. The jovial atmosphere of the streets was in sharp contrast to the historical proportions she was staring at. "Can we do something else?"

"Too much?" Randy asked. He, too, was feeling flooded and dazed.

"What time is it?" Rachael asked.

"Almost five."

"Let's get a glass of wine and decide what and where we want to have for dinner."

"Excellent idea." He hooked his arm around Rachael's and said, "Come, my lady. We shan't want you to have the vapors."

The temperature was in the upper fifties, and most of the outdoor cafés had heaters. They stopped at the first one that had a table available. As soon as the waiter appeared, Rachael blurted, *"Vino, per favore!"*

Randy snickered, "Your Italian greatly improves with wine!"

"Ha! And to think I haven't even tasted it yet!"

It took several minutes for the waiter to return with an unlabeled bottle and two glasses.

"Antipasto? Cheese?"

"What do you recommend?" Randy asked.

"Salumi, provolone."

"Well, as the saying goes, 'When in Rome!' Sounds divine."

"*Assolutamente!*" the waiter replied, and retreated into the café.

Randy crossed his arms and leaned back. "I think that meant absolutely."

Rachael mimicked him, leaned back, and crossed her arms. "*Assolutamente!*"

When they finished their wine and apps, they took another long stroll to the hotel. Neither was in the mood for more food, wine, musicians, or ruins, and they decided to call it a day, maybe order room service later, and watch a movie. Exhaustion had fallen upon them.

Sometime around eleven, Rachael got a second wind. "Hey, want to see what the Romans do at this hour?"

"Are you serious?"

"Well, do you?"

"Yes, but do we have to do it now?" he moaned.

"That's what it means when you say, 'at this hour,' bucko. Come on. Don't be a party pooper."

"But I'm not even dressed."

"That's never stopped you before!" Rachael cackled.

"Oh, stop. I'm really tired, Rachael. I can't believe you want to go out after the long day we had today."

"Well, you can't let me go out by myself. Who knows what trouble I might get into." Rachael was now standing over Randy as he lay on his bed.

"Alright. Alright. But you're gonna owe me for this."

"Understood." Rachael checked her face in the mirror. "Good enough. Your turn," she called out to Randy.

He moaned and groaned his way off the bed, slipped on his jeans and a polo shirt, and hooked his finger in his jacket and slung it over his shoulder.

"Where to?"

"Let's just go for a walk and make up our minds while we stroll. A Zen kind of thing."

"You sound like Frankie," Randy said, pouting.

"Why are you such a sourpuss?"

"Because I. Am. Tired. *Capisce?*" He really was beginning to sound very cranky.

"Fine. I'll go alone."

"Oh, no you won't. God forbid something happens to you. Frankie will kill me."

Rachael crossed her arms and began tapping her foot. "Move it!"

"Now who's cranky?" He stuck out his tongue at her.

"Ha! We're in Rome. Let's enjoy as much of it as we can."

Randy swung the door open, waved his arm, and bowed. "After you, your highness."

They asked the concierge where they might find some night-life nearby. He told them about a retro bar with live music that was a few blocks away.

"That sounds perfect." Rachael smiled. "Come on, Spanky," she said as she yanked Randy by the sleeve.

Randy turned to the concierge and rolled his eyes. "That's not really my name."

"*Sì*," he replied with a grin.

The streets were still lively.

"Talk about a city that never sleeps," Randy observed. "No wonder they usually have dinner at eight-thirty."

"And take a nap in the afternoon!" Rachael hooted.

A man on a unicycle whizzed by, juggling several balls. "I wonder what his day job is," Randy joked.

"Maybe he's in the insurance business."

"Well, I hope he has some!" Randy quipped. "Liability, at the very least." He watched as the man swerved in and out of the crowd, with people scurrying out of his way.

On one of the side streets, they saw a sign that read RETRO.

"That must be the place." Randy pointed to the small neon sign.

The small bar was packed to the brim with people laughing and chatting, while a small jazz trio played. The atmosphere was lively, but it was difficult to talk without shouting over the din. There was a crowd in front of the bar that would require some elbowing to get through.

"You wait here. Don't get yourself into any trouble," Randy shouted at Rachael.

She gave him a salute.

He moved through the swarm, excusing himself over and over. No one seemed to mind and made small openings for him to waggle through. He ordered two Negronis and held them over his head as he maneuvered his way back to where Rachael was standing.

He wasn't gone for more than a few minutes, and there she was, chatting it up with a very beautiful woman in her late thirties.

"And who do we have here?" Randy asked as he handed the drink to Rachael.

"This is Sienna Brown."

Randy held out his free hand. "Randy."

"Benvenuti a Roma!" Sierra replied. "How long will you be staying in our beautiful city?"

"One more day," Randy replied.

Sierra eyed Randy up and down. "Such a shame. I would like to take you to see the many special places of Roma."

Randy was a little uncomfortable with this obvious flirtation. "Maybe next time." He smiled.

"Sì. Perhaps." Sierra took the hint and moved on.

"What was that all about?" he asked Rachael.

"I think she was interested in you."

"So it appeared," Randy replied.

That's when Rachael burst out laughing. "Randy, it was a dude!"

"What?" Randy was stunned.

"She's a drag queen."

"Get out of here."

Rachael laughed again. "She told me she's in a show at a club up the street, and all the performers come hang out here after their show."

"Wait. All these beautiful women are drag queens?" Randy looked around incredulously. "This bar is even more fabulous than I thought!"

"I don't know if they are all drag queens, but the Italians are certainly beautiful people," Rachael quipped.

After one more round of drinks, they decided to call it a night and head back to the hotel. When they got back to the room, Rachael called the front desk and asked for a six o'clock wake-up call.

"As in morning?" Randy questioned her.

"Yes! They say early morning is one of the best times to visit the Trevi Fountain. Fewer people and great lighting."

"Well, you know how I feel about great lighting," Randy said, turning his face back to catch the light from the wall sconce.

"I knew that would encourage you," Rachael laughed. "Now get some sleep. We have another big day ahead."

"Yes, ma'am."

"We should probably hit the Spanish Steps first, then the fountain, and then the Pantheon. After that, we can take a cab to Trastevere."

"You're beginning to sound like Ms. Bossy Pants."

"I learned from the best. Nighty-night." Rachael hit the switch that turned off the lights.

The phone jostled them out of bed at six as requested. Shortly thereafter came a loud knock on the door.

"Who can that be?" Randy pulled the blanket up to his chin.

"Room service. I ordered cappuccino and brioche to get us started."

"I will have to thank Frankie for bringing you up to bossy-speed."

"What's so bossy about coffee?" Rachael threw the covers off and scurried to the door.

"Your organizing skills, madame," Randy called out, ducking completely under the covers.

"*Buongiorno,*" a man with a rolling cart greeted her.

"*Buongiorno,*" Rachael replied, and held the door open for him. He handed her a small black folder. She signed the check and gave him a tip in euros.

"*Mille grazie,*" he thanked her, and left.

Randy peeked out from the covers. "How much did you tip him?"

"I have no idea," Rachael said. "What's a euro in U.S. dollars?"

"Right now, the euro is slightly less than the dollar."

Rachael's eyes went wide. "Then he got a twenty-dollar tip. Well, it's the holidays. Merry Christmas to him. Now get up!" she said, yanking the covers off him.

It took them about an hour to get themselves ready, taking turns in the shower and all the other morning rituals.

It was just before eight, and they planned to cover the Spanish Steps and the fountain before nine. As they made their way to the famous steps, people were beginning to fill the streets. Some on their way to work, while others worked the streets with their wares, music, and art.

Once there, both Rachael and Randy were awed by the magnificence of the sight before them. The polished stone of the Spanish Steps were as spectacular as everything else they had seen so far. Even though it was December, and the steps were void of the beautiful pink azaleas that adorn them in April and May, one could still appreciate their magnitude. Built in 1723, the wide Baroque steps were funded by a French diplomat, with the purpose of connecting the Bourbon Spanish Embassy with the Spanish Square below.

Randy gave Rachael a stern warning: "Do not sit on the steps. Not any of the one hundred thirty-eight of them."

"What if people get tired?"

"Then they should take the lift, or not bother and go shopping." He noticed the area was dotted with boutiques from Gucci, Dolce & Gabbana, Prada, Dior, and Bulgari.

"Of course you would notice that." Rachael laughed.

"Of course I would."

As they stood at the bottom, Randy recalled a scene from *Roman Holiday* starring Audrey Hepburn and Gregory Peck. "Such a delightful film."

"Fairytale."

"Right. Because we need fairytales to get us through rough patches." Randy nodded.

"So, should we attempt to traverse them?"

"Just a couple. Then we'll browse some of the local merchants." He raised his eyebrows.

"How did I know you were going to say that?"

"You know me so well." Randy chuckled as they linked arms, walked about twenty steps, and then turned around.

They window-shopped the designer boutiques and then made the ten-minute walk to the Trevi Fountain. As they approached the eighty-five-foot-tall landmark, Randy swept his arm out, inviting Rachael to behold the marvel before them. "The Trevi Fountain is considered an eighteenth-century masterpiece and was finished in 1762."

When Rachael raised her eyebrow in surprise, Randy retorted, "I did a little homework, missy." He handed her three coins. "Turn your back to the fountain and throw the first coin with your right hand, over your left shoulder. That will assure you will return to Rome."

Rachael followed his instructions.

"Now the next coin will bring you love."

She whipped that one over her shoulder with gusto. "And the last one is for marriage."

Rachael hesitated and turned to Randy. "Seriously? Do I want to get married again?"

"If it's the right person?" Randy suggested. When he saw she wasn't buying it, he sighed, "Just humor me."

She threw the coin half-heartedly. "Okay, your turn."

Randy followed suit.

"What happens to the money?" Rachael asked.

"From what I've read, it's gathered at the end of the day and helps the local soup kitchens."

"More factoids from the Randroid."

He huffed, then went on to discuss two films that made the landmark famous worldwide. "There's the obvious *Three Coins in the Fountain* with Clifton Webb, Dorothy McGuire, Louis Jourdan, and Rossano Brazzi. And there's also the groundbreaking film *La Dolce Vita*, by Fellini, starring Anouk Aimée, Anita Ekberg, and Marcello Mastroianni."

"Well, aren't you the cinephile?" Rachael looked at him with awe.

"Just from 1950 to 1960. The best decade for film."

"You really think so?" Rachael was curious.

"The industry was still evolving with Panavision. Think about it. People had to be creative with limited resources. They were inventing as they went along."

"Good point."

"And did you know that *La Dolce Vita* was what put Italy on the map for filmmaking? It's considered an Italian masterpiece, even though the Italians did not submit it for an Academy Award."

"Why didn't they?" Rachael asked, as she leaned on the stone railing and gazed into the pool of water.

"They thought it already had too much publicity."

"Well, that kinda stinks," Rachael responded, still staring at the fountain's sculpture.

"What stinks even more, in my humble opinion, is that Fellini was nominated for Best Director but lost to Robert

Wise and Jerome Robbins for *West Side Story*. Don't misunderstand me. *West Side Story* was a great movie, but it was a musical first. Fellini also co-wrote *La Dolce Vita*."

"No wonder Nina has a bad taste in her mouth about Hollywood."

"Obviously Fellini wasn't deterred, and the collaboration with Marcello Mastroianni was epic."

"Mastroianni was gorgeous," Rachael added. "I think he was kinda the Cary Grant of Italian film."

"Interesting observation," Randy mused. "But did you know he was arrested and sent to a German prison camp during World War II? Thankfully, he escaped."

"Thankfully, indeed."

"Do you know how many films he made with Sophia Loren, another gorgeous piece of art from Italy?"

"No, but I have a feeling you're going to tell me."

"Seventeen," Randy said smugly.

"You are a wealth of information, my friend. I am impressed."

"As you should be."

"Shall we move on now that I begrudgingly wished for marriage?"

"Oh, stop it."

"By the way, I arranged for a guided tour of the Pantheon."

"You are the pushy planning lady today, aren't you?"

"It's a tough job, but someone had to do it."

The minute they had arrived in Rome, Rachael realized having tickets for some of the most famous attractions was necessary and had asked the hotel concierge to arrange for them.

She checked the time. "Come on!" She yanked him along. "We're going to be late."

When they arrived at the Pantheon, a guide began to tell

them the history of one of the top ancient sites in Roman history.

"It is a monument that has sustained two thousand years of history and is the largest unreinforced concrete dome in the world. Thought to be built by Hadrian, it was a Roman temple until the seventh century BC, when it became a Catholic Church."

The guide continued, "The interior dome rises to one hundred forty-two feet, the exact same measurement as its diameter. At the top is twenty-seven-foot oculus, a central opening to the sky. By design, it can withstand rain due to a slight slope of the floor, with twenty-two holes that help the water drain away.

"The rotunda walls have eight recessed spaces: three are tombs, four are chapels, and the high altar." She pointed to the walls. "The walls are decorated with marble, tile, mosaics, and open space is surrounded with columns."

Then the guide told them to also take note of the floor that consisted of fine marble squares and circles that formed a pattern from the center central disc. "The same disc that carries the rainwater into the drains."

The building was an architectural and engineering feat, filled with beauty and wonder.

Like most visitors, Rachael found it hard not to look up at the big hole in the ceiling. She stood with her mouth agape. "How in the world did they do this?"

"How indeed, considering we can't build something to last more than twenty years."

"And they did this without most of the tools we have today. I mean, like, as in big tools," Rachael responded. She was getting dizzy looking and contemplating the mind-boggling feat.

Randy could tell his pal was fading. They had been on their feet for four hours. "Come on, toots. We need to get you some fortification."

Rachael did not protest and linked arms with her buddy. They thanked the guide and worked their way back to the street.

"Trastevere?" he asked, knowing the answer.

"How about we rest a bit and go to dinner, instead?" she suggested.

"Perfect. I could use a siesta myself."

"It's called *pennichella* in Italy."

"You say tomato, I say tomahto. I concur nonetheless."

The two bedraggled tourists went straight to their room to recharge their batteries. Rachael set the alarm on her phone. As she understood it, a *pennichella* should not last more than thirty minutes; otherwise, you may be groggy instead of refreshed.

"We're just resting our eyes," Rachael reminded him.

Before they could count too many sheep, Rachael's alarm was beeping. "What the heck?" Then she remembered it was only supposed to be a short nap. She must have fallen into a deeper sleep than she expected. She had to admit she was tired. *How can anyone do Rome in two days, let alone one?* There were a dozen more things they could have seen or done, but it was time to pull in the reins. Just the few things they visited were a lot to absorb, especially if you considered when they were built and the millennia they survived. Throw in a few dozen wars, conquerors, famines, disease, floods, and volcanoes, yet these structures were still standing. It was rather extraordinary. And it wasn't just one building. It was dozens. Hundreds.

Rachael looked over at Randy. He was still in slumberland. Too bad. It was time to get up; otherwise, his body clock would be worse.

"Yo, Rand-man. Rand-droid. Up and at 'em."

Randy rolled over and whined, "I'm still sleeping."

"You are not. Time to rally, dear boy." Rachael got up and

slapped him on his hiney. "I'm going to take a quick shower. I expect you to be vertical when I get back."

He saluted and rolled back over.

After Rachael got out of the shower, she couldn't help noticing that Randy was still horizontal. For the second time that day, she yanked the covers off him.

"Stop it!"

Rachael burst out laughing. "Nice. Scream like a girl, why don't ya?"

"Ugh," he grunted, and tried to pull the blanket back on top of him, but Rachael wasn't letting go.

"Come on, Randy," she whined back at him.

"Remind me never to sleep with you again," Randy sassed.

"Like that might happen, never," she laughed.

He finally rolled himself off the bed and walked into the bathroom, turned on the shower, and began to sing "That's Amore" at the top of his lungs.

Rachael banged on the door. "Is someone being murdered in there?"

He sang even louder. Rachael hoped no one could hear him. Dean Martin, who made the song popular in the 1950s, would be rolling in his grave.

Rachael realized the more she protested, the more he continued, so she stopped. Then he went quiet. *Men are so predictable. What's that expression? Let them chase you until you catch them? Or was that dogs? Same difference. No. Dogs are often better.* That's when Rachael realized some of Frankie, Amy, and Nina's crazy love for animals was rubbing off on her. *A dog!* Why hadn't she thought of that? When they returned to the States, she was going to get a dog!

Randy exited the bathroom wearing a robe, with the waft of Versace Eros following him into the room. "Well, at least you smell good."

"And what's that supposed to mean?" His arms were akimbo.

"Nothing. You smell good."

"You said, 'at least.' That's a preamble to something else."

"What are you talking about?"

"At least. As in less."

"What? Oh, for heaven's sake. Do you realize we're starting to sound like an old married couple?"

Randy's mouth dropped open. "Oh, my. Well, darling, perhaps we should consider a divorce."

Rachael wasn't sure if he was kidding or not. Not that they *could* divorce, but was he implying that they should get separate rooms?

Instead, she took it in a lighter direction. "But what about the children? Who'll get the station wagon?"

Randy stopped and thought for a moment. "The kids go with the station wagon."

"But with whom?" Rachael asked impishly.

"Who cares, as long as we get rid of them!" Randy howled, and Rachael echoed his delight.

"Now aren't we really having fun?" she asked.

He sat down on the bed across from where she was sitting. "Rachael, this has been an incredible trip so far. Sorry if I was cranky. It's been quite overwhelming. As in all of it. The traveling, the sightseeing, the time zone."

Rachael smiled. "I'm sorry, too. I know I have been dragging you all around. I just wanted to make sure you had a fabulous time and saw all the sights." The friends hugged, and when they pulled apart, Rachael said, "How much more time do you need to get ready?"

"I'll be ready lickety-split." Randy took out a pair of trousers from the closet, and a long-sleeve polo shirt and a crew-neck sweater from his open suitcase. "Be right back."

Rachael pulled on her good pair of boots. They weren't planning on any more walking around except from the hotel to a cab to Trastevere, where they had a dinner reservation at a restaurant called Otello. Maybe they'd walk a block or so after dinner, but no tourist hikes to, from, in, or out of ancient ruins.

Randy emerged, looking rather spiffy. Rachael decided to make up for the *at least* comment. She made a mental note to be more conscientious in her choice of words. She had meant nothing by it, but in hindsight, she could see where someone could take offense.

"You are looking quite handsome, Randall Wheeler."

"Thank you, dearie. You're looking rather fetching yourself." He swung the door open. "Shall we?"

The cab ride to Trastevere took less than fifteen minutes. It was the old working-class area of Rome. The bohemian section of the city was filled with ancient buildings, narrow cobbled streets, pubs, and trattorias. It was on the western side of the Tiber River, south of Vatican City.

The restaurant was everything they were told it was. Warm, cheerful, and if the food was as good as it smelled, and as people touted, then it was going to be a delectable meal.

The waiter brought a bottle of wine. It seemed as if that was part of the custom. He welcomed them and rattled off the many specials of the evening.

Rachael batted her eyes and said, "Why don't you bring us whatever you recommend. The only thing I will not eat are internal organs."

"Ditto," Randy chimed in.

"*Bene.*" The waiter smiled and retreated into the kitchen. Several minutes later, he appeared with two small plates of fresh mozzarella with sliced tomatoes and basil. From there, they were served deep-fried artichokes, then spaghetti cacio e pepe, a black-peppery pasta dish. Their second course was beef tagliata, marinated sliced beef served with arugula.

Randy decided he could live in Rome. "Don't you just love

this place? Not just the restaurant, but all the restaurants. The food. The wine. The people. *La dolce vita!*" He raised his glass.

"*Cin cin!*" Rachael said in return. "But I hear it's very expensive to live here. How would you make a living?"

"Whatever it takes, honey. Whatever it takes!"

Rachael laughed, then stopped. "Seriously, would you ever consider moving out of New York?"

Randy paused, fork in midair. "If there was a good enough reason. I left Tahoe."

"Do you ever miss it?"

"Tahoe? My friends, yes. The job? Absolutely not. Kowtowing to spoiled rich people who treat you like you are beneath them? No, thank you."

"But that's how we met, and look at us now!" Rachael was serious.

"Oh, and may I remind you, the reason we met was because you were being naughty."

"And you helped. Which reminds me, what kind of pranks can we pull on everyone this year?"

"You mean you didn't get that out of your system last year with the elves and mistletoe?" Randy dabbed his mouth with his napkin.

"That was because they didn't know I was going to be there."

"So why the pranks now?" He dug into another slice of meat.

Rachael thought for a moment. "Maybe it isn't such a good idea. We have no idea where we will be most of the time."

"Didn't Ms. Bossy Pants put an itinerary together?"

"Yes, but would you know how to get from one piazza to another? Your Italian isn't very good."

He tapped his phone in his breast pocket. "Translator app, dearie. We've been using it since we got here."

"Ah, technology. But you can't expect to communicate that way forever."

"For as long as I want." He gave her a shrug.

"Whatev," Rachael replied, and went back to her dish.

"Is that smoke coming out of your ears?"

"What?"

"I can see something burning in your brain."

"Just trying to decide if we should buy up all the mistletoe in Rome and bring it to Naples."

"You're not serious."

"Not really, but, oh wait! I have an idea."

"Uh-oh." Randy folded his arms and leaned back.

"How many of us will there be on New Year's Eve?"

"I'm not sure. Why?"

"Thinking." Rachael tapped her temple.

"I'm afraid to ask."

"Then don't. I'll let it percolate and then fill you in."

"You're not planning on kidnapping an elf or a jester, are you?"

"No. That would be illegal." Rachael's eyes were twinkling. "But I have to come up with something."

"Do you really? I mean, Giovanni, Marco, and Frankie are going to great lengths to make this a great holiday for us. Do you have to do anything?"

"How will they know I'm there?" Rachael said sardonically.

"Oh, gee, I have no idea. You're so laid-back and reserved."

Rachael let out a guffaw. "I need to work on that."

The waiter asked if they wanted dessert, to which both groaned a "no thank you." Randy picked up the check and settled the bill.

As they moved through the restaurant, everyone they passed wished them *"Buon Natale! Buon Anno!"*

Randy noticed how friendly everyone had been. "Seriously, Rachael. This city is special."

"From what I've heard, the entire country is special. I'm glad we did this." She hooked her arm through his again.

"You know, if you keep clinging to me, you are going to make it very difficult for me to meet a handsome Italian," he said to her, half-joking.

She pulled her arm out. "You're right! Neither of us are going to meet anyone if they think we're a couple!" She chuckled.

"We're a couple, alright. A couple of dancers and mischief makers," Randy reminded her, as they came upon another trio playing lively music. Rachael took Randy's hand, gave him a look that he understood rather well, and they immediately started to shimmy and shake. People began to gather around, and soon others joined them. Before they knew it, it became a dance-block-party. The musicians continued to play several more songs with a similar beat, and the group grew bigger. It was a good fifteen minutes of foot-stomping and hand-clapping before everyone took a bow. Shouts of "Bravo! Bravo!," whistles, and clapping reverberated off the stone streets. Strangers were hugging each other as if they were all old friends. It was a wonderful send-off for their final night in Rome.

"That was so much fun!" Rachael blurted as they got in the cab.

The driver turned to them. "It was you that made the jam in the traffic?"

Rachael slid down in the seat. Randy fessed up, "We're dancers. Sorry. Did we cause a lot of trouble?"

"Trouble? Rome knows trouble for thousands of years. You? Dance? Music. Dance. Art. That's what makes our city alive. So, no trouble. We wait, and then we go."

"Thank you," Randy said to the driver.

"You see the Vatican?" The driver looked in the rearview mirror.

"Unfortunately, no. We did see the Trevi Fountain, the Spanish Steps, the Parthenon, the Colosseum, the Forum, and the Palatine Hill and Gardens," Randy recited, and turned to Rachael. "Right?"

The driver asked if they were in a hurry to get back to the hotel. Rachael and Randy gave each other a look of apprehension. "Why do you ask?" Randy inquired.

"I can drive to Vatican City so you can see some of it," he said. "Takes an extra fifteen-twenty minutes."

"Will we be able to see anything?"

"We can drive into the city, but you cannot go into the buildings without tickets. It is beautiful at night."

"As long as we don't have to walk anywhere, that's fine with me," Randy said as he looked in Rachael's direction. "What say you?"

"Let's go!" Rachael said. "I'd much prefer a drive-by at this point."

The driver was more than happy to oblige. He had the proper credentials and made a sweep around the perimeter, pointing out the various buildings, including St. Peter's Square.

"Too bad we didn't meet you when we first got here," Randy said.

"Next time," the driver replied. "You go to Trevi Fountain? You toss coins?"

Both answered "yes" in unison.

"Then you will return." He reached up to the visor and pulled out a card. He passed it back to Randy and repeated, "Next time."

When they pulled in front of the hotel, they thanked the driver for the detour and completing their visit. He waved. *"Ciao! Arrivederci!"*

"Ciao!" Both waved as he drove off.

Rachael was eyeing Randy. "You really like it here, don't you?"

"There is something compelling about it."

"Maybe you were a gladiator in a previous life," Rachael joked.

"Well, I was certainly visiting the baths, if nothing else," he retorted.

Once they got to their room, they agreed they were bone-tired. Their train to Naples left at noon. It was a little over an hour ride on the high-speed transport, but they wanted to give themselves enough time to find Amy and Peter.

The plan was for Amy and Peter to catch a taxi at the airport and then pick up Randy and Rachael at the train station. Then the four of them would head to Pompeii to hook up with Nina, Richard, Frankie, and Giovanni at four o'clock at the address Giovanni gave them. He had arranged for an eight-passenger SUV to take everyone on the pizza tour, and then to Baronissi, where everyone else would be staying and where he left his car.

Rachael packed her bag, leaving out the clothes she intended to wear the next day. Randy did the same. They were ready for the next round of Italian fun.

PART III

Chapter 19

Welcome to Campania

During the hour-long train ride, Randy was transfixed as the high-speed train swiftly passed the fields, farms, and hillside. The train itself was impressive. Clean, modern, fast. A big difference from what they were used to. Rachael struck up a conversation with an American couple sitting across the aisle who were visiting family for the holidays. They traded impressions of the sights they visited in typical Rachael animation. Get Rachael excited about something, and you'll be exhausted soon enough. But in a good way.

The hour went by quickly. Once the train came to a stop, Randy wrestled his luggage onto the platform and then gave Rachael a hand with hers. They wished their fellow train-travelers a *Buon Anno* and looked for the exit where they were to meet up with Amy and Peter.

As soon as they exited the terminal, they spotted Amy hanging out of the passenger window of a taxi, waving cheer-fully and calling their names!

"Woo-hoo! Rachael! Randy!" Amy clapped her hands with glee.

Peter got out of the taxi, shook Randy's hand, kissed Rachael on the cheek, and helped with the luggage. The back of the vehicle was now packed to the brim.

Rachael yanked the door open and popped into the waiting car and gave Amy a big hug around the neck. "Professor! So good to see you!"

"Likewise!" Amy replied. "How was Rome?"

"Fabulous. Really, really fabulous. I wish we had more time, although my dogs were barking after the second day of walking around."

"Dogs? Barking? You don't have a dog, do you?" Amy was confused until Rachael explained it was a euphemism for "my feet are tired, and they hurt."

"Oh," Amy replied.

Rachael was always surprised at Amy's lack of knowledge of colloquialisms. She guessed it was because Amy was busy learning about biochemistry and subatomic particles. But that was one of the things that made Amy so charming: her unawareness of things less important.

"So, Amy, how was the big bang thing?" Rachael asked.

Silence.

"Hello?" Rachael mocked.

"Well, let's just say it didn't go exactly as planned," Amy answered sheepishly.

"What do you mean?" Rachael prodded.

Peter decided it was going to be Amy to tell the story and kept his mouth shut.

Amy let out a heavy exhale. "I kinda got lost."

"Lost? How? Don't they have security? What are you talking about?" Rachael was firing off questions.

"I mistakenly went with the wrong group."

"Okay, and?" Rachael pushed.

"And they were on a general tour. They were from Germany."

"And?" Rachael felt like she was pulling taffy.

"And I just kept following them until the end."

"So?"

"So, I got on a transport bus thinking we were going to another part of the facility."

"But?"

"But they were on their way to another tour."

"So why didn't they just turn around and bring you back?"

"Because they were on a tight schedule. I had to sit on the bus until the driver let them off and could go back to the center."

"Well how long did it take for you to get back?"

"Three hours." Amy hung her head. "Plus, I didn't have my phone. They made me hand it over to security."

Peter could tell Amy was done with her part of the story, so he finished up for her. "She asked the driver to call the center and then asked someone to retrieve her phone. She gave them her code so they could call me and let me know what was going on."

"Oh my gosh! You must have been totally freaked out!" Rachael said with alarm.

"More like totally embarrassed," Amy chimed in. "I felt like such a dodo."

Rachael couldn't help but chuckle. "And this is another reason why we love you, Amy. You're the smartest dodo we know."

With a total straight face, Peter said, "I'm thinking of having a microchip planted in her wrist."

"Don't kid around. I think there is a certain billionaire who wants to do that with his employees. Science fiction isn't so fiction-y anymore," Amy added.

"How was Rome?" Peter asked.

"Ooh. Ooh. Tell them about our spree on the streets of Trastevere!" Randy encouraged Rachael.

"You guys didn't get into any trouble, did you?" Amy asked.

"Why do you think I'm the one always getting into trouble?" Rachael asked. "I believe you just told us a story about a certain person getting lost at a nuclear center."

"I didn't get into trouble. I simply got a little turned around." Amy looked at Rachael. "Okay, I was lost, but I wasn't in trouble."

Peter broke in, "She was lucky because from what I experienced, the Swiss have an accuracy thing going on."

"As in watches?" Rachael asked.

"As in pretty much everything. Precision is in their DNA."

"No wonder they make such good watches." Randy smirked. "Go on, Rachael. Tell them how we started a dance party in the middle of the street."

"You did?" Amy perked up.

"There was a trio playing. There are trios and musicians everywhere, but this one in particular was playing something we could dance to, so I grabbed Randy's hand, and he started spinning me around. Then people began to gather. Then other people joined us. It was such an impromptu thing. So. Much. Fun.

"Next time, make a right turn at Geneva and go straight to Rome. There is so much to see and do."

"And eat!" Randy added. "The people are full of life. Joy. Rachael is right. There are street musicians, street performers, and artists everywhere."

Rachael recounted their sightseeing adventures, concluding with the kind cab driver who made a loop through Vatican City. "We just couldn't do one more thing."

"Especially after dancing in the street," Randy inserted into the conversation. "We put a few hours of walking in during the day, took a siesta, and then went to dinner."

"It's called a *pennichella*," Rachael corrected him again.

"Potato, potahto. It's an Italian nap."

"Supposed to be no longer than twenty or thirty minutes. But Mr. Cranky Pants wanted to stretch it out."

"It's true. Anything longer than forty minutes will put you

into a deeper sleep, which makes it harder to rally. Under thirty will refresh you," Amy agreed.

Randy folded his arms. "My disco naps were always around an hour."

"Goody for you. We're experiencing a different culture." Rachael made a face. Randy made one back at her.

"So, tell me more about where you went," Amy entreated.

Rachael and Randy took turns talking about the sites they visited. "It was awesome," Randy added.

"And kinda overwhelming," Rachael said. "You read about these places, you see them on TV and in films, but when you are standing in the middle of the Pantheon, I have to tell ya, it's mind-boggling to think about how they built those structures."

"And how they survived all these years," Randy said. "Well, kinda. They are called 'ruins' for a reason, but so much of it has been preserved. Like I said to Rachael, we can barely build anything to last more than a couple of decades. Oh, and the train? Amazing. Fast. Clean. Prompt."

"Makes you wonder if Italy can do it, why can't we?" Peter reflected. "Although that's more of a rhetorical question, because we could put a list of reasons together rather quickly."

"True," Amy agreed, and wanted to avoid any negative conversation. "And how was the food?"

"A-mazing," Randy answered. "Rome is a gastronomical wonderland."

"Well, we'll see about the pizza here." Peter snickered.

"Peter and Giovanni have a little difference of opinion about pizza, and Giovanni is going to bring us on a pizza tour this afternoon."

Rachael looked at Peter. "You challenged Giovanni to a pizza throwdown?"

"I couldn't bring any Boston pizza with me, but I packed my taste buds," Peter joked and tapped his cheek.

Rachael looked at Randy and then at Amy. "Is he serious? He's going to compare Boston pizza with Neapolitan pizza?"

"What do you expect from an accountant?" Amy teased.

"My profession has nothing to do with my palate."

"We shall see about that." Amy pursed her lips. "I, for one, can't wait to taste the perfection."

"Whose side are you on?" Peter joked.

"Margherita's," Amy answered.

"Who's Margherita?" Rachael asked, then got it—"Oh, duh. Margherita pizza! Good one!"

As the car approached a turn in the road, the driver pointed ahead. "Vesuvius."

Silence fell throughout the vehicle.

"It's massive," Randy finally remarked.

"*Sì*," the driver agreed. "You go to Pompeii today, no?"

"We're meeting people there, but the four of us won't be going through the ruins."

"Because?" he asked.

"Because we don't have a lot of time here," Amy answered. "We'll be staying in Baronissi, and our friends have everything planned."

"Maybe next time you go," the driver suggested.

"We threw coins in the Trevi Fountain, so we're supposed to come back," Randy said gleefully.

"How many coins?" the driver asked.

"Three. Each." Randy pointed to himself and Rachael.

"Ah, you find love and marriage."

Randy whispered slyly, "But not to each other."

Both Peter and Amy laughed at his comment. Within a half hour, they were at the entrance of the site. The street was crowded with tourists, cars, vans, and buses.

Amy spotted Frankie and Giovanni standing near a large passenger van. "There they are!" Amy squealed. She rolled down the window and started waving wildly.

Frankie was the first to spot her and mimicked Amy's gestures. The driver pulled as close to them as possible without running over any sightseers. They thanked the driver and wrestled their luggage from the back.

He called out, *"Arrivederci!"*

There was a lot of commotion going on outside the vehicle. Hugs, yelps, handshakes, and Amy jumping up and down.

"Nina and Richard are on their way. They're retrieving their luggage," Frankie read the text.

Then Amy spotted them about a hundred yards away. "There they are!" More jumping up and down.

Everyone watched as Nina and Richard threaded their way in and out of the crowd, pulling their rolling suitcases behind them.

More shouts, hugs, yelps, kisses, handshakes, plus Amy's normal jumping up and down.

"Benvenuto!" Giovanni was smiling from ear to ear. They actually pulled it off. Here they were in Italy for their annual New Year's Eve celebration. It started as an idea, and it came to fruition. He knew he had to thank Frankie for talking them into it, but he also knew it wouldn't take a lot of convincing, especially if Frankie was in charge.

"How has everyone's trip been so far?" Frankie asked.

Naturally everyone started talking at the same time.

"I think we're going to have to take turns, kids. Who wants to go first?"

Of course it was Rachael who jumped at the question. "I do! I do!"

"Why am I not surprised?" Frankie poked fun. "The floor is yours."

Rachael recounted the places they visited and almost every morsel of food they enjoyed.

"Don't forget about the dancing," Randy reminded her, and Rachael continued.

Next was Nina's turn. She described her brief visit with

Jordan, how they were going to work on a project, and of course, the fabulous food.

"Amy? How was Geneva?" Frankie asked, noticing Amy was unusually quiet.

"Let's save that for later while I'm investigating this pizza claim Giovanni has insisted on."

"And what about you guys?" Nina asked, referring to Frankie and Giovanni.

"Busy. Very, very busy. But good busy. More food than I can describe."

"And Mr. Parisi's wine." Giovanni chuckled.

"Oh, yeah. Mr. Parisi's wine. It takes homemade wine to another level, compared to the swill my grandfather used to make."

"He produces about fifty cases every year. New Year's Eve, he opens a few bottles and shares with friends. We are invited to sample this year's vintage, and then we will go back to the house for a party."

"Sounds fab!" Rachael said.

"And my friend Jordan will be joining us," Nina added. She could see Richard bristle. *Ha.*

"More on that later. How was Pompeii?" Frankie asked.

Richard began, "For Christmas, Nina gave me a private guided tour with an archaeologist. Obviously, she inserted herself." He chuckled. "It was shocking, startling, and mind-blowing."

"Did any of it creep you out?" Frankie winced.

"It was certainly a tragedy, but such insight into how people lived two thousand years ago was fascinating. The ruins of the city are what you could call an 'open-air' museum. It was a wealthy city with private luxury homes. Luxury for that time. Walls are covered in mosaics, and paintings. They surmise there were approximately eleven thousand residents and a theatre that could accommodate five thousand people at a time." Richard paused. "Even though there has been some question as to what time of year it actually took place, there is evidence it occurred during the Festival of Augustus, which attracted over a thousand more people, and that caused the toll to rise."

"But didn't they feel any kind of rumbling?" Randy asked, thinking about the size of the volcano they had recently passed.

"Apparently the day before was another celebration called Vulcanalia, honoring the god of volcanoes. The partygoers thought rumbling was a sign the gods were pleased."

"If I felt the ground trembling under my feet, I'd hightail it outta there," Randy said with wide eyes.

Amy broke in, "It took less than twenty-four hours for Pompeii and Herculaneum to be covered in ash, but the gases and the heat alone would have killed everyone."

"Okay! Fun times! So, Amy, we haven't heard from you yet," said Frankie, trying to change the subject.

"Later, please."

"What happened?" Frankie looked Amy directly in the eye.

"I kinda, sorta got lost."

"Lost? How? Didn't you get to the collider?" Frankie asked.

"Yes."

"And?" Nina pushed.

"And I got mixed up with a group of tourists from Germany. I got to see a lot of it, but not with the people I was supposed to meet."

"Amy took a tourist van excursion to the Jet d'Eau."

"Why?" Frankie asked.

"Because I got on the bus thinking it was going to take us to another part of the facility, but they were headed to the fountain, which, by the way, I had already seen." Amy sighed. "I had to go along for the ride until the driver could bring me back to CERN, which was where Peter was waiting for me."

"Oh, Amy, that's terrible. You were so looking forward to it."

"I know, but honestly, it's fine. I got to see a lot of it, and now I can say I was there." The disappointment was fading, and Amy was embracing the positive.

"How was what you saw of it?" Randy asked kindly.

"Pretty awesome." Amy smiled.

"It just occurred to me that our little group here has experienced a wide swath of humankind. From ancient Rome to beating up subatomic particles. Past and future. Pretty cool," Richard interjected.

"Let's not forget about the present," Frankie reminded them. "Speaking of presents . . ." She turned her head to reveal the stunning diamond earrings Giovanni gave her.

"Wow!" Rachael exclaimed.

"Holy sparkly rocks, Batman!" Randy added.

"Gorgeous!" Nina tossed in her opinion.

"You're making us look bad, Giovanni," Richard chastened him in jest.

"Richard got me season tickets to the opera and is taking me to dinner at Le Bernardin, Eleven Madison Park, and Per Se," Nina said, making sure Richard knew she appreciated his gift.

"That's not too terrible," Rachael pointed out.

"Peter bought us tickets to go to Albuquerque for the hot-air ballon festival and a weekend in Santa Fe."

"Very nice," Frankie said. "It sounds like everyone had a jolly holiday."

"And it's not over!" Amy squealed. "Pizza! Pizza! Pizza!" she chanted.

"First, we go to the house. You leave your suitcases, wash your face, and then we go," Giovanni instructed.

"Yay!" Amy shouted.

The chatting continued for the next thirty minutes as they drove through the hills of Campania. People on Vespas whizzed by.

"Oh, that looks like fun." Randy craned his neck. "Can we do that?"

"Rent a Vespa?" Giovanni asked.

"Yes? Can we? I mean, is it possible?" Randy asked.

"I think it's okay. Where do you wanna go?" Giovanni asked.

"I dunno." He looked over at Rachael. "You up for a spin?"

"Of course!" she immediately jumped in.

"Tomorrow we go to the Amalfi Coast, and dinner in Sorrento," Giovanni spoke from the front passenger seat.

"How about the day after?" Rachael asked.

"Sure. Day of New Year's Eve? Everyone wanna Vespa?"

"Not me," Amy said, and turned to Peter.

"Me, either. If the few people we've seen so far are an example of it, I'd rather be in an enclosed vehicle."

Nina looked at Richard, who replied, "I'm with Peter on this. Let's sit back and let someone else do the driving."

"*Bene!*" Giovanni said. "I'll take you to the rental agency in Salerno, and then the rest of us can have lunch."

"What about the party?" Frankie asked. "How much prep work is involved?"

"Not too much. The lentils and sausage are ready. I'll make steak on the grill, slice, serve with arugula."

"Oh, we had something like that last night for dinner! It was de-lish," Rachael commented.

"So you like tagliata?" Giovanni asked with a grin.

"Absolutely!" Randy put his two cents in.

"You sure you wanna again?"

"When in Salerno . . ." Randy chuckled.

"*Bene.* Plus, we have some cheese, dried sausage, prosciutto."

"Antipasto, yes?" Nina was more pleading than asking.

"Of course! Bruschetta, too. Simple."

"For you!" Randy chuckled. "I don't mind being the taste tester, by the way."

"I make. You test!" Giovanni clapped his hands together.

"You make whatever and I shall enjoy."

"What else?" Frankie asked. "Do you need me to do anything?"

"Help me find the recipe." Giovanni shook his head.

"What recipe?" Amy asked.

"My mother's recipe for panettone. It is different, and it's *molto bene*."

"And she won't give it to you?" Peter asked.

"No, and we cannot ask." Giovanni frowned.

"Why is it a secret?" Amy pushed on.

"Because it won many prizes for generations."

"Well, aren't you a generation?" Amy asked innocently.

"Yes, but it is in the estate. So, we will not see it until after she passes. I don't wanna wait that long!" Giovanni gave a slight chuckle. "Besides, I wanna make one for her to see how good I can do it. As good as she can."

"As in competition?" Rachael couldn't help herself. Competitions were part of her life.

"No. No. So she could be proud." Giovanni's eyes saddened. "Now. So she could be proud now. So I can see the look on her face when I can do something that's been in my family for generations."

Frankie could tell Giovanni was getting emotional. Maybe all this confusion, travel, people, was wearing him down. "Gio, your mother is proud of you no matter what you do."

Nina jumped in, "Look at the business you and Marco built. The restaurant is busier than ever."

Then it was Richard's turn: "Listen, Giovanni, you made it through the pandemic, and the slow return to whatever normal is now."

"Yes. Yes. Sorry. I not meant to bring family matters to you. We are here together to enjoy each other!" Giovanni was slightly embarrassed by his emotional flare-up. Then he went on to say, "Marco and I have been trying to find the recipe. We don't know where she hides it."

Frankie added, "Yeah. One night I went into the kitchen

to fix a cup of tea, and I saw the light under the pantry door. It was Marco and Giovanni sampling the panettone, trying to scribble down what they thought was in it."

"Oh, and yes, Frankie was going to hit us over the head with a frying pan!" Giovanni's mood lightened.

"For eating cake?" Amy asked.

"No, because, well, I didn't know what I was going to find and wanted to arm myself." Frankie snickered.

"Have you ever watched those stupid babysitter movies where she goes down into the basement with a hammer?"

"Well, duh," Frankie answered. "You never know what you're going to do when you're faced with a situation."

"Write this down. When you hear a strange noise coming from a closet, the basement, or otherwise, get as far away as you can and call the police." Nina shook her head. "Understood?"

"*Capisce*." Frankie was equally embarrassed that she pulled such a stupid stunt.

"What if there really was a burglar in the pantry? Then what?" Rachael huffed.

"Then I'd be toast," Frankie admitted.

"French toast!" Giovanni joked. "Why they call it French toast in Italy, I do not know."

The ride to the house in Baronissi went quickly with all the chatter and laughter going on. It was a small town between the foothills north of the city of Salerno. It was chock full of stucco and cement homes with terracotta tiled roofs. Many of the villages or communes looked similar, many surrounded with lemon and olive trees. It was an interesting mix of vegetation with evergreens, boxwoods, and an occasional palm tree. Most of the architecture was older by hundreds of years, but as you got closer to the university, smatterings of new houses were tucked into the scenery.

The vehicle pulled into a large U-shaped driveway and stopped in front of a large two-story house. Another one for the ages. It was similar to Giovanni's family house in many ways. The tiled floors. A second kitchen on the lower level; slab, stone walkways. Patio in the back. The only thing that was significantly different was the view. Giovanni's family house sat on a hill overlooking the city and the sea. The Baronissi home had a view of the forests and hills.

Everyone *ooh*ed and *aah*ed as they surveyed the property where they would be staying.

"You said they're professors?" Amy asked.

"Yes. They are," Giovanni answered.

"And they can afford a place like this? Or do they only live in part of it?"

"Like many houses, it has been passed on from one generation to the next. Upkeep is very expensive, and sometimes the family can no longer afford to do it and they move," Giovanni explained. "Some families will rent a room to a student for extra income. Baronissi gets many exchange students that want to live among a family, immerse themselves."

"That's very cool," Amy responded. "We do that sort of thing at home, too. When I was in high school, a young girl from Switzerland came for a year. They graduate earlier than we do, and she wanted to spend a year with an American family. Her plan was to go into the hospitality business when she went back to Switzerland. Oh, and did you know that women there didn't get the right to vote until 1971?"

"Wait. What?" Nina was surprised. "I thought they were a very modern country."

"That depends on what you consider modern," Amy responded. "They are very regimented; I found that out for sure. It might have taken ten extra minutes to drive me back instead of making me sit on the bus for three hours."

Nina put her hand on Amy's shoulder. "Amy, try to let it go." Then she quickly turned to Rachael. "Please do not sing."

"What?" Rachael didn't get it right away. "Ah. The song from *Frozen*! Let it . . ." she began to sing.

"Let's forget about Switzerland for now," Frankie jumped in, cutting off Rachael. "We are in beautiful southern Italy. Let's get you guys settled," Frankie said.

"And then we go for the pizza!" Giovanni gave Peter the thumbs-up. "Come. Bring the suitcases upstairs."

As they climbed the stairs, Rachael realized she hadn't given much thought to the sleeping arrangements. She knew there were four bedrooms, and then wondered how things would work out with her and Randy. But then she remembered Frankie and Giovanni were staying at his family's house.

It was as if Randy were reading her mind. He cleared his throat and looked at Rachael. "Good thing there's another bedroom. No offense, dearie, but sleeping with you for two nights is all I can stand." He pursed his lips, waiting for a response. He enjoyed trying to get Rachael's goat.

"As if I would ever consider it again," she mocked in response. Then she addressed the rest of the group. "Do you know he sings in the shower?"

Peter raised an eyebrow. "Oh, really?"

"Oh yes. And terribly, too," Rachael mugged. "I thought someone was trying to kill him. The screeching. It was horrifying."

Randy let out a huff. "Okay, you win this one, dearie."

"Glad to see the two of you are getting along as well as ever," Nina said drolly.

"Oh yes. We were discussing marriage on the train."

Amy looked puzzled. "Marriage? To whom?"

"Certainly not each other," Randy shot back.

"So why did the subject come up?" Amy asked.

"Because we threw three coins in the Trevi Fountain. One,

so you will return to Rome, the second for love, and the third for marriage," Rachael explained.

"Marriage? You? I thought you swore off the stuff," Nina quipped.

"Well, as someone pointed out, if the right person comes along, that could change things." Rachael winked at Randy.

"See? We really are friends." He smiled from ear to ear.

They stood in the hallway, deciding who was going to take which room. The modest rooms were similar in size and style. There was enough room for a decent-sized bed, an armoire, and dresser, with a small chair in a corner. There was just enough room to move around. The windows were slightly open, allowing the crisp, clean air to fill the rooms.

"Is it me, or does the air smell different here?" Frankie asked. "As soon as we got out of the airport, I noticed it."

"Ancient air, perhaps?" Amy said, and she began the science lesson for the day. "Think about this. We breathe air that's made of oxygen and nitrogen gas, with traces of other gases. All those molecules are perpetually rearranged and recycled through bio and geochemical processes."

"Thank you, professor," Nina nodded.

"I'm just sayin' that it's highly likely that there is an infinitesimal amount of molecules that were here thousands of years before, mingling inside your body right now."

Once everyone claimed their space, Giovanni and Frankie went to the first floor and checked the kitchen. There were breakfast pastries in the pantry; fruit in the refrigerator; cream, cheese, and salumi; and several types of freshly ground coffee. Giovanni remembered Peter liked beer, so he made sure to stock the fridge with a six-pack of Peroni and one of Moretti. There was a bottle of white wine chilling, and a bottle of red on the counter.

They looked at each other and nodded. "We could open a B and B," Frankie postulated.

"Ah, no, *cara*." Giovanni thought she might be serious for a minute.

"Ah, *sì*, no. But we would be good at it." She winked.

The group finally reconnoitered on the patio off the living room. Randy was leaning on the railing. "I think I could live here," he sighed.

"But you said that about Rome," Rachael corrected him.

"Yes, I mean I think I could live here in Italy," Randy waxed dreamily.

"As I said, you'd have to figure out what to do for a living."

"If you recall, I was a concierge at a fancy-schmancy resort. I could always find a job doing that."

"But you said you hated it."

"Maybe *hate* was a bit strong, and maybe I was a bit bored. But it could be very different doing that job here."

"Tourists are tourists," Rachael tossed at him.

"Oh, just let me dream for a few, dearie," he yearned.

Rachael noticed the change in his demeanor. He was much more mellow. Maybe this is why so many Europeans call it a "holiday," and not just for the holidays. A holiday from your regular, boring life.

Giovanni broke into her speculation, saying that they would be going to three different pizzerias. "This way you can have a choice, and Peter will not win."

Peter knew he was never going to win a "Boston has Better Pizza than Naples Contest." Italians invented it, although some disagreed with the origin. But considering where the best mozzarella is made, and where the San Marzano tomatoes are grown, it's no contest at all. They were in the heart of pizza country.

They piled into the transport vehicle, and Giovanni gave the driver the three locations.

The first was a hole-in-the-wall in a town on the way to Salerno. Inside was a long counter in front of a stone pizza oven. Two men and a woman were working with dough. Another woman greeted them. Giovanni ordered two pizzas, one regular, the other with pepperoni.

"We start simple," he explained to the crew.

They took their seats at a long wooden picnic table. Within a few minutes, the steaming hot, delicious-smelling pizza was on the top of the counter. The woman brought a stack of paper plates and napkins.

"*Birra?*" she asked, pointing to a glass-front refrigerator that contained bottles of beer.

Everyone raised one hand as they tried to handle the hot slice with the other.

Giovanni took over. "You fold the slice down the middle, like so." He creased the triangle in half. "And then you eat." He took a bite. "But sometimes you eat with a knife and fork. Neapolitan pie is very messy."

Peter elbowed Amy. "See, I told you they eat pizza with a fork and knife here."

"But you eat Boston pizza," Giovanni reminded him. "You'll see. You taste."

The table fell silent as everyone folded and savored the food. Giovanni got up and asked for a few more napkins. He told the woman his friend never ate pizza before. She cackled at the absurd remark. "Who no eat-a-the pizza?"

Everyone at the table roared. Peter simply shook his head and picked up a third slice.

"You have room for more?" Giovanni asked.

"You bet!"

"So? What do you think about our pizza?" Giovanni eyed him.

"I don't believe I can make an accurate assessment without properly reviewing other assets," Peter cracked an accountant joke.

The second pizzeria was a few blocks away. It was a little fancier and was located on one of the side streets. It was a little more comfortable than the previous one, but Giovanni explained that their first pizzeria is where people pick them up or just grab a quick slice. It was Southern Italy's version of fast food.

The second pizzeria had a dozen tile tables and murals painted on the walls. Giovanni had phoned ahead and asked if they could accommodate eight people. They said they could if they didn't mind putting several small tables together. This time, he ordered a pizza with prosciutto, burrata, arugula, and shaved parmesan. When the waiter brought it to the table, it garnered compliments reserved for a work of art.

"*Bellissimo!*"

"Gorgeous!"

And then Nina actually said the words: "It's a work of art."

"*Mangia!*" Gio helped serve the slices while others passed them around the table.

Again, more napkins were needed, and this time they required a fork and knife.

Each of them polished off two pieces each, and one slice remained. Giovanni leaned over and looked at Peter. "We share?" he said.

"How many more pizzas are we going to have?"

"Two, three maybe."

"Okay. We'll share." Peter cut the slice and served it to Giovanni.

For the next hour, most of the sounds they emitted were groans of delight, or "I'm stuffed. What's next?"

That phrase became the slogan of their trip.

The final pizzeria was for dessert. Giovanni ordered a dozen zeppoli, half with crystalized sugar, half with powdered sugar. Then he ordered a light-crust pizza with cream fraiche and fresh fruit, and another thin crust with figs and goat cheese.

They gorged themselves and then sat back, fully sated. "I feel so gluttonous," Nina confessed.

"I think it's unanimous," Richard added.

Giovanni turned to Peter. "So, *signore*, what is the verdict?"

Richard chimed in, "I shall make closing arguments for you, Mr. Lombardi." Richard recapped the variety of flavors they experienced that took their taste buds to nirvana.

Then all eyes were on Peter.

"I concede. Giovanni Lombardi, you have dismantled all I had ever thought of Boston pizza."

Everyone applauded. Then someone at a nearby table asked, "What is Boston pizza? Does it have beans?"

That elicited more laughter and a few snorts. Then the group gathered their belongings and shuffled to the waiting transport. It was about twenty minutes back to the house. The van looked like it was filled with bobbleheads, everyone resisting dozing off. When they got to the house, they said their goodnights and thanked Giovanni profusely for the delectable evening, and for claiming his win over Peter. He reminded them to get a good night's sleep, explained about the food in the kitchen, and that they would be back to pick them up at ten o'clock the next morning.

He and Frankie got in his own car and released the driver for the night.

"That was great, Gio! Everyone had so much fun!" She patted his shoulder and blew him a kiss.

"I hope they enjoy tomorrow the same. And remind me to reserve a Vespa for Randy and Rachael for the day after."

"Really? You're gonna let them do that?" Frankie was dubious about the idea of the two zipping along very curvy roads with steep cliffs, with neither of them knowing where they were going.

"They want to do it. I cannot stop them."

"I know. It just makes me nervous."

Giovanni picked up her hand and kissed the back of it. "*Cara*, they are grown-ups. They are responsible for themselves."

"That's just it. Rachael? Responsible?"

"I think you do not give her enough credit. She's smart. Savvy."

"She's also wild and likes to take chances."

"What kind of chances they take? She's not going to jump into the volcano, no?"

"You're right."

"Relax, *cara*. Your friends are here. I am here. We are here."

The house was quiet when they entered. It was almost eleven o'clock. Marco, Anita, and the children left earlier that morning to go back to New York. Rosevita and Lucia were probably long gone into dreamland. Giovanni took Frankie's hand. He put his finger in front of his lips. "Shush. Follow me."

"Where are we going?" she whispered.

"The pantry."

"Not again," she whined.

"Shush."

They tiptoed into the kitchen and then into the pantry. Giovanni shut the door and turned on the light. He pulled out a step stool and climbed until he was eye level with the top shelf. He carefully reached up for the small, five-by-five, square wooden box where his grandmother had kept her recipes. The box had to be over a hundred years old. Just as he handed it down to Frankie, the door was pulled open. It was Rosevita.

"Giovanni? What are you doing?"

Frankie thought fast, turned, and held the box behind her back. "Changing the light bulb."

"But why? It's working."

"So you won't have to worry about it when I go back to New York." Giovanni caught on quickly.

Rosevita waved him off. *"Pazzo!"* Rosevita thought her son was getting a little goofy. She shook her head and turned around.

Frankie and Giovanni stood frozen in the pantry and listened for Rosevita's retreating footsteps. Instead, she was puttering around in the kitchen.

Frankie mouthed, "Now what?"

Giovanni pulled up the back of his shirt. "Put it here." He gestured to the lower curve below his waist. Frankie held it in place while Giovanni tucked his shirt back in.

"Giovanni! How long does it take to change a light bulb?" Rosevita called out.

Giovanni and Frankie exited the pantry together.

"Mama. Canna I have a little time with my beautiful Frankie?"

Rosevita rolled her eyes. *"Capretti!* Kids!" Then she smiled. It was good to be young and in love. Well, young-ish. Both were staring ahead at forty. She wondered if Giovanni was going to ask Frankie to marry him. She hoped so. This one was a keeper.

Frankie got behind Giovanni and put her arms around his waist. "Sorry, Rosevita. I hope we didn't embarrass you. Or us!" She chuckled.

Again, Rosevita waved them off and went back upstairs.

They didn't move an inch until they heard Rosevita's door close.

Like thieves in the night, Frankie and Giovanni padded their way down the hall to the room Frankie was staying in. Giovanni locked the door and then pulled the box out from his waistband and put it on the bed.

Frankie could barely contain herself. She bit her lip to keep from laughing too loud. "We're such criminals."

Giovanni gently removed the dozens of folded pieces of paper and cardboard from the box and laid them in order, for when he would return them. If he knew his mother like he did, she knew exactly where each recipe was in the pile of scraps of paper.

The two got on their knees and began to survey the decades of family treasures.

"Wow. There's everything from risotto, to bread, to a half-dozen kinds of meatballs. Ew, here's one for tripe." Frankie gagged at the idea of eating stomach lining. Liver was bad enough. She was definitely a "no internal organs" kind of gal. That was one thing she and Rachael agreed on.

"Anything that resembles a panettone recipe?" she asked.

"Nothing." Giovanni sat back on his heels.

"Do you think she uses one? I mean, doesn't she know it by heart at this point?"

"There is a recipe on paper. I remember seeing it when I was a kid. She would use a clothespin to hang it on the shelf."

"Maybe it's still in the kitchen?" Frankie suggested.

"Maybe." But Giovanni was crestfallen. He really thought he might have unearthed the cherished recipe.

"Come." He grabbed Frankie's hand, and they stealthily worked their way back to the kitchen. "You wait here."

He opened the pantry door, pulled out the stool, and returned the treasure chest to its perch. Except there was no treasure.

Once the box was safely back in its space, he went back into the kitchen. Frankie had been noodling around the stove, carefully and quietly opening and closing the cupboard doors. She shook her head.

Giovanni began investigating the drawers. They must have spent the good part of an hour combing every nook and cranny of the kitchen. Giovanni sighed heavily. "It's no use."

"Why don't you just ask her?" Frankie said, once they got back into her room.

"I can't. It's not something we do. If someone wants to give you something, they give it to you."

"Does she know you want it?"

"Of course. She keeps saying it's not *her* secret, it's Santa's secret."

"So, she's waiting for permission from the North Pole?"

"Could be." Giovanni pulled Frankie into an affectionate hug. "*Mille grazie.* You are a good sport."

"And you are a good son." She touched her earrings. "And a pretty, pretty, pretty good boyfriend." She gave him a big, smacking kiss on the lips, and patted him on the fanny. Giovanni returned the kiss before he made his way to the lower level, where he was assigned his sleeping quarters.

Chapter 20

December 30th
The Amalfi Coast

Frankie was up unusually early. Her excitement for their day trip to Positano and Sorrento had her all atwitter. She had seen photos, videos, and movies, but to see it in person would be spectacular. As she quietly padded her way into the kitchen, she could smell coffee. Someone must have gotten up before her. Giovanni? She checked the clock above the sink. It was only 6:00 a.m. She fixed a cup of cappuccino and decided to sit on the patio and watch the colors of the sea change with the morning light.

She spotted Lucia, who was already on the patio with something on her lap. Frankie approached her and whispered *"Buongiorno!"*

Lucia was taken aback. She hadn't heard Frankie approaching.

"Oh, *buongiorno*, Frankie. *Come stai?*"

"Molto bene. You are up early," Frankie stated, then noticed Lucia had the shawl Frankie had given her on her lap. She didn't know what to say next. *Do you like it? Do you*

hate it? Should she say nothing? She also noticed a wadded-up tissue in Lucia's clenched hand.

Frankie put her hand on Lucia's shoulder. "Everything alright?" Frankie could see Lucia had been crying.

"Yes. Fine." Lucia sniffled.

Frankie decided this was the moment to dig into Lucia's puzzling moods. "May I join you?"

"Of course." Lucia gestured to a chair.

Frankie decided the only way to approach this was to take it head on, like she did with most things.

"Lucia, I'm sorry to impose, but I couldn't help noticing that you sometimes seem unhappy. Is it because we have invaded your home?" Frankie thought that could be a good possibility. "A hoard of people descending upon your quiet, peaceful life can be disarming."

"No. No." She shook her head, but still didn't reveal her melancholy.

Frankie put her hand on Lucia's. "Can you tell me what you are upset about? Maybe we can fix it?" Frankie spoke softly. Compassionately. Then she decided to ask about the shawl. "Do you not like your gift?" Frankie knew no one would cry over a shawl, but thought it might prompt more conversation.

Lucia sniffled again. "It's *bellissimo*. I have not received something so beautiful in many years."

Frankie looked into the woman's eyes. She could tell Lucia wanted to bear her soul. Maybe not to Frankie, but to someone. *A priest, perhaps?* "I know somewhere inside you are hurting. Can you tell me what it is? Do you want me to call a priest?"

Lucia's head jerked up. "A priest?"

Frankie couldn't help but laugh out loud. That suggestion didn't land the way she expected it would. She shrugged.

"What man understands a woman? *Nessuno di loro.* None of them!" Lucia was becoming animated.

"So, tell me, Lucia. What is causing you so much pain?" Frankie knew she was on a slippery slope, but she thought she might be making some headway.

"Marriage." Lucia appeared to be more engaged in the topic.

"Marriage?" That came out of the blue. Frankie knew there were a lot of words on the tip of Lucia's tongue. Now if she could pry them off.

"When Rosevita told me you were coming here, I wondered who was going to sleep where."

Interesting. Frankie's initial concerns were not far off.

"We want to respect you and the family," Frankie said.

"I know. And I appreciate."

Frankie felt a *but* coming.

"But who am I to judge?" Lucia said, to Frankie's great surprise. "People should live their life. Too many people are *infelice.* Unhappy. The church makes rules. Too many rules."

Frankie was invigorated by the direction the conversation was going. "I think people still believe in God, but they don't believe in the rules that men put in place."

"*Esattamente*! Exactly!"

Frankie gave her a conspiratorial eye. "Any rules in particular?"

"My husband. He cheat on me many times." Lucia's mood went from sorrow to anger.

Frankie almost fell off her chair. This was not what she was expecting.

"I go talk to the priest and he tells me he is my husband, and I must look the other way."

"Uh boy," Frankie exhaled.

"For years, I put up with this cheat, but we cannot get divorced." Lucia was spilling her guts. "One morning when he left for work, we had a big-a fight. He slapped me, and I said for him to *cadere morte*—drop dead—and later that day, guess what?" She shrugged and opened her hands. "He did."

Frankie didn't know how to react. She wanted to laugh out loud, but it wasn't funny. Ironic, yes. Funny? Not so much.

Lucia continued, "Now I blame myself. All these years."

Frankie grabbed Lucia's hand again. "Don't be ridiculous! It's not your fault."

"Maybe yes, maybe no."

Then Frankie recalled Lucia reminding her of Strega Nona, who used magic.

"Definitely no." Frankie paused. "What did he die from?"

"Heart attack." Lucia sighed.

"You know what I think? I mean if you want my opinion."

"Please."

"I think all that running around, behind your back, that's what killed him. Not you. He brought this on himself." She patted Lucia's hand.

"You know, I never told this story to anyone before." Lucia looked at Frankie with puppy-dog eyes.

"I am flattered and happy you could share this. You cannot blame yourself. You were a good wife and mother."

"*Sì.* Some people knew about his *fidanzata,* his girlfriend, but I held my head high. *Stupido.*"

"So, you didn't get divorced, and he died."

"*Sì.*"

"Did you ever think that it was God who saved you from your terrible marriage?"

Lucia furrowed her brow. "No."

"We have a word for it. It's called karma."

"*Sì.* Yes. Karma." Lucia's face brightened.

Frankie tugged at Lucia's sleeve. "I think it's time for you to shed these widow clothes. You have suffered and grieved enough. If you think about it, you were grieving your faithless marriage long before your husband passed."

Lucia nodded. "Yes, I grieved for five years before he died."

"Well, I think you have paid your grieving dues. And who

is to decide how long one should grieve? It's all very personal."

They hadn't noticed Rosevita standing in the doorway. She made a slight rustle to announce her presence.

"Rosevita! *Buongiorno!*" Frankie said with surprise.

"*Buongiorno!*" Rosevita replied. She went immediately to Lucia and hugged her. "Why didn't you tell me?"

"You hear everything?"

"I heard enough. Frankie is right. And enough is enough."

"So I can wear pretty clothes again?" Lucia asked hopefully, her eyes brimming with tears.

"Absolutely!" Frankie said, wondering if this was a good time to approach Rosevita with the same option.

Rosevita pulled out a chair and sat across from them. "You know, the other night when I saw Giovanni in his father's suit, I realized the suit has moved on, and so should I."

Frankie held her breath before she made the next big suggestion. "I have an idea! Mr. Parisi is having his party tomorrow night, right?"

"*Sì.*"

"How about if my friend Nina and I help the two of you get ready for the party? Let's go into town and buy new dresses for you. Nina and I will do something with your hair."

"And a little makeup?" Lucia said coyly. Then she looked down at her feet. "What about-a the shoes? Can I get new shoes?"

"Absolutely!" Frankie was over the moon. "This is going to be so much fun!" She paused. "And we cannot forget red underwear!"

"No!" Lucia gasped. "I'm too old."

"You are never too old to have some fun. Plus, I hear it's a tradition. We're all going to wear red underwear!"

"Do you think we find my size?" Lucia could barely get the words out.

Frankie leaned in and whispered, "Even if we have to find boxer shorts."

Lucia was so overcome with relief, the welled-up tears streamed down her face. She was laughing and crying at the same time. Rosevita had a similar reaction. It was time for them to move on and enjoy life again.

The three women had a group hug and exclaimed, *"Vivere, ridere, amare!"* Live, laugh, love!

Frankie could barely contain her excitement and ran downstairs to tell Giovanni. When she barged into his room, he woke with a start.

"Everything okay? What's happened?"

"Everything is *molto bene!* Tomorrow, Nina and I are going to take Lucia and your mother shopping for new dresses."

Giovanni bolted upright. "What? New dresses? What happened?"

"Just a little girl talk." This time, it was her turn to kiss him on top of the head. "You'll be on your own with Peter and Richard. Maybe Amy." Then Frankie jumped up and hooted, "Woo-hoo!" before she scrambled up the stairs.

Giovanni and Frankie headed over to the house in Baronissi to pick up the rest of the crew. Nina proudly presented the package to Giovanni. "I was so immersed in pizza heaven, I forgot to give this to you last night." She handed him the shopping bag that contained the shirt and blazer. "A token of our appreciation."

Giovanni was taken aback when he saw the name Armani on the bag. He had several items from the renowned designer, so he knew that whatever was inside was of value and quality, and a bit pricey.

"Oh, Nina, this is not so necessary."

Frankie gave him a sideways look that said, *accept the gift with grace.*

"But I appreciate it very much. Can I open now?"

"That depends. How many days have you been wearing the same shirt?"

"I wash every night," Giovanni said defensively.

"Open the bag." Nina stood with her arms folded.

Giovanni removed the perfectly wrapped items with the Armani logo sticker on the tissue. *"Bellissimo!"* Giovanni remarked. "I need a shirt!" Then he opened the packaged blazer. He let out a whistle. "Wow! *Fantastico*!" He immediately removed the one he had been wearing for the past several days and tried on the new one. It fit perfectly. He grabbed Nina and kissed her on both cheeks. *"Mille grazie*! This is too much!"

Frankie elbowed him. "And I love it!" he continued.

"Speaking of clothes, have they found your luggage yet?" Richard asked.

"I think it took the train," Giovanni joked. "Maybe tonight. But I don't need it now!" He was smiling from ear to ear. *"Andiamo*! We have places to go, sights to see, and food to eat!"

Giovanni explained the area as they drove west. "There is much to do here. You can hike, swim, and sail. Of course, eat and shop." He continued to describe the coastal communities. "The Amalfi Coast is a UNESCO World Heritage Site, protected by the United Nations."

"Yes, I read about this. Plus, Frankie gave us a little geography lesson," Amy interjected. "It's a place on earth with historic and cultural value. There are just under two thousand designated sites in the entire world," she continued in her professorial cadence. "It's situated in Southern Italy's Campania region, and stretches for approximately thirty miles, with towns and villages connected by the SS 163 highway."

"Very good, Amy!" Giovanni applauded. "We will experience one of the most magnificent driving routes in all of Eu-

rope. It can be a little, how you say, breathtaking." Giovanni
ran down the list of the waterfront towns. "The most popular is Positano, but they are all beautiful. From west to east,
it starts with Vietri sul Mare, then Cetara, Maiori, Minori,
Atrani, Amalfi, Conca dei Marini, and Praiano. Up on the
hills are Ravello, Tramonti, Furore, and Agerola."

"And you get an 'A' in geography," Amy clowned around.

"*Sì*. For one, I grew up here, and for two, we had to know
this in school. So, yes, I get an 'A.'"

As they began the journey on the highway, everyone noticed how narrow the road was, and how fast people were
driving. It was more than breathtaking. It was breath-holding.
It was hard to tell where the *whoa*s, *yikes*es, and *oh my*s were
coming from amongst the passengers.

When the vehicle finally stopped in Amalfi, their legs were
like Jell-O as they exited the van.

"That was more like an amusement park ride," Amy blurted
as she clung to Peter's arm. "Wow. People do this every day?"

"Pretty much." Giovanni grinned. "Come, we'll have some
coffee."

"I don't know if I can handle caffeine after that. Do we
have to go back the same way?" Amy asked.

"No, we'll be in Sorrento, and there is a calmer highway
back." Giovanni slapped Peter on the back. "She okay?"

Peter looked at Amy. "You okay?"

"Yes. I'm good. I guess I wasn't expecting such a serpen-
tine ride."

"Ah, and you said you did your homework," Giovanni
teased. He didn't mention they hadn't really started the journey. It was only going to become more of a white-knuckle
ride.

"It looked different on paper." Amy pouted.

Amalfi is situated at the mouth of a deep ravine at the base
of Monte Cerreto, with coastal scenery amid the high cliffs.
It was once an important trading port and a place of power

in the Mediterranean in the years between 800 and 1200. The group started their walking tour at the port and the arsenal Piazza Dante, passing fountains, and the Amalfi Duomo. Most of the towns along the coast were vertical, with buildings situated in the cliffsides. Rows of homes were terraced from the beaches to over twelve hundred feet of bluffs.

They meandered through the covered streets and finished their tour at the Paper Museum. Fashioned after the Chinese invented paper, Amalfi became one of the world's premier producers of paper. Frankie was especially intrigued by the history and process and purchased authentic Amalfi paper goods to bring back to work. She bought several boxes of note cards of different sizes. "These are perfect to send with an Advance Reading Copy or BLADs."

"What's a BLAND and an Advance Reading Copy?" Randy asked.

"It's BLAD. B.L.A.D stands for 'basic layout and design.' We do it for cookbooks and other artsy stuff. Most other books, like fiction or nonfiction, get a very limited printing of the first pass. They're uncorrected proofs. We need to get those to reviewers four months ahead of when the book goes on sale. I always write a personal note. You know, 'hope you like this' or tell them how excited I am about an upcoming title."

"Aren't you supposed to be excited about every upcoming title?" Randy tilted his head and batted his eyes.

"Let's not overstate the obvious." Frankie chuckled. "We *have* to be excited. It's the unspoken rule of corporate."

Rachael and Nina also purchased several boxes of the luxurious handcrafted paper.

"I love the deckled edges on them. And the watermark. Impressive," Rachael stated as she ran her hand across the soft texture.

After they paid for their goods, the travelers returned to the van and moved on to Praiano to take another look at the spectacular scenery and the statue of Christ the Redeemer, the second largest statue in the world, after the one in Rio de Janeiro.

On the drive to Positano, they were awed by the magnificent landscape. Terraced among the rocks and greenery, neutral-colored buildings with tiled roofs were surrounded with lemon groves, olive trees, and Mediterranean scrub. Once they arrived, they decided to give themselves two hours to meander the streets and eventually meet up at a restaurant Giovanni recommended.

Nina, Frankie, Rachael, and Randy were in shopping mode, while Amy, Richard, and Peter were in sightseeing mode. Giovanni offered to show them around the scenic, famous town while the others watched local cobblers make shoes right in front of them.

"You know I am going to have to get a pair of those," Nina said.

"To go with your sweatpants wardrobe?" Frankie joked.

"Listen, since I've been here, I have an entirely new appreciation for fine fabric and clothing," Nina said.

"Hallelujah," Rachael cracked. "Although I have to say, you *have* been looking a bit spiffier since you got here."

"You can thank Jordan for that. He fashion-shamed me."

"Oh, I'd love to meet the person who disgraced you into real clothes!" Randy said.

"And you will. I've invited him to the party tomorrow," Nina replied.

"Excellent. Anyone with good taste in clothing is at the top of my list," Randy said gleefully.

Nina eyed Frankie. Randy might just have a new playmate. They were going to have to figure out something for Rachael. She wouldn't get jealous, just miffed that she wasn't getting Randy's full attention.

"Who else is coming to the party?" Nina asked.

"I'm actually not sure who Giovanni invited besides us. I'll have to ask him later," Frankie answered.

"Maybe we can rent a date for her."

"I think that's called a gigolo."

"Didn't Italians invent them?" Nina gave Frankie a playful nudge.

"No, the French."

"Figures," Nina scoffed.

"The French what?" Rachael sidled up to the girls.

"Invented brioche," Frankie replied with a straight face.

Nina sat on the stool in front of the cobbler, who measured her foot. She picked out the style and color, and he told her to come back in an hour.

"Wow. Custom sandals," Rachael marveled. "Maybe I should get a pair." She looked at the man who was cutting the tanned leather.

"Apologies. I can only do-a one pair before we close-a for lunch."

Rachael looked at Frankie and Nina. "Food is definitely a priority here."

"Not such a bad thing." Nina patted her stomach. "Although I think I may have gained a few pounds since I've been here."

"I'm sure we'll walk it off today," Frankie said. "But I don't think you gained weight, honey pie. You're just not used to wearing pants with a waistband."

"Ha, ha," Nina sneered. "But I have to admit, I do feel more upscale than usual."

"Good food, good wine, and nice clothes can do that to you," Frankie commented.

Rachael spotted another artisan making small leather handbags. "Look! I'm going over there." She pointed down the narrow street. "See you in a few."

Rachael automatically flirted with the young apprentice

working with the leather craftsman. "*Buongiorno!*" She gave him one of her winning smiles.

"*Buongiorno, signorina. Come stai?*"

"*Molto bene.*" Rachael tried to be coy with her feeble Italian.

"What can we help you with today?" The young man's eyes pierced hers.

Is every young man in Italy gorgeous? she thought to herself. Rachael was not easily disarmed by men. If anything, she was always in control. At least at first blush. But this guy rattled her. She gathered her composure and asked if he could make a small crossbody bag for her.

"Do you not like any of these?" He brought her inside the shop. There were dozens to choose from, with different silhouettes, colors, and sizes.

"Oh, but I wanted *you* to make one for me." She fluttered her eyes.

"Ah. Signorina, I show you the ones I make." He gently took her elbow and walked her toward a display. She thought she was going to faint. Her eye went to a burnished, burgundy-colored bag with fringe.

"This is beautiful."

He took it off the rack and placed it over her shoulder. "I can make the strap any length for you."

His handsome looks were making her dizzy. For one of the few times in her life, Rachael was speechless. The man was raw beauty. "I . . . I think this is fine." Then she got ahold of herself and said, "But I wanted you to make it especially for me."

The young man smiled. "I cannot do that for you today, but I can make your initial on it. Then you can say it was made for you."

"That would be fantastico!" Rachael exclaimed.

"Come." He walked her to the back of the shop. "Tell me, what is your name, signorina?"

"Rachael." She could barely speak.

"Ah." He gestured for her to hand the purse to him.

He took the front flap and placed it on a large slab of stone on a workbench; then he showed her different styles of fonts. "What you like?"

"Oh, you decide."

The man eyed her up and down. "I think you need something *feminile*." He showed her a sample of script. "You like?"

"*Sì.*" She didn't know what else to say.

He made a fine pencil line of the letter and then fired up the burning tool. Within a few short minutes, the letter *R* was inscribed on the bag.

"*Bellissimo!*" Rachael fussed. She touched his arm. Big mistake. He had muscles from Amalfi to Nova Scotia. She silently scolded herself, *Behave, girl.* Then she noticed a young woman at the other side of the shop, giving her the stink eye. Of course, this man was spoken for. Rachael quickly thanked and paid him and hotfooted it out of the shop before the young woman could say anything or, even worse, do anything. Rachael had watched too many *Real Housewives of New Jersey* not to know what an angry Italian woman was capable of.

She quickly caught up with her pals. "Where's Randy?"

Nina nodded to a millinery shop across the street. The three of them spotted him inside, trying on several fedoras. When he noticed them watching, he called out, "What do you think, girls?"

"I like it," Nina said, and nodded. "I think I like the cream-colored one."

"Not the baby blue?" Randy frowned. "It matches my eyes."

"Nope. Cream." Rachael barged in and said, "He'll take this one." She took it from Randy's hand and gave it to the woman.

"So glad I asked," he *tsk*ed.

"It's on me, cowboy." Rachael handed the woman her credit card.

"Well then, I guess I do like the cream better." Randy raised his eyebrows. He plopped the hat on his head. "Now I really feel like I'm on the Amalfi Coast."

They walked back to the cobbler to fetch Nina's sandals and then through the Piazza del Mulini, where they caught up with the rest of the gang.

They headed toward the beach and up a flight of stone steps to a restaurant perched on a cliff. Boats of all shapes and sizes bobbed in the water below.

The table was arranged with two on each side and four in the middle, so everyone had a view of the sea. Giovanni spoke to the waiter in Italian and ordered Negronis for everyone. When the waiter returned with the tray, he began to spout off the specials of the day. Most of it was fish, all freshly caught.

Giovanni asked if anyone minded if he ordered for the table. Naturally there were no objections. He rattled off his selections: lemon tagliolini pasta with shrimp, ravioli stuffed with tomatoes and ricotta cheese, and grilled zucchini. They were going to share it family-style. Two bottles of wine were brought to the table when the entrees were served. They mostly ate in silence, enjoying the epicurean delights and the view of the sea.

"Giovanni, why did you ever leave Italy?" Rachael asked.

"My family moved to New York when I was twelve. My father took over the restaurant."

"But it's so beautiful here," Amy said in awe.

"True. But remember, when my grandfather first went to America, Italy was not in such good shape, and he wanted to make a better life for his family. And so it goes for many generations."

"Would you ever consider coming back?" Richard asked.

Giovanni looked at Frankie. "Maybe yes. Maybe no. It depends on how life goes."

"I concur," Richard replied. "I never thought I'd open a practice in New York and still keep my practice in Philadelphia." He squeezed Nina's hand under the table. Both knew that it was because of Nina that Richard made concessions in order to spend more time with her.

"I can say the same," shared Randy. "I hadn't considered moving to New York until Miss Dancing Shoes, here, got me a job."

"I went to New York, too," Nina added.

"And I went from Stanford to Boston," Amy chimed in.

"I guess we're the poster children for 'You Never Know,' right, Frankie?" Nina said with a grin, knowing that was one of Frankie's favorite expressions.

"And here we are. In Italy. On the Amalfi Coast. Who knew?" Frankie quipped.

After their leisurely lunch, Giovanni directed them to follow him to the port and told them that he had made reservations on the ferry to take them to Sorrento. "We cannot get to Capri this trip, but we will pass by, and you can see the rest of the coastline from the water. Nobody gets seasick, no?"

Amy figured it couldn't be worse than the nail-biting ride from Salerno.

A crowd waited to board the ferry. Even though it was winter and the tourist crowd wasn't as vast as it was in the summer, Giovanni anticipated there would be hordes of people and ordered tickets in advance. The boat carried over a hundred passengers, all clamoring to get a seat by a window. Giovanni tipped one of the crew members, who pulled the group out of the waiting line and escorted them to the first row on the boat.

It was a high-speed ferry that would make the trip in just under forty minutes. They swiftly passed the rocky cliffs that jutted into the sea, the hillside dotted with houses, and Medieval structures that looked like forts in a state of disrepair. As the boat approached the far end of the peninsula, it was easy to catch sight of Capri. Voices speaking Italian were full of excitement, as if they were on an amusement park ride.

Once they docked in Sorrento, the group walked to Tasso Square, where large baskets of flowers in wrought iron stands lined the middle of the road separating the flow of traffic. The busy square had a scenic overlook of an aerial view of a gorge created by volcanic activity. They passed the Sedite di Porta, a historic building that once housed prisoners.

Peter noted the town seemed much busier than the previous ones they visited earlier.

Giovanni replied, "*Sì.* It's much easier to get to Sorrento from Naples so, yes, very busy place."

They turned to Corso Italia, a favorite shopping area, closed to traffic but filled with high-end and local artisan shops, where you can find hand-painted ceramics and anything and everything lemon.

He went on to explain that over the centuries, Sorrento was ruled by the Greeks, Romans, Byzantines, French, and Spanish. "You can see the Spanish influence in the architecture and hear it in the dialect."

He ushered them through an alley that brought them to the Sorrento Cathedral. It was built in the Romanesque style in the fifteenth century and is home to many pieces of art from the Neapolitan School from the eighteenth century. "The building was restored in 1933."

They followed him back to Corso when Rachael stopped abruptly.

"Check this out!" She pointed to a small boutique called Shopping Victim. In front of the store was a large cart filled with bags of lemons, lemon candy, lemon juice, lemon balm, lemon-scented candles. "You weren't kidding! Everything lemon!"

She had to buy a bag of the bright yellow fruit. "Do you think I can get this through customs?"

"You could just buy lemons at home," Randy snorted.

"But not Sorrento lemons." She stuck her tongue at him.

Giovanni realized everyone was getting a little cranky. They had covered a lot of territory over the past several hours. Too bad there was no place to take a *pennichella*. Espresso would have to do. "Come. Let's rest a while." He ushered them to an open-air café, where he ordered pastry and heavy-duty coffee for everyone.

Amy sighed. "I am running out of steam."

"Me, too," Nina echoed, and shot a sideways glance at Frankie.

Frankie didn't want to say anything to Giovanni, fearful she would hurt his feelings if she suggested they head home.

Peter and Richard were silent. They didn't want to seem lame, but they, too, were bedraggled.

It didn't take much for Giovanni to get the hint. "I think, if nobody minds, maybe we should go back home after the coffee."

"Oh, but not until we sample some of the limoncello. I've heard this is where it was invented," Randy responded.

"How about we buy a few bottles?" Richard suggested.

"Brilliant!" Peter added.

"So, it is settled. I will cancel the dinner appointment and let the driver know to pick us up soon."

"Didn't he leave us at the dock?" Amy asked.

"Yes, but I tell him to drive to Sorrento to bring us back."

"Are you sure you're not a travel guide?" Richard asked.

"Not such a good one. I make my people tired," Giovanni said solemnly.

Everyone started contradicting him at the same time.

"Don't be ridiculous!"

"Are you crazy?"

"*Pazzo?*"

"Insane?"

"Pul-lease!"

He held up his hands. "Okay. Okay. I'm not such a bad tour guide."

Frankie threw her arms around his neck and gave him a big kiss on the cheek. Randy was sitting on the other side of him and did the same.

"*Mille grazie,*" Giovanni said, blushing.

"I'm not trying to rush anyone, but when will the car be here?" Randy asked.

"Half hour. Maybe a little more," Giovanni answered.

"Then there *still* is time to have some limoncello and bring some back to the house, and back to home, home." Randy clapped happily. "I saw a place right around the corner."

"Excellent!" Richard said. "I'll go with you."

The two men got up from the café table and walked to the shop.

"Oh my gosh. As Rachael would say, 'my dogs are killing me,'" Randy quipped.

Richard gave him a curious look. "Your what?"

"Dogs. Feet. Don't ask. I have no idea where that expression came from."

They walked quickly to the store and bought six bottles. While the cashier was wrapping them, they sampled the famous elixir.

"Oh. My. Gosh. Is this the tastiest thing you've ever had?" Randy exclaimed.

"I'll tell you, I haven't had one bad thing since we've been here." Richard downed the sample, and the cashier poured another into his paper cup. "Is it safe?" he asked.

The woman cackled, "You are in Sorrento. Everything or nothing is safe. It's up to you!"

They gathered their procurements and thanked the woman.

"These people have such a great attitude, don't they?" Randy remarked.

"Most definitely. Before we got here, I watched something about Naples, Pompeii, and Vesuvius. Evidently, the threat of an eruption has given the people an exuberance for life."

Randy pondered that for a moment. "That actually makes sense. But it shouldn't take living in the shadow of a volcano for us to appreciate life."

Richard became pensive. "I am beginning to understand the meaning of 'Every moment is a gift.' Sometimes it takes a change of scenery to figure it out. Would that be considered literally, or metaphorically?"

"Oh, who cares? Maybe it was just a pun." Randy held up the paper cup the woman had refilled for them. *"Cin cin!"*

When they returned to the café, Amy's head was on Peter's shoulder. He whispered, *"Pennichella."*

Chapter 21

New Year's Eve Day
Shopping for a Cause

By the time they made their way home the night before, everyone was disheveled and bone-tired. It was nine o'clock, and they had put twelve hours under their tourist belts. Dinner in Sorrento would have been lovely, but it still had been a perfect day.

Giovanni was the first up in the morning. He made a cup of cappuccino for Frankie and brought it to her room. He gently knocked and then heard her soft voice, *"Sì?"* Giovanni slowly opened the door. There was Francesca, looking beautifully rumpled. A Mona Lisa smile on her face.

"Buongiorno, bella." He handed her the steaming coffee.

"Buongiorno," she replied with a smile, then quickly switched gears. "What's up?"

"I've been thinking about Rachael and Randy renting the Vespa."

"And?"

"And I'm not so sure it's a good idea."

"You were all for it yesterday."

"Yes, but driving on the highway yesterday reminded me how dangerous it can be."

"I'm sure they'll stay off the main roads." She slurped the frothy coffee. "I'm not about to tell them it's not a good idea. You know how defensive Rachael can be when you question one of her decisions."

"This is true." Giovanni kissed Frankie on her head. "Come. I have nice brioche waiting for you in the kitchen."

"Be out in a minute." Frankie was much more interested in the jaunt she and Nina were going to have with Rosevita and Lucia. There would be no arguments there. As the morning fog began to rise from her brain, she wondered what colors would look good on Lucia. She had seen Rosevita in "civilian" clothes many times. She would be easy.

Her thoughts were interrupted by another knock on the door. This time, it was Rosevita.

"May I come in?"

"Of course." Frankie patted the side of the bed. "Sit."

"No. No. I just want to say how much I appreciate what you're doing for Lucia, and for me. It has made me tired being with someone who has a cloud follow them every day. And she never would talk."

"I can understand that. It's too bad she felt that way for such a long time."

"This much is true. I am so grateful, and I look forward to having a, what you call it, 'a girls' day' with you and Nina."

"Me, too." Frankie wanted so much to come out and ask Rosevita for the panettone recipe. *Now would be the time. Or would it? Maybe not. Let's not muddy the waters. One situation has nothing to do with the other.*

Rosevita noticed the faraway look in Frankie's eyes. "Everything okay?"

Frankie blinked. "Oh, yes. I was just wondering what colors would look best on both of you."

"We find out today!" Rosevita got up and clapped her hands.

Frankie was glad she held back from asking about the recipe situation. She wondered why it was such a big secret. Frankie was confused. The Lombardis were very generous people. It was odd that Rosevita wouldn't want to share something that was so important with the rest of the family.

Frankie waved it off. There had to be a good reason. More on that later. Today would be a "girls' day," and she would have another victory under her belt. Frankie often challenged herself. This one was a biggie. Get Rosevita and Lucia to change their outfits? That was one for the record.

She wiggled out of bed, put on a robe, and shuffled to the kitchen. As promised, Giovanni had a fresh brioche waiting for her with a slice of melon.

"Another cup?" He gestured toward the coffee machine.

"Not just yet." She picked up her plate and brought it outside to the patio, where one of the heaters warmed the tile. "Another beautiful day," she said to herself, raised her coffee mug, and toasted the air and the sea.

Giovanni joined her at the table. "What time are you taking Mama and Aunt Lucia into town?"

"I have to check with Nina. I believe Jordan is arriving this afternoon. I want to give her a little more time to sleep in this morning. It was a long, but glorious day yesterday."

She rested her head on his shoulder. "I'm sorry we all pooped out on you and your dinner plans."

"Can I tell you a secret?" Giovanni whispered.

"Of course." She took a sip of her coffee and then said, "Spill."

Giovanni recognized Frankie's word for telling secrets or telling it like it is.

"I was so happy everyone wanted to come back. How does Rachael say it—'the dogs, they bark'?"

Frankie chuckled. "Sorta."

"But, for real. These shoes are not meant for walking on the stone streets all day."

"Right. You're going to have to take them to a cobbler."

"I thought about buying other shoes, but then I thought wearing new shoes for walking all day, maybe not so good."

"Speaking of which, any word on your luggage?" Frankie asked.

"No," he said, and shrugged. "What does it matter now? I have a new shirt and a new jacket."

"Yes, but if those jeans go through the spin cycle one more time, they may not hold up for another day."

"Maybe you are right. I'll buy another pair today. I give up on my suitcase."

They finished their breakfast and watched the colors of the sky change from pale pink to a spectacular azure and royal blue. The contrast to the multi-colors of the turquoise sea made it impossible to choose which shade was more beautiful.

"Giovanni?"

"*Sì, cara.*"

"Would you ever want to come back here?"

"For sure! We come back to visit any time you wanna."

"No, I mean permanently. Move back here?"

"I don't think about it."

"But it's so beautiful here. The people, the pace. *La Dolce Vita.*"

"But we have a business. We have a life. I've been in New York longer than I was here."

"Yet you still have that charming accent."

"I pretend." He chuckled.

She turned to him. "Seriously. Would you consider moving back?"

Giovanni was surprised at Frankie's question. "*Cara*, I don't know if it's possible. What would I do? What would

Marco do? He would not be able to run the restaurant alone." He went on, "What would you do? I mean if you would come here, too."

"I suppose you're right, but it's nice to think there are options."

"True. But now, what is the option? I need to work. You need to work." Giovanni knew Frankie wouldn't want to leave her job. For some editors, they can work remotely. But in her case, it was hands-on, and she needed to be available to her authors, especially with all the charity work involved.

Frankie sighed. "Well, I am going to stick to one of my favorite expressions."

"You never know," they said in unison.

Frankie's phone vibrated in the pocket of her robe. "*Buongiorno*, Nina! *Come stai?*"

"*Molto bene*! I can't remember the last time I slept that well."

"A trip to the Amalfi Coast and some limoncello can do to that to you." Frankie grinned.

"After you guys dropped us off, we cracked open a bottle. It was incredible."

"That's one of the things the town is famous for. Did you leave anything left to bring back?"

"Richard hid his bottle!" Nina chuckled.

"I don't blame him. Is he enjoying himself?"

"Like I've never seen. He's so relaxed."

"Richard always seems pretty chill," Frankie said.

"It's that lawyer thing. Never let them see you sweat."

"And I thought it was a slogan for antiperspirant," Frankie laughed. "My mother always said, 'Never let them see your hand.'"

"Same thing," Nina acknowledged. "I know Richard can seem pretty buttoned-up, but he's learning to let loose."

"I'm sure you have a lot to do with that."

"He appreciates my dry humor."

"Well, I'm very happy he's having a good time."

"And the food? We have a convert."

"What do you mean?"

"Carbs!" Nina laughed. "You can't get away from them here between the pasta, pizza, and bread."

"Why would anyone want to?"

"Exactly."

"So, what time is Jordan arriving?"

"Some time around five. I told him the party didn't start until ten, but that we were going to Mr. Parisi's first."

"Well, before any of that happens, I have a project for us today."

"And what might that be?" Nina asked curiously.

Frankie lowered her voice. "We're going to do a makeover."

"For who? Or is it whom?"

"It's Rosevita and Lucia," Frankie said gleefully.

"Huh? What are you talking about?"

"I had a heart-to-heart chat with them. More specifically, Lucia. I am not going to get into details, but I convinced both of them that every moment is a gift, and a gift to enjoy."

"Wow. Are you sure you're in the right business?"

"What do you mean?" Frankie furrowed her brow.

"Life coach. Motivational speaker."

Frankie laughed. "Just got down to the heart of the matter."

"Care to share?" Nina prodded.

"I'll fill you in later. Suffice it to say, we are going to turn the clock back on these two. New dresses, hair, and makeup."

"And shoes, I hope," Nina added.

"Absolutely. This is going to be so much fun."

"You sound even more enthusiastic than usual, and that's saying something."

Frankie got up, kissed Giovanni on the head, and motioned that she was going back to her room. She didn't want anyone to hear the rest of the conversation. Once she shut the door behind her, she said, "Lucia has been carrying around guilt and grief for too long. She spilled her guts."

"Geez. What happened?"

"Her marriage wasn't the best. He was a cheat. She couldn't get divorced. One morning they had a fight. He slapped her, and she said she wished he would drop dead."

"Don't tell me he did?"

"Yep. And she's been blaming herself for all these years."

"Did you explain karma to her?"

"I did, indeed. I told her she suffered long enough."

"Wow. And she went for it?"

"Honestly, I think she was waiting for someone to give her permission."

"What about Rosevita?"

"She said when she saw Giovanni in his father's suit, it made her realize it was time to move on."

"Very impressive, my friend."

"Well, I hope it doesn't backfire."

"What do you mean?"

"I hope they don't hate the makeover. I hope people don't shun them for discarding the mourning clothes."

"Sweetcakes, I seriously doubt this would be a total failure. And I don't think Rosevita would care what other people think."

"But she's been wearing widow clothes for a while."

"Maybe she did it to make Lucia feel she had someone who was sympatico."

"Good point. I have to tell you, when Giovanni saw his mother when we first arrived, he was shocked. So was I. I am so glad we're doing this makeover, for his sake as well as hers. He was very worried about her."

"I would never have recognized her, so I can understand how he felt. And now we have a Frankie project in the works. You are quite the negotiator."

"Now if I could negotiate Randy and Rachael not renting a Vespa."

"Ah, they'll be fine. You have to stop being the camp counselor."

Frankie laughed. "I know. You are correct. Just part of my Bossy Pants persona."

"So, what time does the grand transformation begin?"

"Let's plan on heading out around eleven. Giovanni will be using his mother's car and is going to pick up Rachael and Randy around ten and bring them to the rental agency. Maybe he can drop you off here and we can take an Uber or taxi or something. They have Ubers here, right?"

"Or something. What are we going to do with Richard, Peter, and Amy?"

"Did Richard indicate what he wanted to do?"

"No, but what if we assign them to Giovanni? He can probably come up with something to keep them occupied."

"Good idea. I'll go talk to him as soon as I get off the phone."

"Roger that. See you in a bit." Nina ended the call.

Frankie got dressed and went downstairs to talk to Giovanni. "When you go to get Randy and Rachael, can you drop Nina off here?"

"Of course. What about the others?"

"That's what I was going to ask you. Could you be their tour guide today?"

"After yesterday, do you think they trust me?" Giovanni was slicking his hair back.

"Of course. They had a great time."

"But I make them tired," Giovanni worried. "Maybe I drive them to some sights. No walking. Then lunch."

"Sounds perfect. When you get to the house, you can ask them what they would like to do."

"Amy not going with you?"

"I didn't ask her yet. I'll call her now so you guys can have a 'boys' day' while we have our 'girls' day'."

"Perfetto." Giovanni gave her a kiss on the top of the head; then he finished buttoning his new shirt.

Frankie pulled out her phone and called Amy. "Hey, honey bunch. We have a mission we need to complete before the parties start tonight."

"Oh? What kind of mission?" Amy was already intrigued.

"A makeover."

"What? I already did that!"

"Not you, silly. Rosevita and Lucia."

"Huh?" Amy pulled the phone from her ear and gave it a curious glance. "Rosevita and Lucia?"

"Yes. It's time for them to move on, and we're going to help."

"That sounds like fun. What about the guys?"

"Giovanni will take care of that. This way, they can have a guy day and we'll have a gal day." She winked at Giovanni. "Shopping and lunch. We'll figure out hair and makeup. I don't know if we can get appointments this late in the game, but I know Nina is good with makeup, even though she rarely wears it."

"Thank goodness for her television experience," Amy added. "What about hair?"

"I think I can handle a box or two of color. Between the three of us, I think we can work a little magic." Frankie's thoughts went back to Strega Nona. She grinned.

"Goody!" Amy exclaimed.

Frankie pictured Amy bouncing up and down.

"Giovanni is driving over at ten to pick up Rachael and Randy, and he's dropping Nina off here so you can ride with them. Once he gets Rachael and Randy sorted, then he'll go back to Baronissi and fetch the guys."

"I like this idea. Tell me the rest of the itinerary."

"Mr. Parisi invited all of us to go to his house at eight. He's going to uncork some of his wine. We'll stay there for an hour or so and then head back here for our party. Giovanni wants to start around ten."

"Whew. Will we have time for a *pennichella*?"

Frankie laughed. "Probably. I suspect we'll be done with our transformations by five. A little nap and then off to Mr. Parisi's."

"Sounds great!" Amy bounced on her heels.

"Okay, honey pie. I shall see you in a bit."

"*Ciao*!" Amy replied and ended the call.

Frankie looked at Giovanni. "Okay. I'm all set. How about you?"

"I know it's cold outside, but do you think they might want to go fishing?"

"Fishing? Interesting suggestion. What are you going to do about clothes?"

"When I drop off Rachael and Randy, I will buy some boots."

"And a new pair of jeans, please?"

"Frankie, these are clean every day."

"I know, but . . . and what about a pair of dress pants?"

"Maybe my suitcase will arrive today?"

"Do you really think so?"

"I am calling them again."

He phoned the airline and was put on hold. He had been waiting over ten minutes and no agent. True, it was New Year's Eve. Still, he wondered why people didn't prepare better if they are going to serve the public? The holidays come the same time every year. He huffed and looked up at the ceiling; then he hung up.

"It's no use. I will have to do a little more shopping."

"Excellent. You'll have a half hour between your taxi jobs." Frankie grinned. "I'm going to put myself together. We have a big day ahead."

"*Sì*. We should expect to be back here around five or six. Go to Mr. Parisi's at eight. Come back by ten."

"Did you invite anyone else besides our crew?"

"Yes. I invite a relative of the people who swapped the houses."

"Oh?"

"*Sì*. He is a *professore* at the college, too. Music. Salvatore Barone."

"You never spoke of him before."

"Because I don't know him. His cousins asked if we could include him in our plans, because this is his first time here for the New Year, and they did not want him to be alone."

"What did he do for Christmas?"

"I dunno. But my job is New Year's." Giovanni grinned.

"How old is he?" Frankie was curious.

"Something around our age."

"Music, eh?"

"*Sì*."

"That could prove to be very interesting. Do you know what he looks like?"

"No. Why?"

"Rachael," Frankie blurted out.

"Ah. *Sì*. It's not my responsibility. I just make the party." He gave her a hug and a kiss. "I'm gonna go get everyone now. *Ciao, bella*."

"*Ciao*. Good luck!"

Frankie went back to her room and slipped on her boots, pulled out a scarf and a pair of fingerless gloves, and stuffed them in her tote. She went upstairs to see how Rosevita and Lucia were coming along.

Rosevita was ready and said Lucia was still pondering which black dress to wear. Frankie knocked on her door. "Lucia? Ready?"

Lucia opened the door. "What should I wear?" She held up two black frocks that looked almost identical.

"Whichever one you can get on and off the easiest."

Lucia nodded and tapped her finger to her forehead. *"Sì."* She went behind the armoire door to change.

"Do you have good undergarments?" Frankie hoped she wasn't pushing it, but a good bra can change everything, as could a bad one.

"I think we need to buy," Lucia called out.

"And red underwear!" Frankie reminded her. She swore she heard Lucia giggle.

Lucia came around the open door, and Frankie asked, "All set?"

"Sì."

Frankie stopped. "Maybe no kerchief?"

Lucia felt the top of her head. "My hair. It's so ugly." She pulled the babushka back a little, revealing a lot of gray hair.

"It's going to come off when you try on the clothes. Come here." Frankie was taking charge. "Take it off, please."

Lucia removed the scarf that was hiding her locks. Her hair was wavy and just below the chin.

"Do you have a brush?"

"Sì." Lucia went to her vanity and handed Frankie the brush.

"Wait right here." Frankie bounded down the stairs, pulled out one of her headbands, and took the steps two at a time back up.

Frankie proceeded to brush Lucia's hair and then placed the headband on her head, pulling the hair away from Lucia's face. Frankie noticed Lucia was rather pretty, but you would never notice with all that black material surrounding her features. She was curious to see what kind of body type Lucia had. The frocks she wore did not reveal any physical characteristics.

"Giovanni is going to bring Amy and Nina here on the way to the Vespa rental agency."

"Who is going to drive it?" Rosevita asked.

"I would imagine Randy." Frankie hadn't given it much thought except how terrifying it could be. But that was Rachael. She loved going over the top. *Bad choice of words, Frankie. Reword that.* She didn't want to put any bad juju into the ethers.

The three women made their way down the stairs as Nina and Amy entered. Rachael and Randy stopped in to say hello.

"*Buongiorno*, Mrs. and Mrs. Lombardi." Randy tipped his new hat.

"*Buongiorno*. Beautiful hat. You buy in Positano?"

"*Sì*. It makes me feel very Italian."

"You maybe should not wear if you are on a Vespa," Lucia remarked. "It-a will blow off!"

"Good point. Maybe I'll just stick to my Gucci sunglasses. Giovanni, would you be so kind to return my chapeau to the house?"

"No, but I will return your *cappello*."

"Frankie is a hat?" Randy said in mocked astonishment. "I had no idea."

"*Cappella. Sì*. I am a hat," Frankie mugged.

"Okay, kids. *Andiamo*!" Giovanni steered the group toward the door.

"Wait. I have a question. If you are from Salerno, why is your name Lombardi?" Randy asked. "Don't the names coincide with the area you're from? Or what kind of labor or craftsmanship your ancestors did?"

"*Sì*, but people travel. People move. Our relatives were originally from the Lombardi region. There was a revolution, and the Austrians came into power, and they moved south in eighteen-forty-eight. Then in eighteen-sixty-one, the peninsula was unified into a single nation. By that time, the family had established themselves in the South." Giovanni looked at his mother. "*Sì?*"

"*Sì,*" she said, and nodded. "And now that you know what

Francesca's name means, I will tell you what Lombardi means."

All eyes were on Rosevita. "Long beard!" she hooted.

"Get out!" Randy blurted. "Well, I am certainly glad that didn't become a family tradition."

"You and me both," Frankie added.

Giovanni ran the back of his hand along his chin and joked, "This face? Never. Come. We have much to do."

Rachael and Randy said their goodbyes, and Giovanni gave Frankie a kiss on the cheek.

Rosevita turned to the group of women. "We ready?"

"You bet!"

"Absolutely!"

"*Andiamo!*" Amy said. She was beginning to enjoy using the few words she learned on her trip.

Frankie suggested an Uber, but Rosevita insisted that she would drive. They piled into the car, and Rosevita turned to the group. "Where do we start?"

"Dress shop," Frankie answered. "We also have to stop at a drugstore."

"*Perché?*" Lucia asked.

"Because we want to make the gray go away."

"Color my hair?" Lucia asked, wide-eyed.

"*Sì*. This is a total makeover!" Nina said.

"*Oh, Dio Mio.*" Lucia was a little nervous, but also very excited.

Rosevita drove to the Cilento Outlet, where there were dozens of designer shops. They were bound to find almost everything they needed there.

"Let's look around before we go into any of the shops. This way, we'll have a good idea what might work," Frankie suggested.

"Listen to Miss Bossy Pants. She knows how to coordinate pretty much everything," Nina told the two older women.

The first store was Goldenpoint, a lingerie shop. Frankie

knew neither of the women would want to go in, so she took charge.

"What size are you?" she asked Lucia.

"Large?" she said hesitantly.

"And you?" She turned to Rosevita.

"I guess large."

"Okay, you wait here. Amy, stay with them. Nina, come with me."

They strolled into the store, and Frankie asked one of the women if she spoke English. The answer was yes, and she spoke it well. Frankie explained they were looking for red underwear for the two women outside. Frankie waved at them. Lucia and Rosevita looked like deer in the headlights and gave feeble waves in return.

The sales associate knew exactly what was needed. "New Year's, eh?"

"*Sì.*"

"I show you a few things." She went to the back of the store and returned with three different styles. All in red. One was a bikini. Definitely not. The other was a brief. Possibly. The third was a boy-short, like men's boxers. Frankie held up the brief to show Lucia and Rosevita. The two women looked over their shoulders to see if anyone was watching. You would have thought they were on some wild heist. Rosevita gave a covert thumbs-up. Lucia wasn't as sure. Then Frankie held up the boxers, and Lucia nodded.

"We'll take one of each in a large, please."

The woman nodded, retreated to the back of the store again, and returned with two boxes, and Frankie handed her a credit card. The boxes were placed in a beautiful shopping bag.

"I'll carry it," Nina offered. She figured neither of the women would want to be seen handling something from a lingerie shop.

"Okey-dokey. That's one thing off the list," Frankie announced as she got back in the car.

"I am so relieved," Rosevita admitted. "I was not sure

about these." She nodded toward the shopping bag Nina was toting.

Next was Sandro Ferrone. Lucia made a beeline to a lilac dress with blouson sleeves, a pleated skirt, and cinched waist. Frankie was intrigued. Maybe Lucia had a figure under her frock.

Lucia took the dress off the rack and held it up to her. "*Sì?*"

"It's beautiful," Nina said. "Pick a few so you don't have to take your clothes off too many times."

Lucia nodded and moved from rack to rack in search of something flattering. She looked giddy. It had been years since she shopped for anything pretty. She picked an apple-green wrap dress with a ruffle hem and a gray, long-sleeved button-down midi dress. All three were completely different. The sales associate escorted Lucia to a dressing room. She was so nervous, she could barely get the zipper open.

"You alright in there?" Frankie asked.

"Fine. Fine." Lucia tried on the lilac dress and stared at herself in the mirror. "*Che sei?*" She asked herself. Who is that person in the mirror? She turned and went out to show everyone.

Rosevita gasped, "Lucia! You look *bellissimo*!"

"You think so?" Lucia turned sideways in front of the three-way mirror.

Amy was the first to agree. "Lucia, the color is perfect."

"It's beautiful," Frankie chimed in.

"Ditto," said Nina.

"Go try on the other dresses," Frankie urged. Frankie's plan was to convince Lucia to find a few dresses, not just one. Giovanni made Frankie promise not to let the women pay for their new clothes. It was going to be his gift to them for their hospitality.

Next was the green wrap dress. Another winner. But everyone agreed the button-down wasn't doing it.

Frankie slipped her credit card to the sales associate and

told her to wrap the two dresses Lucia admired. Naturally, when the shopping bag was handed over to Lucia, a slight spat ensued as to who should pay for it.

"I shall not hear one word. From either of you," Frankie instructed. She looked at Lucia and then at Rosevita. *"Capisce?"*

"Capisce." Lucia smiled and then gave Frankie a hug.

"You're next," Frankie declared, as she looped her arm through Rosevita's.

They moved on to Phard. A fuchsia pantsuit caught Rosevita's eye immediately. It was tailored, but the color exuded femininity.

While she was in the dressing room, Lucia spotted a cobalt midi-dress with an empire waist and blouson sleeves. "I wish I found this first," she sighed.

Nina overheard her. "Try it on," she urged.

"No. No," Lucia protested.

"Frankie, Lucia likes this, but won't try it on."

Frankie walked over to where they were standing, took Lucia by the shoulders, turned her around, and marched her into a dressing room. Nina and the dress followed.

As they were waiting for Lucia to emerge with the blue dress on, Rosevita came out of the dressing room, and everyone stopped.

"You look like a movie star," Amy gushed.

She wasn't far from wrong. It surely added a lot of glamour. Frankie motioned to the saleswoman. "Wrap this up, please."

"But I should look for something else, no?" Rosevita questioned.

"Yes, but you are definitely getting this. You look stunning," Frankie declared. "Come on. Follow me."

Frankie remembered some of the outfits Rosevita used to wear and steered her to a mannequin wearing a long, navy asymmetrical tiered skirt, a silk turquoise blouse, and an animal-print belt. She gestured to the sales associate. "Can you find this outfit in her size, please?"

Rosevita saw it and gasped, "I like this."

"And it will make your eyes pop."

"I donna wanna my eyes to pop!" Rosevita wasn't quite sure what Frankie meant.

"The color of your eyes will stand out."

"Ah. *Sì.*"

The salesperson returned with the three pieces for Rosevita to try on.

Lucia exited the dressing room she occupied. More gasps of delight came from the onlookers.

"That's a keeper," Nina said.

Frankie turned to the salesperson again, who was already anticipating what Frankie was going to say. She waited outside the dressing room for Lucia to hand her the dress.

Soon after, Rosevita reappeared, wearing the mannequin's outfit.

"That, too," Bossy Pants announced. Again, the clerk waited, then brought all three pieces to the counter where the other items were waiting to be wrapped.

After Rosevita put her own clothes back on, Frankie noticed that she was looking at a cream-colored tunic sweater. She nodded at Amy, who knew what Frankie had in mind. Amy edged over to Rosevita, snatched the sweater out of her hand and pushed her towards the dressing room.

It occurred to Frankie that the women would need a few more items. The dresses were beautiful, but some casual items would be necessary for day to day. She gathered her cohorts. "Grab a long black pencil skirt and a pair of black slacks for Rosevita, and a red cardigan."

She thought for a moment about what Lucia might be comfortable wearing on a normal day. "For Lucia?" she asked the group.

"I saw a pretty black-and-white floral pattern dress. Simple styling," Amy offered.

"Great. Go grab it."

"Do you think she'd wear pants?" Nina asked.

"We'll find out. Grab a pair of trousers and two blouses," Frankie answered.

Before the women came out of their dressing rooms, the salesclerk handed them the next batch of clothes.

Frankie could hear Lucia's voice from inside.

"Pantaloons? Maybe. Okay, I try." A few minutes later, she walked out, wearing the pants and the white blouse with the bow collar. She looked casual yet elegant.

Amy clapped. "Oh, you look terrific."

"I never wear pantaloons." Lucia did a twirl in front of the mirror. "I think I like."

"Bravo!" Frankie cheered.

Rosevita was busy trying on the slacks and the skirt. She walked out of the room, all smiles. "Beautiful. My figure, it's not so bad!"

Everyone cackled at the comment, while Frankie settled the tab.

Once all their purchases were wrapped, Amy announced, "Good thing there are three of us!" as she fumbled with the shopping bags.

"Now, shoes!" Frankie proclaimed, pointing to a large store a few doors down.

Rosevita hadn't been wearing the same kind of clunky shoes as Lucia but was certainly in need of something more stylish than the plain black flats she wore. She chose a square-toed black patent leather shoe with a brass buckle, and a two-inch block heel. Dressy, yet practical. She could wear it for a number of occasions. Frankie also spotted a short bootie that could also have multiple uses. They were tan with black goring and a one-inch heel. They would look good with the skirt outfit, and any pair of pants she would wear with the sweater. She asked the salesperson if they had it in Rosevita's size.

Lucia was a bit more complicated. She hadn't worn anything else for years. Nina found a pair of pointed-toe loafers that would work well dressed up or dressed down. She handed them to Lucia to try on.

Lucia looked at them suspiciously. "I'm not so sure." She pointed to the toe.

"Just try them on, please," Nina encouraged.

Much to Lucia's surprise, the shoes fit well and were extremely comfortable. "Soft leather," she commented.

Frankie put her index finger in the air and swirled it around. "Wrap 'em up."

Lucia still needed a pair of normal shoes for everyday wear. Those clunkers were going to disappear when they got back to the house. Amy and Nina perused the section where they had moccasin-type driving shoes with a metallic accent buckle. Amy looked in Frankie's direction and held it up. Frankie gave the *wrap it up* signal.

She pulled out one of her lists. Three outfits for each. Check. Two pairs of shoes for each. Check. Red underpants. Check. Their work here was done.

"*Andiamo*. Time for some lunch," she announced.

Chapter 22

Vespas and Vesuvius and Not So Much Adventure on the High Seas

Earlier that morning, Giovanni brought Randy and Rachael to the rental agency. Randy presented his driver's license, a credit card, and his passport. He signed the waivers and the contract, even though he had no idea what either said.

"I'll be back at five o'clock." Giovanni waved to them. *Be careful.*

Randy and Rachael explained as best they could that they wanted to go to Vesuvius. The young man at the counter looked at them skeptically. He walked them over to a large map on the wall and pointed out the easiest and safest route for them to travel.

"How long will it take?"

"Depends how fast," the young man said in broken English. "Maybe thirty, forty minutes."

"*Grazie.*"

The young man handed each of them helmets, goggles, and talk-back equipment, and then walked them out to the lot, where a row of Vespas were lined up.

"Which one?" Randy asked.

The young man shrugged. He had no idea how good a driver Randy was and left it up to him.

"Let's take this one," Randy said, pointing to a GTS 250 that looked comfortable enough for the both of them.

He hopped on and turned over the engine. He turned the handle grips and revved it up. Rachael climbed behind him.

"*Andiamo!*"

The first few miles on the E45 highway were easy, but when they began to drive north, the traffic got heavy. Rachael's nerves were challenged as eighteen-wheelers zoomed past them. She tried to tap Randy without losing her balance. Then she remembered the earpiece and the microphone.

"Randall."

He didn't seem to hear her.

"Randall!" she yelled louder.

"Yes, dearie?" He sounded cool and calm.

"I think we should take the local roads. These trucks are way too close."

"Okay. I'll get off at the next exit."

A half-mile later, he got off at the sign that said SS18— Pecorari. He brought the scooter to a stop on the gravel side of the road.

"Pull out your phone and Google our location."

Rachael got off the motorbike and reached around her belt. Nothing was there. No fanny pack. Which meant no wallet, no phone. She either left it at the rental place, in Giovanni's car, or at his mother's house.

"Dang! Randy, when was the last time you saw my fanny pack?"

"I wasn't paying attention. Sorry."

"We're going to have to use your phone. I don't have mine."

"Do you want to go back and look for it?"

"How much further until Vesuvius?" she asked.

He tapped his phone a few times until the local map appeared on the screen. "Another half hour, forty minutes."

"We might as well keep going."

"It says west, so we're going in the right direction. I'm sure we'll see signs as we get closer."

"It's kind of hard to miss," Rachael quipped, and got back on the bike.

The local route was much more picturesque, and Randy also had to drive slower. It had never occurred to her that Randy could be a secret speed demon.

Several minutes later, they arrived at a crossroad. It was SS 268 and had a sign for Vesuvio National Park.

Rachael gave him an *atta boy* pat on the back. They'd be there in another fifteen minutes.

When they finally arrived, there were hundreds of people milling about, waiting to do the hike.

"What do you think?" Randy asked.

"I did enough hiking yesterday. Let's just take a spin around it."

Randy revved the engines, proceeded north, and began to circumnavigate the massive mountain of rock and lava. It took about an hour to get all the way around. He pulled onto the side of the road and said, "What do you say we look for someplace to grab lunch?"

"Good idea." Rachael was happy to remove herself from the saddle. Yesterday, her feet hurt; today, it was her butt.

They soon discovered there was nothing in the area and had to drive back around to the other side.

Rachael sighed. Why on earth did she think this was a good idea?

They continued for another twenty minutes until they came upon an exit for the small town of Cercola, which had both a local pizza joint and the ever-ubiquitous McDonald's.

"Now, that's disappointing," Rachael remarked. "I'm surprised they allowed it."

"Someone told me the McDonald's in Mexico makes everything from scratch," Randy said.

"You can't be serious."

"I'm just repeating what I was told."

"Well, I'm not going to find out. It's pizza for me." Rachael slid off the seat. She could barely walk.

"How is it that someone who has danced as long as I have can't get her legs to work?"

Randy hooted, "Well, you're going to have to withstand at least another hour."

"*Mama mia.*" Rachael hit herself on the forehead with the palm of her hand.

They lingered over their pizza for almost a half hour. "How long it is going to take for us to get back?" Rachael asked.

"Figure an hour."

Rachael pouted. "How did I let you talk me into this?"

"Ha! It was your idea, dearie."

"I don't think so, dearie," she sneered at him.

"Let's not fight, or we are going to have to get a divorce," Randy joked.

When it became obvious that there wasn't a crumb left for them to eat, they began their trek back to Salerno.

"Highway?"

"That would still be a no," Rachael said emphatically.

The three men were geared up for a few hours on a fishing boat. Giovanni noticed there were whitecaps on the bay. Not a good sign.

"How far out are we going?" he asked the captain in Italian.

The answer was five miles. In Giovanni's opinion, that was five miles too far. He turned to Peter and Richard. "The sea is rough. It's the wind." He waited for a reaction.

"I'll admit it. I don't have much in the way of sea legs," Peter said, without any shame.

"I'm not exactly Popeye the Sailor either, Giovanni," shared Richard.

"No worries. What if we just go for a little ride around the marina?"

"What if we just go someplace for lunch?" Richard suggested.

"Molto bene!" Giovanni said with relief. Even a short boat ride could turn someone's gills green. "If you like, I can show you the Acquedotto Medieval. It's an aqueduct built in the ninth century. No walking. I promise. Well, maybe a block, but no more."

"Sounds like a plan," Richard said.

"Andiamo."

No one wanted to say it, but all of them were relieved they weren't going to have any hijinks on the high seas. Giovanni's original thought was for them to do something *coraggioso*, manly, with courage. But he had to face facts. They were past the age when physical challenges were not as important as maintaining their health and bones. They could save the machismo for another day. If ever.

Giovanni found a local seafood restaurant that was known to be a hidden gem. "Close enough, eh?"

"Perfetto!" Even Peter was enjoying his three-word Italian vocabulary.

They ordered clams, mussels, grilled octopus, and calamari. Lunch took over two hours, the same amount of time they would have been fishing.

"This was much easier." Richard leaned back in his chair.

"And we didn't have to bait a hook."

"Or clean and cook!" Giovanni remarked.

After lunch, they stopped at a local pastry shop and picked up an assortment of sugary and buttery delights for the party.

When they got back to the car, Giovanni looked at both of them and asked, *"Pennichella?"*

"*Sì! pennichella!*" Richard chortled.

Giovanni drove them back to Baronissi and decided to have his *pennichella* on the sofa rather than drive back to his house.

Before the women went to lunch, Frankie brought all the shopping bags to the car and locked them in the trunk. There were a few cafés in the complex, and they decided to stop in one of them instead of driving elsewhere. They still had to stop at a drugstore for hair dye and makeup.

It was close to two o'clock when they left the outlet center. Frankie pulled out a few file cards and a pen. "Hair will take about two hours."

"I can do Rosevita, and one of you can do Lucia."

"Hair? You color my hair?" Lucia looked alarmed.

"Yes. You are in my power." Frankie chuckled. "What's the point in looking good just from the neck down?"

Lucia was skeptical. "Rosevita? You, too?"

"Of course!"

Amy asked the women, "What color was your hair originally?"

"Me?" Lucia asked. "Almost black."

"I don't think that would look good on you now. What if we go all white?"

"All white?" Lucia looked horrified.

"Platinum." Amy took out her phone and looked up a few photos of women over sixty. She showed her several photos.

Lucia pointed to the picture of the red-headed Sharon Osbourne. "I like that."

Amy looked at the photo and then held the phone up next to Lucia's face. "It could work."

"And you?" Frankie addressed Rosevita. "I remember you being ash blonde."

"Yes. Ash blonde. But maybe I try platinum?"

"Splendid idea."

Rosevita had a blunt cut that skimmed her collar bones. She would look stunning with that color.

They drove several miles to a large pharmacy and headed straight to the hair care section.

"What if I no like?" Lucia was having second thoughts.

"Then you can wear your black babushka," Frankie cackled.

It took the good part of a half hour for all of them to agree on shades of red and blond. Once that was out of the way, they went to the makeup section of the store. They let Nina handle the shades of foundation, blush, eyeshadow, and lipstick, and she piled everything into the shopping basket.

Amy was getting excited about what she considered a "human renovation experiment," but she wasn't going to use those words in front of the two women, who had entrusted their appearance to them.

It took two trips to bring their booty into the house. Amy brought the bags upstairs and hung the dresses on the hooks of their bedroom doors, while the other two began to set up the kitchen to be their makeover salon.

When Amy returned to the kitchen, she spread newspaper on the floor and placed two chairs on top of it. Nina told the women to change into something they wouldn't mind getting hair color on, should that happen. Nina had been coloring her own hair for years and was rather adroit at it, but better to be safe than sorry.

Frankie set up two tray tables, one next to each chair. The older women reentered the make-shift salon and took their seats. Nina wrapped the capes around them as Lucia made the sign of the cross.

Nina put her hand on Lucia's shoulder. "It's going to be fine. If anything, it will be better than this mess of white, gray, and whatever that other color is."

Amy and Frankie mixed the color in the bowls and handed them to Nina one at a time. She quickly brushed the reddish-brown paste into Lucia's hair and then placed a light, disposable shower cap over it. Then she moved on to Rosevita and did the same. Amy set the timer for ten minutes so Nina could check the color. If all was up to snuff, she would leave it on for another ten minutes.

When the timer rang, Lucia jumped. She was definitely on edge.

Frankie asked, "Would you like some tea?"

"Maybe a little sweet and dry vermouth," Lucia said, and trembled. "With a little scotch."

"Coming right up," Frankie answered. "How about you, Rosevita?"

"Sure, why not?"

Amy went over to the refrigerator to fetch the red vermouth. "Do you mix equal parts?"

"*Sì*. With a slice of orange, *per favore*."

Amy put the concoction together and served it. "Is there a name for this?"

"Some say it's a French Kiss, but we call it *Affinità*," Rosevita replied.

It took only one sip, and Lucia's shoulders began to relax. "*Bene.*"

A half hour later, they were ready to be shampooed and blown out. Once all the color was out of their hair, Nina used a little shampoo and then conditioner. She spritzed them with Frankie's styling mist.

"Looks like we might have two fabulous babes here," Nina said confidently. She began to blow out Lucia's hair and styled it similarly to Sharon Osbourne's, with hair parted on one side and behind one ear.

"Wow!" Amy squealed.

"Spectacular!" Frankie added.

"Can I see?" Lucia asked.

Frankie went into the bathroom and brought back a hand mirror.

Lucia gasped. "I look-a ten years younger! *Bellissimo!*" She couldn't stop staring at herself.

"You're next!" Nina pulled the blow-dryer over to Rosevita and began to finish the job. More sounds of approval filled the kitchen. When she was done, she took the mirror from Lucia, who was still staring at herself.

"You'll get it back." Nina grinned.

Rosevita had the same reaction as Lucia. "I love it! You make me look so glamorous!"

"And we're not done yet," Nina said proudly.

The kitchen clock was ticking past six. "I wonder if Randy and Rachael are back yet," Frankie considered. "I'll give Giovanni a quick call."

"Do you think they caught any fish?" Amy wondered out loud.

Frankie chuckled. "If I know Giovanni, he talked them out of it."

Giovanni answered his phone. *"Pronto, cara!"*

"Hey there. How was your day?"

"Very nice."

Frankie gave her phone a curious glance. "How much fish did you catch?"

"We found some clams, and mussels."

"Oh?" Frankie's gut was telling her they did not go clamming. "How many bushels did you rake?"

"No rake. Eat!"

"Ha! You can tell me all about it later. Have you heard from Rachael and Randy?"

"No. I thought maybe you."

"Not here. I hope they're okay."

"Don't worry. They will show up." Giovanni didn't want to express any concern, but it was dark, and the roads could be treacherous, day or night.

"How is the make-things-over?" Giovanni asked.

"The makeover is going quite well." Frankie turned and

looked at the transformed women. "We have a little more to do. When will you be back?"

"About an hour. I have to pick up some things," Giovanni said. "I tell Peter and Richard we will pick them up on the way to Mr. Parisi's."

"But Nina and Amy still need to get ready."

"Okay. I come now, bring them here, and then go to the store. Tell Nina her friend arrived. Jordan is here."

"Oh, good." Frankie knew she was probably running Giovanni ragged. "I'm sorry. I wish I could drive them myself."

"Ah. I'll call Fredo. Tell him to come now. He can bring the girls here and then wait. Then he'll go to our house."

"You're becoming quite the planner." Frankie smiled.

"I learn from the best," Giovanni answered.

"Ha! Okay, I need to get back to work." She looked over at Nina. "How much more time do you need?"

"An hour."

Frankie turned back to the conversation. "Send him here in an hour."

"*Sì*. I will be there soon, Fredo in one hour. *Ciao*."

Once they ended the call, Frankie turned to Nina again. "Jordan is at the house. Will you have enough time to get ready?"

"Oh, I almost forgot about Jordan!" Nina winced. "Well, it will give him and Richard a little time to get to know each other."

Frankie checked the time again. Things were running smoothly. Good.

"Okay, ladies. Time to decide what you are going to wear tonight." The troupe went up the stairs single file.

"I think I wear the skirt and blouse?" Rosevita suggested.

"Try on the pantsuit, too, and see which one you like with your new 'do," Nina suggested. "Lucia, why don't you try yours on, too?"

Lucia had already decided to wear the cobalt-blue dress. "Make my eyes pop!" She giggled.

Rosevita slipped into the pantsuit. It was stunning. Then she tried the skirt and turquoise blouse. It was a toss-up.

"I think the skirt and blouse is more party type," Nina decided.

"Okay. Party!" Rosevita agreed.

"Get dressed, and I'll do your makeup," Nina instructed.

They bought two extra capes to drape over their outfits to be sure their new wardrobe would be free from any spills or powder.

Nina did Lucia's face first. The foundation matched her skin tone perfectly, and the light peach blush blended well with her new hair. A touch of brown eyeshadow, eyebrow pencil, and a pale coral lipstick finished off the look.

Rosevita's foundation was also a perfect match. Nina chose a pink-tone blush, a purple-brown eyeshadow, and a cotton-candy-pink lipstick.

When she removed the capes and allowed the women to see her handiwork, they were stunned.

Lucia clutched her chest. "Who is that?" She stared in the mirror.

"That's you, Lucia. The Lucia that's been hiding under the black cloud. Welcome to the new light!"

Rosevita was also blown away. "I cannot believe I look so good."

"Don't either of you start to cry," Nina warned. "I've gotta go, and you need to look as perfect as you do now." She gave both of them air kisses. "You look spectacular!"

Fredo pulled the transport into the driveway, and Amy and Nina made haste.

Lucia and Rosevita kept staring at each other. "Who knew we could be so glamorous?" Lucia asked.

"Frankie." Rosevita put her arm around Frankie's waist. "This was a wonderful gesture. I cannot thank you enough."

"And you opened your home to us, so this is our way of thanking you."

Frankie realized she, too, had to get her act together and get ready. She had an hour before they were supposed to leave for Mr. Parisi's. She phoned Giovanni again.

"Any word from Rachael and Randy?"

"No. Nothing." Giovanni was now quite worried.

Frankie let out a huge sigh. "Okay. Keep me posted."

"I'll be back at the house in half an hour," he said, trying to keep the anxiety out of his voice. "*Ciao, bella.*"

"*Ciao.*" Frankie turned to Rosevita. "No one has heard from Randy and Rachael."

"Not to worry." Rosevita patted Frankie's hand. "I'm sure they are fine. Maybe got a little lost."

Frankie knew that was entirely possible with that duo, but still, no phone call from either of them. She knew there was nothing she could do about it, so she went to her room and began her own transformation.

Chapter 23

New Year's Eve
Parties and Missing Persons

By the time Fredo returned, there was still no word from the two vagabonds. "What should we do?" Frankie asked Giovanni.

"What *can* we do?"

"Call the police? The hospitals?" she suggested.

"Okay, I call the metro police. Ask if there were any accidents." He kissed her on the forehead and went downstairs to finish getting dressed in his new slacks, re-soled shoes, a fresh white shirt, and the new blazer.

When he phoned the main number of the police station, he asked if there had been any accidents involving a Vespa between Salerno and Vesuvio. The answer was no. He wondered where they could be. He didn't want to think they had gone off a cliff and no one had found them. It sent shivers up his spine. Maybe they simply ran out of gas. That was the explanation he decided to lean on rather than something terrible.

Frankie exited her room wearing leggings, knee-high boots, and a black jacket with gold brocade. Her hair was in a French braid over one shoulder.

Giovanni thought she looked more beautiful than ever. *"Bellissimo!"* he said as she entered the living room.

"And you look quite dashing yourself."

"Where's Mama?"

"She'll be down in a minute. But I must warn you," she said with a stern face, "she looks, well, different."

Giovanni furrowed his brow, but before he could say anything, the two women descended the staircase. Giovanni stood slowly. He barely recognized his own mother, but he would never have guessed the other woman was his aunt.

"Wow! *Bellissimo!* You both look so beautiful. Elegant! *Spettacolare!* Spectacular! I don't know if we should let you out in public. Too many men will be chasing you!"

Giovanni walked over to his mother and took both her hands. "I cannot tell you how happy I am to see my mother again."

Rosevita made a face. "What do you mean? You are here over a week." Then it occurred to her. "Oh, me? *Sì.* I understand now." She did a little twirl.

Then he turned to Lucia. "Aunt Lucia. I have never seen you look so lovely. Stunning. I mean it; the men will be all over you." Giovanni could not believe the transformations the girls pulled off in one day.

"Frankie's crew. *Molto bene!*"

When Nina returned to the house, she found Jordan, Peter, and Richard yakking it up. *So much for the jealousy. But it was reassuring to know Richard was capable of those feelings.*

She gave Jordan kisses on both cheeks. "So glad you made it!"

"Thank you for inviting me. I didn't know how I was going to handle my first New Year's alone, but you changed all that."

"Happy to be of service." She gave a slight bow. "If you'll excuse me, I have some primping to do. You boys keep busy."

Back in her room, she rummaged through her suitcase,

kicking herself for not being better prepared. She tossed sweaters, a jacket, and slacks on top of the bed. She knew Frankie was wearing a brocade jacket and leggings. Maybe she should do something similar. Actually, she really didn't have many options. Then she spotted one of Richard's blazers hanging in the armoire. It was a black and white sport coat. She tried it on. It came to mid-thigh.

She called out, "Richard, are you dressed for the evening?"

"Yes. Why?" He looked at the two other men. All had jackets of one kind or another. Jordan was wearing a moto-jacket, Peter in a navy-blue blazer. Richard was wearing a dark brown plaid.

"I may need to borrow something," Nina shouted.

Again, he glanced at the other two and shrugged. "Okay!"

Nina pulled on a pair of leggings, a black camisole, and topped it off with Richard's sport coat.

"Pretty nifty," she said as she looked in the mirror. "Now the hair." She decided to let it all hang out. She rubbed some Moroccan oil in her palms and tousled her hair. She added blush and a cat-eye liner to her eyes.

"Yep. Nifty." She pulled on her short booties and walked into the living room.

"Where's Nina?" Jordan kidded.

"Maybe you should consider a life in comedy instead of drama," Nina quipped back.

"You look rather fetching, darling. Glad to see some of my fashion influence has rubbed off on you."

"More like *my* fashion influence," Richard corrected him. "That's *my* sport coat she's wearing."

"Well, it works!" Jordan applauded.

Fredo pulled into the driveway and then rang the doorbell.

"Where in the world are Randy and Rachael?" Nina wondered.

"They weren't at Giovanni's?" Peter asked.

"No. No one has heard from them."

Nina phoned Frankie. "Any word from the dynamic duo?"

"No. Giovanni phoned the metro police, but there haven't been any accidents involving a Vespa reported."

"Well, if she's not dead, I am going to kill her," Nina huffed.

"There isn't anything we can do for now," Frankie said.

"You're right, as usual." Nina tried to shake off any concerns, but it wasn't going to be easy. Rachael never missed the opportunity for a party.

They climbed into the transport and headed to the Lombardi house. Richard and Peter helped Rosevita and Lucia into the rear seat.

"You look beautiful," Richard said to both of them.

"*Grazie.*" Lucia was smiling from ear to ear.

"Nina does good work," he continued.

"*Sì.*" Rosevita nodded in agreement. She, too, had a smile on her face. Rosevita whispered in Lucia's ear, "Wait until Mr. Parisi sees us! He's-a gonna faint."

Lucia giggled in response. They felt like schoolgirls.

Giovanni couldn't help but stare at the panettone his mother was holding on her lap. It was the last one from the batch. Frankie could read his mind and squeezed his hand.

There was a variety of conversations taking place in the vehicle. No one mentioned the missing persons, but the elephant in the room was hard to ignore.

Finally, Nina blurted out, "What are we going to do about Rachael and Randy?"

Giovanni reiterated his conversation with the local police. "No accidents."

"So, what should we do?" Nina pressed. "Both of their phones are going to voicemail."

"We cannot look for them, because we do not know what roads they took. I told the desk sergeant if he could please contact me if there are any reports."

Giovanni knew it was a terribly worrying situation, but there really wasn't anything they could do at the moment.

"Please, let's try to enjoy ourselves. I am sure they will phone soon."

The main area in the front of Mr. Parisi's house was lit with over a thousand lights, and they were greeted by a man dressed like Santa holding a tray with glasses of prosecco.

"*Felice Anno Nuovo!*" Mr. Parisi shouted, walking out to greet the arriving guests.

He looked at Rosevita and held out his hand. "*Buona sera.* I am Elio Parisi."

"Hello, Elio. I am Rosevita Lombardi." She suppressed a grin.

He blinked several times. When the shock finally wore off, he responded, "Rosevita. *Sei molto bella stasera!*" He told her how beautiful she looked that night.

"*Grazie.*" She smiled. "You know my sister-in-law, Lucia."

Again, a look of surprise washed over his face. "*Mama mia!* I am surrounded by so much beauty!"

Nina, Frankie, and Amy were beaming. *Mission accomplished.*

Mr. Parisi showed them into the house and introduced his brother, Anthony, to everyone. It was obvious there was an immediate connection between Lucia and Anthony, and the affection Mr. Parisi had for Rosevita was undeniable. The three younger women could not have asked for a better outcome. Lucia had broken free from her guilt, revealing an elegant, confident, beautiful woman. Rosevita just needed a little nudge, and it, too, was worthwhile.

After two hours of celebration, the crew said their goodbyes, thanking their host, who gave everyone a bottle of his wine to take with them. When they piled back into the van, they debated what to do next.

"We should go back to the house and have the party. We cannot waste the food or the wine," Giovanni recommended.

"Plus, Salvatore Barone, a cousin of the people who own the house, is coming."

Everyone agreed and hoped they would have some information about Rachael and Randy before the stroke of midnight.

Frankie decided to call Rachael's phone again. Little did she know it was in her fanny pack that was in the back of Giovanni's car, which was in the driveway of the house.

At one point, it became abundantly clear to Rachael that they had taken a wrong turn back to Salerno. She was ready to cry. She didn't have her phone, and Randy's was out of juice.

As they went around a hairpin turn, another Vespa whizzed past, almost knocking them over. Rachael shouted expletives in return.

When the road straightened, they noticed a car on the narrow shoulder. The driver was also shouting expletives. Randy thought they should go over and see if he needed any help. At the very least, they could share their disdain for the reckless Vespa driver. However, the automobile driver wasn't interested in a conversation. He had phoned the police, who arrived within minutes. The driver of the car accused Randy of running him off the road.

Randy protested, trying to explain they too almost collided with the Vespa, but the police officer wanted to hear nothing more. He asked for identification. Randy was able to show his, but Rachael could not. It was in her fanny pack! She attempted a very poor justification, but that, too, fell on deaf ears. The police officer ordered them to get in his patrol car, leaving the Vespa on the side of the road.

Rachael was beside herself, yammering at the officer driving the patrol car. His English was poor, so he ignored her. Someone at the station could handle the wild thing in the back seat.

Randy sat dumbfounded. How could this be happening?

When they arrived at the one-room, one-cell station, they tried to explain what happened. Randy repeated that it wasn't them who caused the other car to swerve. Some crazy Vespa driver had whizzed past them, too, almost causing an accident.

The officer listened carefully. "But you have no identification," he said to Rachael.

"Correct. I mean I do have identification, but I misplaced my bag."

The officer assumed she was telling the truth. She was very emotional, especially toward her friend. Indeed, they were tourists, not terrorists. He explained in the best way that he could that there was no judge available because of the holiday, and they would have to wait until morning.

"You mean we have to spend the night here?" Rachael didn't know if she should scream, throw up, or cry.

"Don't we get to make one phone call?" Randy was at his wit's end.

"This is not-a *Law and*-a *Order*, Mr. Wheeler. Usually we wait for a judge, then you make-a the phone call. But since you are visiting our country, I do not want to make it unpleasant for you and you think we are not hospitable." He picked up the phone that was sitting on his desk. "Who do you wanna me to call?"

Randy looked at Rachael. "Giovanni. Do you have his number?"

"In my head? No," Rachael sputtered.

"Oh, wait," Richard said. "It's probably in my recent call list." He looked at the officer. "Do you have a charger? This way I can find the number."

"Your phone, no work?"

"Dead battery."

The officer nodded and opened a drawer. He handed the cord to Randy and plugged it in. As soon as it fired up, Randy got excited, until he realized there was little or no cell service. But maybe the number was stored in the phone. He scrolled through the numbers and let out a whoosh of air. He rattled off the number to the officer, who dialed the phone.

Salvatore Barone had no idea what he was getting into when he stepped onto the patio of the Lombardi home. Introductions were made, and they welcomed the stranger into their circle.

He immediately pitched in, helping to get the food and beverages set up outside.

They were putting the finishing touches on the display when Giovanni's phone vibrated in his pocket. The caller ID said *Albori Polizia*. He dreaded answering it, but perhaps this was the key to the big question of the night.

"*Pronto!*" he said, and waved for everyone to keep the noise down. He listened carefully, then responded, "*Sì*, Rachael Newmark. Randall Wheeler."

Frankie rushed up to Giovanni, fearing the worst. He gave her a weak smile as he thanked the police officer and hung up.

"Everybody, listen, please. Randy and Rachael are okay. But they are in jail."

"What?" was the resounding response.

"What in the heck happened?" Frankie asked.

"A misunderstanding on the road. They cannot release them until they can find a judge. Maybe tomorrow, but it's a holiday."

"Now what do we do?" Peter asked.

"We do what we usually do. We make the party."

Richard and Peter looked at each other and then at Giovanni. "We're not going to have to cook again, are we?"

Giovanni laughed for the first time in several hours. "No. We pack everything, and we bring the party to the jail."

A very confused Salvatore asked, "Will they let us do that?"

"I think if I make a nice antipasto, they will not be able to say no." Giovanni grinned. He dialed Fredo and asked him to come back and take them to Albori. He would pay him double.

"*Andiamo!*"

Peter packed up the confetti cannon and the sparklers. Richard took charge of the champagne. Frankie, Nina, and Amy wrapped the food. As they were leaving the house, Frankie ran back inside and pulled out two old pots. When she got back to the van, she held them up.

"Do you think your mother will mind?"

Giovanni laughed out loud. "After today, I don't think she will mind."

During the forty-minute drive, Giovanni explained what happened. Salvatore listened intently. It wasn't exactly what he thought a typical New Year's Eve party in Italy was like.

When they arrived at the small police station outside of Albori, Giovanni suggested, "Let me go in first."

He opened the door to the one-room facility and immediately saw a deflated Rachael and freaked-out Randy sitting in the jail cell. They were thrilled to see him.

Giovanni approached the officer sitting at the main desk and rattled off who Randy and Rachael were, the purpose of their stay, the party they planned, and asked if they could please celebrate in the jail.

The officer said they could not have a party in the jail, but if they wanted to use the roof, they could, as long as no one tried to escape. He laughed at his own joke.

Giovanni went back to the transport and explained why their friends were detained, but that their New Year's party would still be happening, albeit in this unexpected location. Cheers and shouts bounced off the interior of the van. Then Nina said, "Do I strangle Rachael before or after midnight?"

"Ah. It's a holiday. No fighting allowed," Giovanni reminded her.

Each of them carried the supplies into the station, where the officer directed them to the narrow circular steps that led to the roof. If nothing else, the view was spectacular. They could see the city of Salerno in the distance, and the lights along the Amalfi Coast.

The police officer gave them a folding table that Richard and Peter wrestled up the steps. Once everything was set up on the roof, Giovanni went back downstairs and waited as the officer released Rachael and Randy.

As soon as the cell door opened, Rachael and Randy both started talking at the same time.

"*Basta*! Enough!" the officer said, and motioned for them to go upstairs.

Giovanni tried again to get the police officer to just release his friends. The officer apologized but explained that he needed the signature of a judge before he could let the two go. It was all about the paperwork.

Giovanni knew any further negotiation would be fruitless, so he thanked him for being hospitable and asked if he wanted to join them for some food.

"Sure. Why not?" the officer said. He locked the front door and picked up his walkie-talkie. If there was an emergency, he'd know about it.

As usual, Giovanni had a delectable spread ready to devour. He checked his watch. It was almost eleven.

Giovanni introduced Randy and Rachael to Salvatore. "Here are the criminals."

Once again, Rachael's legs were wobbly, but not because she had been sitting on a motorbike for hours. Another stunning-looking man stood in front of her.

"How did you get sucked into this chaos?" she asked him.

"Because of you," he teased.

Was he flirting? "I have a habit of creating chaos," Rachael flirted back.

"Good. I could use a little of that."

Nina introduced Randy to Jordan.

"Jordan Pleasance?" Randy cooed. "As in *the* Jordan Pleasance?"

"Guilty. Oops. Wrong verbiage."

"I have seen every one of your films."

"You have not." Jordan had heard that line many times.

"Quiz me," Randy challenged him.

Sure enough, Randy was able to answer all the questions Jordan rattled off.

"So, you really have seen all of them."

"Uh-huh," Randy said proudly.

Rachael was standing close by. "Oh, you should have heard him when we were in Rome. Every movie that was filmed at the Trevi Fountain, the Pantheon, the Spanish Steps. He's a true cinephile."

She was getting a vibe that there was a connection between the two men and decided to step aside. Plus, she wanted to coochy-coo a little more with the newbie.

Giovanni took out a tablet and speakers from a small bag. "A party needs music!" He looked at the officer, who was chowing down a sandwich of prosciutto, mozzarella, tomato, and basil. He nodded his approval.

That's when Rachael got an idea. She walked back over to Randy, pulled Nina and Frankie into the mix, and whispered something. They nodded in agreement. Then Rachael went over to Giovanni's tablet and pulled up a song. Within seconds, the familiar, "Doh . . . Doh-Doh, Doh-Doh-Doh" rang out, followed by the horn section announcing the opening of Mark Ronson and Bruno Mars's recording of "Uptown Funk." Randy and his three dancing partners lined up and did their routine. It took less than a minute for everyone else to join them, some stumbling, others catching on quickly. Jordan thought it was hilarious, but also quite good. It was obvious that Rachael and Randy had a little more practice, but Nina and Frankie did a pretty good job keeping up.

The playlist continued, with dance music ranging from

Donna Summer; to Earth, Wind & Fire; to Kool & the Gang. There was definitely a party going on here.

While Randy was boogieing, he got the feeling Jordan was staring at him. Then Jordan noticed Randy noticing him.

"Sorry, mate, but you do look familiar."

"I hear that all the time," Randy jested.

"No. I've seen you before." Jordan eyed him up and down. "Your dance moves are quite keen."

"Thanks. I do it for a living, actually."

"Were you in that musical, *Brothers in Arms*?"

Randy was taken aback. No one ever noticed him in plays. "Why, yes. But it was a small part."

"You did exceptionally well. Rather brilliant performance."

Giovanni checked his new watch. It was almost midnight. Time to pour some champagne. He handed everyone a glass, including the officer. It was Italy. It was New Year's Eve. And it was only one glass.

The fireworks display began along the coast, with each town offering their own spectacle that could be enjoyed by many. Miles and miles of colors filled the sky and reflected off the sea. Giovanni shot off several rounds of confetti, and Frankie threw the pots off the roof.

Everyone was hugging and kissing one another. It was a celebration on many levels. Rachal and Randy were rescued, new friends were made, and Lucia and Rosevita got their license to enjoy life renewed. Giovanni called his mother to wish her a Happy New Year and to make sure she was having a good time.

There was no doubt about it. Rosevita was dancing the night away. He told her where they were and why, how Rachael couldn't find her passport and phone, and it was a case of mistaken identity.

She couldn't help but snicker, "You always have such interesting celebrations!"

"As they should be! *Buon anno!* I love you, Mama!" Giovanni ended the call and kissed Frankie passionately.

By two o'clock, the party was waning. The next puzzle would be where everyone would sleep. They couldn't leave Randy and Rachael at the jail. While they were debating their next move, the officer saw a vehicle pull in front of the station. He couldn't imagine who it could be. There was nothing on the police radio. He excused himself and headed down the stairs.

When he opened the door, two couples stood in front of him. It was Rosevita, Lucia, Elio, and Anthony.

"*Buon anno. Come posso aiutarti?* How can I help you?"

"We are here to help *you*," Anthony answered. "I understand you have two prisoners here."

The officer looked a little puzzled; then he realized they were talking about Rachael and Randy. "Ah. *Sì.*"

Anthony took out his credentials. *Giudice di Circuito.* And no, he wasn't related to one of the *Real Housewives of New Jersey*. He was a circuit judge.

Rosevita produced Rachael's fanny pack that she rescued from Giovanni's car before they made their way to Albori.

While the two hooligans were being processed, the rest of the partygoers cleaned up any remnants of their party.

Finally, the duo was released from custody, with more cheers from the crowd.

As they were walking to the car, Rosevita noticed two old pots on the gravel. "Ha. I have two pots that look like that."

"No Mama, you *used* to have two pots that look like that."

Epilogue

It was practically sunrise by the time they got back to the house. New Year's Day was one of recovery but mostly gratitude.

Rachael invited Salvatore to join them for brunch when she discovered he was only in Italy for one more semester and then planned to move back to New York for a teaching position at Columbia University in New York.

Randy and Jordan were already making plans for Jordan's next trip to New York, when he would meet with Nina to discuss the new project.

Richard confessed that he had been jealous of Jordan. He also confessed that he was in love with Nina and suggested they consider making more permanent plans.

Amy and Peter won an international competition with their one-thousand-piece Large Hadron Collider puzzle.

On the flight home, Giovanni and Frankie agreed that in spite of the chaos, they could not have asked for anything more. Well, just one thing: the recipe.

Back home, when Giovanni was unpacking, he went through the pockets of his blazer and found a small envelope. Inside was a note in his mother's handwriting:

Fluff the flour and soak the raisins in rum for two days.

Buon appetito. –Santa

Note to Reader: If you are ever at a baggage claim in an airport and there is one lonely suitcase circling an otherwise empty carousel, it's probably Giovanni's.

FEAST OF THE SEVEN FISHES

MENU

Steamed Mussels

Clams Oreganato

Scungilli Salad

Calamari Marinara with Linguini

Scallops Oreganata

Baked Stuffed Cod

Shrimp Scampi

Steamed Mussels

- 2 lbs. mussels, cleaned (see note)
- 3 tablespoons extra virgin olive oil
- 1 cup onion, chopped
- 3 cloves garlic, finely chopped
- $\frac{1}{4}$ teaspoon crushed red pepper
- 2 plum tomatoes, peeled, seeded, diced
- $\frac{1}{4}$ cup dry white wine
- 2 tablespoons fresh breadcrumbs
- 2 tablespoons fresh parsley, chopped

1. Heat the oil in a large pot over medium heat. Add the onion and sauté until soft and translucent. Add the garlic and continue cooking until fragrant. Stir in the crushed red pepper, the wine, and the diced tomatoes. Turn up the heat and bring the liquid to a boil. Add the mussels and cover immediately. Cook for about 3 minutes, shaking the pan every 30 seconds. Uncover and check to see if most of the mussels have opened. If not, cover again and continue to steam for another minute.

2. Once the mussels have opened, use a slotted spoon to transfer them to a serving bowl. Stir the breadcrumbs into the still simmering pan juices, then add the parsley. Pour over the mussels and serve.

Serves 4

Recipe Note: To clean the mussels, scrub the shell lightly with a soft brush, rinse thoroughly, and drain. Trim the "beard" (rough brown fibers) with kitchen shears.

Clams Oreganato

- 2 dozen littleneck clams
- $\frac{1}{2}$ medium shallot, finely chopped (about 1 tablespoon)
- $\frac{1}{2}$ medium red bell pepper, finely chopped
- 2 tablespoons dry white wine
- 1 tablespoon fresh parsley, chopped
- $\frac{1}{4}$ cup seasoned breadcrumbs

1. Position a rack in the middle of the oven and preheat the broiler for at least 5 minutes. Line a baking pan with aluminum foil and arrange the clams in a single layer.
2. Broil for 5 to 7 minutes, using tongs to remove clams one at a time as they open to avoid overcooking. Pour the juices that have accumulated into a small bowl.
3. Once the clams are cool enough to handle, remove and discard the top shells, then use a paring knife to cut through the connecting muscle to loosen the meat from each. Return clams to the pan and set aside.
4. Turn off the broiler and heat the oven to 400° F.
5. In a sauté pan, sauté the shallot and bell pepper just until the bell pepper is tender and the shallots are fragrant, about 3 to 4 minutes.

6. Deglaze the pan with the white wine, scraping up any browned bits on the bottom of the pan. Stir in the reserved clam juices and continue cooking until the liquid has evaporated, about 2 to 3 minutes. Stir in the parsley and remove from the heat. Add breadcrumbs and stir.
7. Spoon some of the mixture over each clam and return to the oven just long enough for the clams to heat, about 5 minutes. Serve immediately.

Serves: 4

Scungilli Salad

- ½ pound scungilli, fresh if possible (may use canned or frozen, but defrost first)
- 2 stalks celery, peeled and thinly sliced
- ½ medium onion, thinly sliced
- ¼ cup extra virgin olive oil
- 2 tablespoons red wine vinegar
- 1½ tablespoons lemon juice
- 3 cloves garlic, finely chopped
- ½ teaspoon crushed red pepper
- 1 teaspoon salt
- Freshly ground black pepper
- 2 tablespoons parsley, finely chopped

1. Place the scungilli in a large pot and cover completely with cold water. Bring to a boil over high heat, then reduce to a steady simmer.
2. Cook the scungilli until it can be easily pierced with a knife, about 45 minutes to an hour.
3. Drain and allow to cool enough to handle.
4. Slice the cooled, cleaned scungilli as thinly as possible and place in a bowl.
5. Add the celery and onion.

6. Combine the remaining ingredients in a separate bowl, add to scungilli, and toss to coat well.
7. Taste and adjust the salt and pepper, if necessary.

Serves: 4

Recipe Note: Best made a day in advance and chilled until serving.

Calamari Marinara with Linguini
- 2 tablespoons olive oil
- ½ medium yellow onion, finely diced
- 1½ teaspoons kosher salt, divided, plus more as needed
- 3 garlic cloves, minced
- 1 tablespoon dried oregano
- 1½ teaspoons red pepper flakes, plus more for garnish
- ¼ cup tomato paste
- ½ cup full-bodied red wine, such as Cabernet Sauvignon
- ½ cup clam juice, or chicken broth
- 1 can whole peeled tomato, drained
- 1 lb calamari rings and tentacles, cleaned
- ¾ lb uncooked linguine
- 2 tablespoons lemon
- ½ cup fresh Italian parsley, roughly chopped, divided

1. To make the sauce: In a large pot, heat the olive oil over medium heat until shimmering. Add the onion and ½ teaspoon salt and sauté for 4–6 minutes until the onion is soft and translucent. Add the garlic, oregano,

and red pepper flakes and sauté for 1 minute, until the garlic is fragrant.

2. Add the tomato paste and mix until evenly combined with the aromatics. Cook for 6–8 minutes, stirring occasionally, until the tomato paste has darkened and thickened. Some of the paste may stick to the bottom of the pot—this is okay. Deglaze the pan with the red wine and clam juice, scraping up any browned bits. Simmer for 4–6 minutes, until the liquid is reduced by half.

3. Add the whole peeled tomatoes and, using a potato masher, break up the tomatoes into bite-sized chunks. Bring the sauce to a simmer.

4. Add the calamari and stir to coat in the sauce. Reduce the heat to medium low and simmer for about 25 minutes, until the calamari is very tender and the sauce has thickened. Season with the remaining teaspoon of salt, plus more to taste.

5. While the sauce is simmering, bring a large pot of well-salted water to a boil. When the calamari has 6–8 minutes cooking time left, drop the linguine into the boiling water and cook until not quite al dente. Drain the pasta, reserving ¼ cup of the pasta water.

6. Transfer the linguine directly to the calamari sauce. Add the reserved pasta water and toss well to combine. Cook for 2–3 minutes, until the linguine is al dente and well-coated in the sauce. Remove the pot from the heat and stir in the lemon juice and half of the parsley.

7. Transfer the pasta to a large serving platter and garnish with remaining parsley and red pepper flakes.

Note: If Fra Diavolo/spicy sauce is preferred, add cayenne pepper, according to taste.

Serves: 4

Scallops Oreganata

- 2 lbs. scallops
- ½ cup clam juice
- 6 tablespoons fresh lemon juice
- ½ cup seasoned breadcrumbs or add 1 teaspoon oregano to unseasoned
- Sweet paprika for sprinkle
- 2 tablespoons butter cut into small cubes

Directions

1. Preheat oven to 450° F.
2. Pat scallops dry and arrange them in a single layer in the dish. Add clam juice.
3. Bake for 16 minutes until scallops become translucent.
4. Turn oven to broil.
5. Add butter to tops of scallops. Sprinkle with breadcrumbs.
6. Broil 2 minutes until breadcrumbs become crispy.
7. Sprinkle paprika to finish.

Serve hot.

Serves: 6-8

Baked Stuffed Cod

- 4 cod fillets, about 1 inch thick (approximately 1 to 1½ lbs total)
- 4 tablespoons freshly squeezed lemon juice, divided
- 4 tablespoons extra virgin olive oil, divided
- Salt and freshly ground black pepper
- 3 tablespoons butter
- 3 cloves garlic, minced
- ¼ teaspoon crushed red pepper

- ¾ cup fresh breadcrumbs
- 2 tablespoons fresh parsley, chopped

1. Preheat the oven to 400° F. Coat a baking dish with nonstick spray and add the cod fillets in a single layer.
2. Drizzle each fillet with 1 tablespoon of the lemon juice and 1 tablespoon of the olive oil, then season lightly with salt and pepper and set aside.
3. In a skillet, heat the remaining olive oil together with the butter over medium heat.
4. Add the garlic and crushed red pepper and sauté just until garlic begins to turn golden (do not brown).
5. Remove from the heat, stir in the remaining lemon juice, the breadcrumbs, and parsley.
6. Spread the crumb mixture evenly over the fish and bake for 12 to 14 minutes, or until the fish flakes easily.
7. Serve immediately.

Serves: 4

Shrimp Scampi
- 2 tablespoons butter
- 2 tablespoons extra virgin olive oil
- 4 garlic cloves, minced
- ½ cup dry white wine or broth
- ¾ teaspoon kosher salt, or to taste
- ⅛ teaspoon crushed red pepper flakes, or to taste
- Freshly ground black pepper
- 1¾ pounds large or extra-large shrimp, shelled
- ⅓ cup chopped parsley
- Freshly squeezed juice of half a lemon
- 6 cups of cooked linguine or a loaf of crusty bread

1. In a large skillet, melt butter with olive oil. Add garlic and sauté until fragrant, about 1 minute.
2. Add wine or broth, salt, red pepper flakes, and plenty of black pepper and bring to a simmer. Let wine reduce by half, about 2 minutes.
3. Add shrimp and sauté until they just turn pink, 2 to 4 minutes, depending upon their size.
4. Stir in the parsley and lemon juice and serve over the linguine or accompanied by crusty bread.

Serves 4

SANTA'S SECRET**
PANETONNE (CHRISTMAS BREAD)

Ingredients

For the bread:
- 7 Tbsp raisins
- 3 Tbsp rum or rum extract
- 4 Tbsp warm milk
- 1 Tbsp dried yeast
- 8 Tbsp sugar
- 2 sticks butter, room temperature
- 2 tsp vanilla extract
- grated zest of 1 lemon
- grated zest of 1 orange
- 5 large eggs, beaten
- $3\frac{1}{2}$ cups flour plus extra (up to $\frac{1}{2}$ to $\frac{2}{3}$ cups more)
- pinch of salt
- 2 Tbsp candied lemon and orange peel, finely chopped
- butter for greasing pan

For the topping:
- 1 Tbsp egg white
- 1 Tbsp icing sugar
- more icing sugar for dusting

Equipment:
- panettone mold or an 8-inch-deep round cake pan
- mixing bowls
- hand mixer
- silicone brush
- large spoon
- small saucepan

Instructions:
1. Two days before: soak the raisins in rum for two days.
2. Grease a panettone pan with softened butter.
3. Place the warm milk in a bowl and add the yeast and 1 tsp of sugar. Mix well and let sit for a few minutes.
4. Put the remaining sugar in a large bowl and, using a hand mixer, blend with the butter and vanilla extract until light and creamy.
5. Add lemon and orange zest and mix.
6. Add the eggs, one at a time, and mix until all are well incorporated.
7. If the mixture starts to curdle, add a tablespoon of the flour and beat in with the eggs.
8. Place the flour in a second large bowl, fluff, and mix with a pinch of salt.
9. Make a well in the center of the flour and add the yeast mixture, then the butter and egg mixture, folding in with a large spoon to make a soft dough.
10. Knead the dough in the bowl for 5 minutes, until the mixture starts to come together. It will be sticky.
11. Put the dough onto a floured surface and knead for another 10 minutes, sprinkling flour onto the dough with

your hands as needed to prevent it from sticking. Knead everything until you get a soft, stretchy dough.

12. Place the dough in a lightly greased bowl and cover with plastic wrap. Keep it in a warm place for 2 hours or until the dough has doubled in size.

13. When the dough has risen, tip it out onto a lightly floured surface and knead for another 5 minutes. Gradually knead in the soaked raisins and chopped candied peel.

14. Shape the dough into a ball and put it into the prepared panettone mold or cake pan. If using an 8-inch deep cake pan, wrap a layer of baking parchment around the outside of the tin, to come up about 2 inches above the rim, and secure the paper with string. This will help contain the dough as it rises.

15. Cover lightly with plastic wrap and leave to rise for another hour until it has risen to the top of the pan or paper.

16. Preheat the oven to 350° F.

17. Mix together the icing sugar and egg white and gently brush over the top of the panettone.

18. Place the panettone in the oven and bake for 50-55 mins or until golden and risen. Insert a skewer into the middle of the cake to test if done.

19. Leave to cool in the pan for 10 minutes before turning out onto a cooling rack.

20. Leave to cool completely before dusting with icing sugar.

21. Cut into wedges to serve.